Praise for the Downward Dog Mystery series

Pre-Meditated Murder

"Weber's yoga-inspired series regulars hit the road… Light on yoga and heavy on complex relationship dynamics."

—*Kirkus Reviews*

"Lots of red herrings and potential motives eventually lead Kate to a surprising killer. Cozy fans will cheer her every step of the way."

—*Publishers Weekly*

A Fatal Twist

"If you're a fan of yoga, dogs, childbirth, and murder cases, then Tracy Weber's *A Fatal Twist* is just what the fertility doctor ordered."

—*The Seattle Times*

Karma's a Killer

"Weber's clever assemblage of suspects is eliminated one by one in her entertaining novel."

—*RT Book Reviews*

"*Karma's a Killer* continues Tracy Weber's charming series."

—*The Seattle Times*

"[Weber's] characters are likeable and amusing, the background is interesting, and the story is ultimately satisfying."

—*Ellery Queen Mystery Magazine*

"Weber keeps readers guessing and populates the action with plenty of kooky characters."

—*Mystery Scene*

"Crazy, quirky critters and their odd yet utterly relatable human counterparts make *Karma's a Killer* an appealing story. But when you add the keep-you-guessing mystery with both laugh-out-loud one-liners and touching moments of pure poignancy, the result is a truly great book!"

—Laura Morrigan, national bestselling author
of the Call of the Wilde mystery series

"Tracy Weber's *Karma's a Killer* delivers on all fronts—a likably feisty protagonist, a great supporting cast, a puzzler of a mystery and, best of all, lots of heart. This book has more snap than a brand-new pair of yoga capris. Pure joy for yoga aficionados, animal lovers … heck, for anyone who loves a top-notch mystery."

—Laura DiSilverio, national bestselling author of
The Readaholics book club mysteries, two-time Lefty finalist
for best humorous mystery, and Colorado Book Award finalist

"Yogatta love this latest in the series when Kate exercises her brain cells trying to figure out who deactivated an animal rights activist."

—Mary Daheim, author of the Bed-and-Breakfast
and Emma Lord Alpine mysteries

A Killer Retreat
"Cozy readers will enjoy the twist-filled plot."

—*Publishers Weekly*

"[Kate's] path to enlightenment is a fresh element in cozy mysteries … [A]n entertaining read."

—*Library Journal*

"Weber's vegan yoga teacher is a bright, curious sleuth with a passion for dogs. A well-crafted whodunit with an intriguing mystery and a zinger of a twist at the end!"

—Krista Davis, *New York Times* bestselling author
of the Domestic Diva and Paws and Claws Mysteries

"An engaging mystery full of fun and fascinating characters and unexpected twists. An intriguing read that includes yoga lessons and feisty dogs."

—Linda O. Johnston, author of the Pet Rescue Mystery series

"Weber's second yoga mystery, *A Killer Retreat*, is as delightful as her first. Readers will love the setting, the complex mystery, and the romance of Kate's second adventure. Especially noteworthy in this popular series is the appealing combination of strength and vulnerability that Kate and Bella share. Enjoy!"

—Susan Conant, author of the Dog Lover's Mystery series

"Whether yoga instructor Kate Davidson is wrestling her hundred-pound dog, her new love life, or trying to solve a murder, *A Killer Retreat* is simply a killer read! Witty, fun, and unpredictable, this is one cozy mystery worth barking about!"

—Shannon Esposito, author of the Pet Psychic Mystery series

"Fun characters, a gorgeous German Shepherd dog, and a murder with more suspects than you can shake a stick at. *A Killer Retreat* is a must-read for cozy fans!"

—Sparkle Abbey, author of the Pampered Pet Mystery series

Murder Strikes a Pose
An Agatha Award Nominee for Best First Novel

"Cozy fans will eagerly await the next installment."

—*Publishers Weekly*

"*Murder Strikes a Pose*, by Tracy Weber, is a delightful debut novel featuring Kate Davidson, a caring but feisty yoga teacher ... Namaste to Weber and her fresh new heroine!"

—Penny Warner, author of *How to Dine on Killer Wine*

MURDER
LIKES IT HOT

········

A DOWNWARD DOG MYSTERY

········

TRACY WEBER

MIDNIGHT INK
WOODBURY, MINNESOTA

FIRST EDITION
First Printing, 2019

Cover design by Kevin R. Brown
Cover Illustration by Kim Johnson / Lindgren & Smith

Midnight Ink, an imprint of Llewellyn Worldwide Ltd.

Library of Congress Cataloging-in-Publication Data
Names: Weber, Tracy, author.
Title: Murder likes it hot : a Downward Dog mystery / Tracy Weber.
Description: First Edition. | Woodbury, Minnesota : Midnight Ink, [2019] |
    Series: A Downward Dog mystery ; #6.
Identifiers: LCCN 2018037596 (print) | LCCN 2018039694 (ebook) | ISBN
    9780738755885 (ebook) | ISBN 9780738750699 (alk. paper)
Subjects: | GSAFD: Mystery fiction.
Classification: LCC PS3623.E3953 (ebook) | LCC PS3623.E3953 M85 2019 (print)
    | DDC 813/.6—dc23
LC record available at https://lccn.loc.gov/2018037596

Midnight Ink
Llewellyn Worldwide Ltd.
2143 Wooddale Drive
Woodbury, MN 55125-2989
www.midnightinkbooks.com

Printed in the United States of America

ACKNOWLEDGMENTS

This book would never have been possible without a wonderful network of people who helped with research, gave feedback, and supported me every step of the way.

First of all, thank you to editor Sandy Sullivan at Midnight Ink. Your keen eye for detail has improved my writing many times over. Thanks also to my agent, Margaret Bail, and editor Terri Bischoff at Midnight Ink, who both worked with me as a newbie author and believed that a dog-crazy yoga teacher could, indeed, plot murder.

Special thanks go to three lovely women: Heather Jaynes, Katie Arrants Okun, and Jill Corddry. Heather helped me understand the joys and challenges of working with homeless teens. Katie shared her experiences teaching yoga to at-risk youth through Street Yoga in Seattle. Jill graciously and openly spoke with me about her personal experiences with IVF. Of course, any misperceptions, errors, or misinterpretations are strictly my own.

Physical therapists and practical jokesters Ed Elder and Lonnie Sellers get full credit for the inclusion of rats in this novel. I'm delighted to incorporate both of these gentlemen in my work in such a fun way. They're the reason I'm healthy enough to keep typing.

Hubby, Marc Martin, and German shepherd pup, Ana, get extra special bonus points for keeping me smiling, being my inspirations, and generally making life worth living.

Finally, I know I've said it before, but it bears repeating. Thank you—so much—to my readers. I appreciate every Facebook post, email, note, kind thought, and review. You're the reason I keep writing.

To the real Ed and Lonnie.
Thanks for keeping me moving all these years.

ONE

THE EMPTINESS ROLLED IN quietly, like a thick, cold fog. A hollow ache of longing so insidious that I didn't notice its arrival until I'd been consumed by it. The yoga teachings give it a name: dukha. An empty cavity. A hole in the heart.

In my case, dukha was a black hole I never knew existed. It hadn't existed, in fact, until the day I witnessed the birth of Rene's twins, Alice and Amelia. Since then, dukha had grown into a yawning cavern that devoured all of my enthusiasm—all of my passion. A cavern I desperately hoped to fill.

Tonight.

Michael and I sat on the couch, knees inches apart but not daring to touch. He raised his hand to place a reassuring palm on my shoulder, and I involuntarily flinched. He stopped, pretended to examine his wedding band, and then lowered the hand back to his lap. I pretended not to notice.

We were stuck in a painful *Groundhog Day* loop six times in the running. I felt oddly detached, yet painfully present. The sofa's worn fibers chafed the backs of my thighs, making my skin itch. The yeasty scent of Michael's half-consumed Guinness invaded my nostrils. The mantle clock's tick, tick, tick drummed against my eardrums. No, not drummed. Pummeled. Like Poe's tell-tale heart, pounding out each second of the longest two minutes of my life.

Why hadn't we gotten this over with on Monday?

We'd waited three extra days this time, in superstitious agreement that if we pretended to have more patience, the outcome would be different.

It wouldn't.

I went through the motions for Michael, but I already knew the outcome of our charade. We'd get the same answer we'd gotten the last five times. If it was different, I'd know, wouldn't I? I'd feel the life burgeoning inside me. I'd feel some connection. Some tickle of nausea not caused by apprehension. Some achiness in my breasts. Some... something. But my trickster mind toyed with me. Taunted me. Gave me false hope. *Maybe not, Kate. Every pregnancy's different. You expect too much.*

The timer on the end table dinged. My heart fluttered. My trickster mind stopped teasing, suddenly dumbstruck.

Michael flashed a reassuring smile, but worry clouded his blue-green eyes. "Are you ready?"

Answer? No. Of course not. If I didn't look, the possibilities were endless. If I didn't look, I could go on pretending. Like with Schrödinger's cat. If I didn't look, Mr. Whiskers would be both alive and dead. I would be both pregnant and not pregnant. If I didn't look, I'd never know. I'd never be disappointed.

I gave him a tentative nod, closed my eyes, and said a final quick prayer to the universe. *Please?* I read the answer on Michael's face before I glimpsed the single blue line. Negative. Again.

Michael tried to hide his disappointment, but the tremor in his voice gave him away. "It's okay, Kate. We'll keep trying. Next month will be different."

A familiar refrain—a mantra—said by my wonderful husband over and over and over again. What was once reassurance now felt like a dirge. Deep down inside, I knew he was wrong.

I forced on an empty smile. "I know." I went to the kitchen, poured a goblet of Chardonnay, and drained it in two large gulps. I refilled the glass before I rejoined Michael in the living room. "I'm exhausted. I'm going to bed."

For the sixth month in a row, Michael didn't follow me upstairs.

TWO

FIVE MONTHS AND AN equal number of negative pregnancy tests later, I stood outside the entrance to Infant Gratification, trying to gather enough courage to enter.

The flagship store for Rene's no-longer-online-only infant accessory business had opened three months ago. The space—which used to house Zorba's Greek Deli—was next door to my yoga studio, Serenity Yoga. I'd dropped by a grand total of four times since she'd opened the store, which was four more times than I'd wanted to. I'd been avoiding Rene and her husband, Sam, and I had a feeling she knew it.

It was time to put on my big girl pants and talk to her, but what was I supposed to say? How could I explain my reluctance to spend time with my best friend when I barely understood it myself?

I should have been happy for Rene's astounding success. I should have been ecstatic to have her and her twin toddlers within whispering distance. At the very least, I should have been grateful for the clientele she passed my way. I'd needed to add a third Mom and Baby Yoga class to keep up with demand.

And I was.

But watching Rene's customers stroll past my business was like being subjected to a perverted form of Chinese water torture.

Smiling, twenty-something brunette cradling an infant in a Baby Bjorn.

Drip.

Baby Booty exercise class thundering by to check out Rene's new line of infant workout wear.

Drip.

Tuesday afternoon Mothers of Multiples group, pushing multi-child strollers.

Drip.

Swollen-bellied, exhausted woman herding three toddlers while wearing a T-shirt proclaiming, *This is my last one. Seriously.*

Drip, drip, drip.

So I tried not to look. I spent hours in the studio's back room arranging and rearranging the toilet paper. I managed the studio from home, much to the delight of Bella, my hundred-pound German shepherd. When I taught, I skulked in and out of the back entrance like an accused pedophile afraid of facing the press.

Today, I couldn't avoid it anymore. Today, I needed to talk to my best friend.

If she was still speaking to me.

I glanced through the window into Rene's light-filled space. She sat at the checkout counter, waving goodbye to a customer pushing a baby stroller. My stomach lurched.

Drip.

Maybe stopping by the store wasn't such a great idea.

I turned to leave, but I'd hesitated too long. The blonde, thirty-something woman backed through the door, pulling the stroller behind her. She collided with my back.

"Oops! Sorry. I swear, I need to install a rearview mirror on this thing."

"No problem," I replied. I held the door open while she maneuvered the stroller and two large cloth shopping bags through the opening. One bag read *Gratified Mom*. The other, *Gratified Baby*. The newest of Rene's marketing swag.

"Thanks, Rene," the woman whisper-yelled over her sleeping infant. "See you next week."

Rene wiggled her fingers in reply. She looked gorgeous, as always. Her dark, shoulder-length hair fell in elegant layers, and her makeup had been applied with the usual natural-looking perfection. When she spied me, her hand dropped to her lap. Her expression turned Barbie-doll plastic. Friendly, but too stiff to be genuine. "Well, if it isn't a blast from the past. The elusive Kate Davidson. How nice of you to drop by. Finally."

I slinked through the doorway, avoiding eye contact by taking in the space. "Wow. You've made some upgrades." The last time I'd visited, the walls had been eggshell white. Now they were painted in a palette of summer-day blues accented with white puffy clouds. To my right was a safari-themed area, decorated with balloons sculpted into giraffes, monkeys, and a surprisingly detailed lion. Twin Town, an area of the shop dedicated to all things multiple, was to my left. Brightly colored signs highlighted displays of baby accessories that were labeled *Identical, Coordinated*, and *Consciously Clashing*.

Rene had started her business with a small line of custom-designed pacifier purses and quilted infant stilettos. Eighteen months later, Infant Gratification was rapidly becoming the Tiffany's of the toddler crowd. Jewelry included, as evidenced by the glass case in front of me, which was filled with platinum infant ID bracelets, teeny-tiny toe rings, and matching mother-and-daughter necklaces. Nursery-themed jewelry boxes decorated its top.

I pointed to a pair of impossibly small tennis shoes with soles made of pink Swarovski crystals. "No self-respecting baby would ever walk in those."

"Don't be ridiculous, Kate. They're designed for newborns! Babies don't start walking until ... " She paused and narrowed her eyes. "You're teasing me, aren't you." It was an accusation, not a question.

I grinned, and for the first time in weeks, the expression felt genuine. "Gotcha." I lifted my heels in a tennis-shoed Tadasana and peered at the space behind the desk. "The girls aren't with you today?" The prior times I'd visited, Rene's sixteen-month-old toddlers, Amelia and Alice, had been at the store wreaking havoc. "I thought they were your designated models."

"Having the girls here was a disaster. Once they started running, I couldn't keep track of them. I used to think Ricky and Lucy were hard to control." She shuddered. "Believe me, labradoodle puppies have nothing on twin toddlers. Sam and I finally gave up and enrolled the girls in toddler school from nine to noon. The nanny picks them up after school, feeds them lunch, and babysits the whole menagerie until one of us gets home."

"Toddler school?"

"Don't mock me, Kate. It's never too early to start preschool prep." She frowned. "You'd already know all of this if you'd come around lately." She didn't disguise the hurt in her voice.

Honestly, I didn't blame her for chastising me. Rene and I had been inseparable since we were teens. My avoidance of her had to feel like a betrayal, especially since I'd kept my fertility issues a secret. I knew that hiding Michael's and my troubles was unhealthy, but until today, I hadn't been able to make myself talk about it.

"You're right, and I'm sorry," I said. "I've been a terrible friend, but I need to talk to you. Can you spare a minute?"

Rene didn't reply for several seconds. Long enough that I thought she was about to say no. Then she pulled a sign out from underneath her desk and looped her purse over her shoulder. "I'll give you thirty of them." She held up an index finger. "On one condition."

"Name it."

"You're buying coffee."

Five minutes later, I sat across from Rene at one of Mocha Mia's outdoor tables, relishing Seattle's rare autumn sun on my shoulders. Rene stirred extra sugar into her double-whip, double-chocolate mocha, then plunged her fork into her version of health food: an extra-large slice of Dutch apple pie à la mode. I sipped a soy cappuccino and stared across the street at the four-story brick building that housed both of our businesses.

The newer, mixed-use building contained shops at street level and housing units above. Serenity Yoga, Infant Gratification, the Phinney-Wood Grocer, and my husband's pet supply store, Pete's Pets, occupied the four business suites. The upper three floors consisted of a mixture of studio and one-bedroom apartments, some with fabulous views of the Olympic Mountains. The Yoga over Fifty class was in session, so Serenity Yoga's lobby was empty. A woman pushing a baby carriage stopped at Rene's storefront and read the sign taped to the door.

"I never understood signs like that," I said. "How is it useful to say *Back in thirty minutes* when customers don't know what time you left?"

Rene licked ice cream-laced pastry off her lips. "It's genius, actually. If customers think you'll be back soon, they hang around the area and keep checking back. And if they don't know what time you left, they can't complain if you're late."

It actually made sense, in a demonic, Rene sort of way.

"Are you sure you should be away from the shop right now?" I pointed at the woman, who was pushing her stroller toward the parking lot. "I'm costing you business."

Rene shrugged. "I'm on lunch break. Like the sign says, I'll be back in thirty minutes. If she doesn't stick around today, she'll come back tomorrow. Besides, if I don't snag you now, you might make like a groundhog."

I flinched. Groundhog's Day, of course, was what my Kate-torturing mind called pregnancy test day. Could Rene have intuited that somehow? I pretended confusion. "Groundhog?"

"See your shadow and disappear for another six weeks." She scowled. "I was beginning to think the Great Kate Disappearing Act was going to be permanent. I haven't heard from you in weeks, and you didn't return my last five phone messages. Not that anyone's counting."

I swallowed.

"We've been friends for years, Kate. I shouldn't have to scour Facebook to make sure you're still alive."

"I know. I'm sorry. Things have been tough lately."

Her voice grew irritated. "Tough? That's your excuse?" She made a repeating series of finger quotes. "Things were 'tough' when your father died. They were 'tough' when I almost lost the babies. They were 'tough' when Dharma showed up and then got arrested. They were 'tough' when you found out Michael was married to Gabriella. We've seen each other through plenty of difficult times. You've never ghosted me before."

"Ghosted you?"

"Dumped without warning. Disappeared." She made fists and quickly opened her hands as if performing a magic act. "Poof!"

I opened my mouth to defend myself, then closed it again. "What did I do? Was it opening the store? Did I invade your turf somehow? If you wanted that retail space for yourself, you should have said something." Rene pushed her dessert to the side, a move so uncharacteristic that it shocked me out of my silence.

"Invade my turf? You think I'm acting territorial?" I smiled, hoping to lighten the mood. "Better be careful or I'll pee on your onesie collection."

Rene's jaw hardened. "Whatever's going on, you've been acting petty and jealous. It's not attractive, Kate."

She was right about the jealousy, of course. Simply wrong about the reason. "I swear, Rene, it's not about you. I love that Infant Gratification is doing so well, and it's great knowing you're close by."

"Could have fooled me. You've clearly been avoiding me."

"You're right. But it's not because you opened the store, though I can certainly understand why you'd think that." I reached across the table to take her hand. "The timing is just all screwy."

She pulled her fingers away, but the anger in her eyes dimmed. "What timing? Kate, would you please tell me what's going on?"

I bit my lower lip to keep it from trembling. "Michael and I recently had our first wedding anniversary."

"I know. I called and left a message asking if you two wanted to get together with Sam and me to celebrate. You never called back."

I ignored the well-deserved gibe, but I felt my face flush. "Michael and I started trying to make a baby shortly after the wedding."

Rene's energy softened. "I know you wanted to have kids right away, but sometimes it takes a while. Sam and I were married for five years before we had the twins."

"You were on birth control, remember? I tossed the pills in the trash as soon as we said 'I do.'"

Rene remained silent.

"We waited for a couple of months to let the hormones clear my system, but after that, it was all baby-making, all the time." I yearned for those days. Back then, sex was so uncomplicated. So free. Now it was performed on demand. Timed so that Michael's swimmers would have the perfect opportunity to strike. "At first we figured it was taking a while for my system to adjust, so we kept trying. Nothing happened. We finally called to make an appointment at a fertility clinic, shortly after you opened the store."

"And?"

I stared down at the table. "I got the newest test results yesterday. Michael and I have issues. Big ones."

THREE

"I'm so sorry," Rene said. "I wish you'd told me sooner."

"Honestly? I do too. The fertility specialist confirmed my biggest fear." I grinned, but it felt like a grimace. "Michael's swimmers are ready for the Olympics. My eggs, on the other hand, are scrambled."

Rene didn't grin back. "Nothing about this seems funny. What exactly did the tests show?"

I took a long drink of my soy cappuccino, drowning what remained of the chocolate heart floating in the foam. "My egg supplies are dwindling, and the ones I have left aren't healthy. The doctor says I have something called Primary Ovarian Insufficiency."

"What does that mean?"

"It means my number of viable eggs is minuscule. As if that wasn't bad enough, one of my fallopian tubes is scarred shut, so half of the eggs will never make it to my uterus."

"Is getting pregnant out of the question for you?"

"Not completely. We have options." We had options, all right. None of them great. Most of them expensive. I ticked them off on my fingers. "One. Michael and I can keep trying to conceive naturally. The doctor says that about ten percent of women with Primary Ovarian Insufficiency get pregnant naturally. My chances are less than that, but it could still happen."

"Would fertility drugs help?"

"Not enough. The doctor says drugs alone almost never work with women with my condition." I added a second finger. "Option two. I can shoot myself up with different customized fertility drugs, have minor surgery to retrieve as many good eggs as we can, and go straight to IVF."

"In vitro fertilization?"

"It's our best option, if we want children that are genetically ours. There are no guarantees there, either. My number of viable eggs is *tiny*. If I were a chicken, I'd be stew meat."

Rene ignored my lapse into gallows humor. "What about using an egg donor?"

I shrugged. "That's option three. The doctor says an egg donor is by far our best chance." Using an egg donor wasn't feasible, though. Not for Michael and me. The costs would quickly become untenable. Depending on the number of attempts required, upwards of seventy-five thousand dollars worth of untenable. Michael and I couldn't afford IVF using our own genetic material, and that was considerably cheaper. "Option four is adoption. But Michael and I talked about it, and we want a child that we made together."

"So, go straight to IVF."

"IVF is expensive. Even if we can come up with the money, I'd experience significant side effects. According to the literature they gave me, it's like the worst case of PMS you've ever experienced. Can you imagine what that would look like with my temper?"

Rene's right eyelid twitched.

"Exactly," I said. "And homicidal mood swings are only the start of the fun. Less than forty percent of women my age conceive on the first IVF attempt, and conception won't necessarily result in a live birth. Given my low egg quality, even if I do get pregnant I could easily lose the baby. I don't know how many failures I can take and still keep my sanity."

"What does Michael think about all of this?"

"I don't know."

"You don't know?"

"Not really." I shrugged. "Michael treats me like cracked glass, liable to shatter at any moment. I can't tell lately if he's telling me the truth or saying what he thinks I want to hear." I shrugged. "I don't blame him. I've been so moody lately, even Bella's giving me a wide berth."

Rene and I sat in uncomfortable silence. I idly stirred lukewarm coffee while she stared at the melted ice cream pooled at the bottom of her dish. After several long seconds, she spoke. "How can I help?"

"I wish I knew. There doesn't seem to be an easy answer. Honestly, all I want to do is hide out under the covers, avoiding people. I can't stand to be around anyone who's currently pregnant, has ever been pregnant, or might ask if Michael and I are planning to get pregnant."

"Kate, that doesn't make any sense."

"Of course it does. If Sam were impotent, would he want to chat about it with everyone he knows? If you were destitute and I won the lottery, would you want to ooh and aah over the Bentley I bought with the winnings?"

Rene frowned, but it looked more like concentration than disapproval.

"If you haven't struggled to get pregnant, you can't understand. I feel like a dried-up old shrew, not woman enough to conceive. I hunger for a baby like a drowning person hungers for air."

"I never thought about it like that."

"I didn't either, until it happened to me. Avoidance seemed like the only reasonable option. It sounds crazy when I say it out loud, but I convinced myself that if I didn't talk about Michael's and my fertility issues, they wouldn't exist."

"How's that working out for you?" Rene asked drolly.

"It's not. It's destroying my marriage. Michael keeps pushing me to get out and be active. I hide out under the covers with a flashlight and a calendar, calculating the next time we should have scheduled sex. If something doesn't change soon, Michael and I are going to end up divorced."

"What does Dharma say about all of this?"

"I haven't told her about it."

"Seriously, Kate? You haven't even told your mother?"

"It's not the kind of thing you chat about over the telephone. I'll tell her when she and Dale come to Seattle in a few weeks." *If the timing feels right.*

Rene's eyes narrowed, but she didn't push me about Dharma, at least for the moment. "There must be something I can do to help." She took a long, slow drink of her mocha. "Will your insurance cover the costs?"

I knew where she was going, but I answered her honestly anyway. "Unfortunately, no. Our plan didn't even pay for all of the fertility testing."

"Then there *is* something I can do. The last thing you and Michael should be stressed about is money. I'll talk to Sam about giving you a loan."

Example number 1351 why I adored my best friend. I'd been prepared for her offer. Heck, part of me had even hoped for it. But I couldn't accept it. "Thanks, Rene. That's truly generous of you. Michael and I will have to get a loan from somewhere, but I can't take that much money from you and Sam. It wouldn't feel right."

"You were willing to borrow money from us to pay off Michael's ex-wife. At least this way we'd be getting a godchild out of the bargain."

Rene pursed her lips. "Sam and I would be the godparents, right?"

"You'd be more than the godparents. You'd be the auntie and uncle, the best friends, the guardian angels, and the designated foster parents if anything ever happened to Michael and me. Honestly, Rene, I'm glad I didn't end up having to take money from you to pay off Gabriella. It would kill me if finances ever got in the way of our friendship. Besides, back then Michael and I had at least a snowball's chance in hell of paying you back. If a baby came along, we'd be even more broke than we are now."

"So what are you going to do?"

"The fertility clinic has some financing options, and we're going to apply for a second mortgage on the house."

"Will you qualify?"

I shrugged. "Honestly? I don't know. It'll be tight. You'd better keep sending me new yoga students. I'll need all the income I can get."

Rene hesitated. "Actually, I do know a way you can make some extra money. Not a lot, but a few hundred a month."

A horrible image flashed through my mind: a five-foot, three-inch yoga teacher wearing yoga pants and a pre-prenatal T-shirt. "Please don't tell me you want me to model some new pre-conception clothing line."

Rene scrunched her perfectly plucked eyebrows. "Where'd you come up with that?" Then she paused, placed her index finger over her lips and tilted her eyes skyward. "It's not a bad idea, though." Another pause. "I could sell it as a *First Trimester and Trying* line. It might open a whole new untapped market."

I groaned.

She placed her palms on the table and leaned forward. "Seriously, Kate. Think about it. Why should pregnancy clothes all be designed for when you're already fat? I could capitalize on the bigger-boobs, still-small-waist-line weeks." Her eyes jumped wide. "Ooh, and easy wash-and-wear outfits for the morning sickness days." She grabbed her purse and started digging. "Layers. We'd need lots and lots of layers."

She pulled out a notebook and pen and started sketching. "Morning sickness made you vomit right before that important business meeting? No problem! Pull off the soiled layer, toss it to the side, and you're good to go." Her smile grew so wide, I could see her back molars. "This is truly brilliant, Kate! I specialize in accessories, so I'll start there. What about eighteen-karat acupressure bracelets for nausea?"

I sipped cold coffee and watched my friend, momentarily captured by her enthusiasm. Somehow I had a feeling that *First Trimester and Trying* would be her next big success.

A few minutes later, she stopped writing and shoved the notebook back inside her purse. "Sorry, Kate. I needed to jot down a few thoughts before I forgot. Back to my moneymaking idea for you. Sam has a potential job for you at Teen Path HOME."

"Teen Path HOME? Isn't that a center for homeless youth?"

"You've heard of it?"

"Yes. I read an article about it in *Dollars for Change*." *Dollars for Change* was a local homeless advocacy newspaper. It shared stories about Seattle-area homelessness and poverty while employing some of its subjects as salespeople. "Since when is Sam involved with local nonprofits?"

She gave me a mock scowl. "You'd know if you ever returned my calls. The center's director, Gabriel Cousins, was Sam's roommate in college. He approached Sam a few months ago and asked for a technology grant. Sam toured the place, met some of the youth they serve, and fell in love. He joined the board of directors shortly after."

Rene leaned forward, attention now completely focused on me. "Gabriel wants to add some stress management classes, and Sam thinks yoga would be perfect. He sort of volunteered you to teach a trial series."

"Sam volunteered me?"

Her cheeks turned pink. "I hope you're not mad. I told him he should have talked to you first, but he's so excited, he got a little carried away."

I wasn't upset in the slightest. I was surprised and, to be honest, a little flattered. Sam had never taken one of my classes.

Rene continued. "It wouldn't have to be a forever thing, more like a trial run. We were thinking maybe a three-week series?"

Champagne-like bubbles of interest percolated beneath my sternum. Sam was right. I didn't have any experience teaching yoga to displaced teens, but I still might be able to help them. More selfishly, I might be able to help myself. At the very least, I'd be forced to get out of the house and focus on something besides my barren uterus for a change. "A three-week series won't be long enough. Let's make it six."

"Are you sure you're up for that long, Kate? Most of the teens you'll be teaching have been pretty traumatized. A lot of them suffer from mental illness and drug addiction."

"That's why yoga's so perfect!" My interest blossomed to enthusiasm. "Yoga has been proven to help veterans with PTSD, and it's a great tool for overcoming alcoholism and drug addiction."

"So you seriously want to do it?"

"Yes. I'm in, at least in enough to learn more. Before I fully commit, I'd like to check out the facility and meet some of the clients."

It seemed impossible, but Rene's smile widened. "Awesome. Sam will be so pleased. I'll have him connect you with Gabriel."

I strode back to my car through the retail parking lot, feeling more upbeat than I had in days. Lighter. Not happy, exactly. Certainly not optimistic. But less desolate. According to *The Yoga Sutras of Patanjali*, yoga's key philosophical text, pain is inevitable. The only thing we can control is how we react to it. Frankly, controlling internal turmoil had never been my strong suit. I *was* good, however, at helping others do so. That's why I dedicated my life to teaching yoga. I might not always be able to find inner peace, but at least I could offer it to my students.

My discussion with Rene had reminded me of something else I'd almost forgotten: I had a great life. Rather than dwell on what I *didn't* have, I'd focus on what I did: an amazing marriage, loyal friends, adored pets, a successful yoga studio. Michael's and my savings account might still be sucking fumes, but business at the studio was on the upswing. I could at least be grateful for that.

I crossed the white-lined lot and wove through the cars, so caught up in cataloguing blessings that I barely noticed the flyers trapped on each automobile's windshield. I paused long enough to wave at Michael's assistant, Tiffany, inside Pete's Pets and took a left into the underground parking garage, where I rented a covered parking space. Bella was deeply immersed in her favorite pastime: guarding my Honda from imaginary intruders.

Bella's separation anxiety had improved significantly since Michael and I had adopted Mouse, her polydactyl calico cat, but I still indulged my German shepherd's fondness for yoga studio ride-alongs whenever I could. On this late-October afternoon, the back seat of my ancient Honda was cool and secluded, and Bella could enjoy a brief respite from her role as a calico's pincushion.

At the sound of my approach, she sat up and pressed her nose against the back window. Her deep brown eyes sparkled. Her brilliant white teeth flashed in the canine version of a smile.

"Hey there, Bella baby," I said. "Want to go for a walk?"

I pulled out the keys to release my happy-looking canine, then paused. A paper was trapped underneath my windshield wiper.

What is it this time?

I was surprisingly nonplussed. Historically, notes left on my car had been harbingers of bad news, but I wasn't worried this time. Someone had obviously covered every car in the area with flyers. Annoying, but not worth the energy to stress about. I slid the folded page out from underneath my windshield wiper and opened it.

I immediately wished that I hadn't.

Above the top fold, a blood-red headline danced at me like a psychotic clown in a Stephen King movie.

Do You Yoga?

The next third of the page displayed a full-color photograph of scantily clad yogis posing in Warrior Two. Their biceps glistened with sweat. I recognized the studio instantly: Some Like It Hot Yoga.

At first I was irritated. How rude for another studio to plaster Serenity Yoga's parking lot with flyers. Irritation melted into confusion. Why bother? The one and only class I'd taken at Some Like It Hot Yoga had been a sweaty, slippery, smelly failure, but I'd been in the minority. Their downtown studio already had a much-greater-than-capacity following. Why would Some Like It Hot Yoga advertise in Greenwood, over five miles away?

My eyes drifted lower, and confusion spiked to alarm. *Opening November 15th. Ten Classes for Ten Dollars!* The address at the bottom was that of a large, newly empty retail space two doors down from Mocha Mia. As in, directly across the street from Serenity Yoga.

I unlocked the car, crumpled the flyer into a ball, and tossed it onto the passenger seat's floor. "Forget the walk, Bella. We're going home."

What could go wrong next?

FOUR

"DANG IT, I'M GOING to be late," I grumbled to no one in particular. I hated being behind schedule, but in this case, it wasn't my fault. I'd left home in plenty of time for my meeting with Gabriel at Teen Path HOME—or so I'd thought. Parking—except for coveted spaces in fifteen-dollar-an-hour lots—had proven to be practically nonexistent, and the center's building didn't have parking except for a couple of staff spots that Sam said were always in use. Most of the center's clients didn't have cars, so it wasn't a problem for them. For me, it meant driving around the area for fifteen minutes until I scored street parking six blocks away.

The last five days had been predictable, if uneventful. After several late nights of discussion, Michael and I had opted to let the universe decide our fertility fate, at least for now. We'd continue to time our lovemaking to coincide with my increasingly erratic cycle and hope to hit the pregnancy jackpot. Some lucky dog has to win, right? In the meantime, we'd start applying for loans large enough to purchase a few IVF cycles using my own eggs. It was the most reasonable option available to us. Provided we could find a bank to agree, that is.

Last week's flyers for Some Like It Hot Yoga had been the prelude to a flurry of advertising activities for its new location, including newspaper ads, radio promotions, and coupon mailings. A new sign mocked me from the storefront across the street: *Yoga—Ten Classes for Ten Dollars!* The *Help Wanted* sign below it mocked me more. At the rate my luck was going, I'd need to score a second job working for them.

But those were worries for another day. As I turned the corner to Third Avenue, I vowed to push all thoughts of fertility treatments, unwanted periods, competing yoga studios, and loan applications firmly to the back of my mind. Dad's voice echoed through my subconscious: *Good luck with that.*

Thanks a lot, Dad.

I stopped in front of a two-story building painted in bright, welcoming colors. Cherry red door, royal blue trim, lemon yellow exterior. The space nearly shouted, *Hope lives here!* The sign above the door read, *Teen Path HOME. Creating a Path out of Homelessness via Outreach, Mentoring, and Education.*

Sam was right. This place was special. I could practically feel positive energy emanating from the siding. The sidewalk in front of the facility was clean, in spite of the downtown location and the homeless youth loitering around it. Three male teens laughed and smoked cigarettes to the right of the doorway. A girl around fifteen huddled on the left, cuddling a red pit bull.

Only one thing darkened the area's bright energy: two teens arguing near a late-model Mercedes that was parked in a loading zone half a block away. The tiny blonde female of the pair gestured wildly with one hand and gripped a cigarette in the other. A dark blue backpack hung from her shoulder. Her gangly male counterpart wore a stony expression. As I watched, their fight escalated.

The male snarled something I couldn't hear and turned to leave. The girl blocked him. He yelled, "Give it a break already!" and pushed past her. She grabbed his arm, and he snapped. He placed his palms on her shoulders and shoved. Hard. She stumbled back several steps, tripped over the curb, and crashed to the pavement. Both her cigarette and her backpack fell to the sidewalk beside her.

I reacted instinctively, like Bella protecting her kitten. "Hey!" I yelled. "Knock it off! Leave her alone."

The young man whipped toward my voice. He growled something to his female companion, then ran. I couldn't hear what he said, but the exchange didn't look friendly. The girl curled into a ball and buried her face in her hands.

I jogged down the sidewalk and crouched beside her. "You okay?"

She slowly unfurled, shrugged her pack onto her shoulder, and stood. "Yes." The tears wetting her cheeks disagreed, but I didn't contradict her. My new friend was around fifteen or sixteen, impossibly thin, and several inches taller than me. The freckles across her nose stood in dark contrast to ivory skin. Her eyes never fully met mine, but they still made an impact. Arresting, gray-blue irises underscored by purple-black crescents.

I smiled and tried to appear nonthreatening. "I'm Kate. Why don't you come inside with me? Maybe I can buy you a cup of coffee."

"No, I . . . I need to go after . . . " She gazed down Third Avenue, but her companion had already disappeared. "That was my boyfriend, Jace. He's not usually . . . It was just an argument." Her lips trembled. "I have to go now. Thank you." She ran down the street after him.

I stared at her retreating shape, willing myself not to follow. Whatever was going on between the two was none of my business. My mother's voice gently chastised me. *Are you sure? She might be in trouble.*

I glanced at my watch, then stared after the blonde. My meeting was supposed to start five minutes ago. Subconscious rebukes notwithstanding, I had no time to chase after strangers. I reluctantly left the loading zone and entered the building.

The entrance opened to a lobby containing a pool table, several video games, and three comfortable-looking couches filled with teenagers slouched over cell phones. The faint aroma of cigarette smoke permeated the air, but the institutional-beige carpet was clean and the walls were decorated with inspirational posters. I glanced around for a reception desk and didn't see one, so I approached a group of teens at the pool table.

"I'm looking for Gabriel Cousins. He's the site director here. Any idea where I can find him?"

A friendly looking teen gestured with his thumb toward a hallway. "First office on the right. I'm pretty sure he's with someone, though. You might want to give them a few."

Since I was now almost ten minutes late, I strongly suspected that "someone" was supposed to be me. I followed his directions to a closed door with a nameplate that read, *Gabriel Cousins, Youth Counselor and Site Director.* I raised my hand to knock, but an angry female voice stopped me. Solid wood muffled the sounds coming from inside the office, but I could clearly make out a heated exchange.

"You can't keep doing this! I swear to god, Gabriel, if you let me down one more time, I'll—"

A male voice interrupted. "You'll what? Show up at my workplace and embarrass me? Newsflash. You already did that."

Ten minutes late or not, now clearly wasn't the time to interrupt. I moved away from the door and positioned myself close enough that I could see when it opened but far away enough that I wouldn't be tempted to eavesdrop. I killed time by examining a display of unframed drawings mounted along the hallway. I assumed they'd been created by Teen Path HOME's clients. The art varied in subject matter and talent, but each work evoked at least one deep emotion. Desperation. Rage. Longing. Surprising optimism. Directly in front of me, a young man's face was locked in an agonized scream. The title? *Self Portrait.*

I continued wandering the hall, studying each work and allowing myself to experience its impact. To my left, a young girl stared into a makeup mirror. A teenage skeleton stared back. The drawing next to it was split into halves. The right half was a remarkably life-like depiction of a child's bedroom, complete with a love-worn teddy bear, princess bedspread, and a light-filled window accented by baby blue curtains. The window overlooked a vibrant rainbow arched across a bright blue sky. The left half was a horror movie image of the same room. Tattered curtains, beheaded teddy bear, bloodstained bedspread, black clouds obscuring a charcoal sky. A blonde teenager with arresting gray-blue eyes stood, trapped, on the horror movie side. The resemblance was unmistakable. It was the young woman I'd spoken with outside.

The teen in the drawing placed her palm against an invisible force field, wanting to cross between worlds but unable to do so. The placard beneath the drawing read, *Another Life.* The artist had signed it *Rainbow.*

The door to Gabriel's office slammed open, and I jumped. A striking woman with caramel skin, straight dark hair, and deep brown eyes stormed through it. She gave a brief glance my direction, then charged through the lobby and crashed out onto the sidewalk. An African-American man emerged from the office and stared silently after her. Gabriel Cousins, I presumed. He was attractive, likely mid-to-late thirties. Not a strand of hair marred anything above his collarbones, including his scalp.

I cleared my throat to let him know I was present.

He jumped as if startled, then turned toward me. His eyes flashed with frustration, then softened. "Sorry, I didn't know you were standing there. You must be my ten o'clock."

"Yes." I approached him and held out my hand. "Kate Davidson. I'm here to talk about the yoga classes."

Gabriel grasped my hand and gave it a firm shake. "Sorry about the wait." He gestured with his head to the lobby. "Even sorrier about the scene you just witnessed. My wife stopped by unexpectedly and … well, we obviously had an argument. Not exactly a great first impression."

I smiled. "No worries on that score. I adore my husband, but we fight like cats. And the waiting's no trouble, either. I was running late myself, and I've been enjoying the drawings." I turned toward *Another Life*, drawn like iron toward a magnet. "This one with two rooms is amazing."

Gabriel joined me. "She's talented, isn't she?"

"She's incredible." I pointed at the girl in the drawing. "Is that the artist?"

"Yes. She includes herself in a lot of her work. I suspect she's re-creating scenes from her life, but that's an assumption. She hasn't said either way."

"You don't ask her?"

He shrugged. "When she's ready to open up, she will."

"I think I met her outside. I'm a little worried about her, actually. She was arguing with another teenager. A skinny guy with dark hair."

Gabriel's face turned to granite. "That would be Jace." He opened his mouth as if about to say something, then closed it again, frowned, and changed the subject. "All of this artwork is impressive, but *Another Life* is especially powerful. I'm trying to talk Rainbow into letting us use it in our next fund drive."

"Sam didn't tell me that the youth here were artists."

"They're not, for the most part. These drawings are part of our new art therapy program. For most of our clients, talk therapy—if they're willing to talk—doesn't do much. But get their hands busy with some pastels, and ... " He pointed to a dark, somehow vulnerable rendering of female genitalia. The sign underneath it read, *My Worth*. It was signed *Echo*. "I mean, look at that. What more needs to be said?" He shrugged.

"The artist can't believe that," I said.

Gabriel shook his head. "Unfortunately, she does. Believe me, she has her reasons. I've been trying to help her, but without much success. As long as she believes she's only worth what she can give sexually, she'll be hard to reach." His jaw hardened. "She's not alone. A lot of our clients have been abused—in more ways than one. Kids like Echo survive by being sex workers. I try to have compassion for all people, but adults who abuse kids ... They deserve a special place in hell."

I shuddered, for multiple reasons. "The artist who drew this is a kid?"

"Chronologically, I suspect she's around nineteen or twenty. Emotionally, she's a lot younger. That's true for most of our clients. We serve ages twelve to twenty-one, but the youth who come here are more like adolescents than adults. We all tend to call them kids regardless of how old they are.

He turned back to *Another Life*. "We've had talented people come through here before, but Rainbow may be the best."

I pointed at the signature. "Is Rainbow her real name?"

He shrugged. "It's what she goes by, anyway. I assume it's a street name. Like I said, she's been coming here for a couple of months, but I don't know much about her. She hasn't opened up to anybody."

"Is that common?"

"It's not *un*common. Our clients don't trust adults easily. Most didn't exactly grow up with the Cleavers. Almost three-quarters of them have been physically or sexually abused. I tell my staff that learning our clients' stories is a privilege that's earned with time, if ever."

"That must make counseling them tricky."

"Definitely. That's one of the reasons I'm so interested in offering yoga here. I've read that movement practices like yoga can help people process emotions physically. It might be a way to help our kids heal from trauma without forcing them to talk about it." He gestured toward the lobby. "But I'm getting ahead of myself. Let me give you a tour of the facility, and then we can talk."

Gabriel led me from the office area to the room with the pool table. His vocal tone changed, as if he were launching into a speech he'd recited many times before. "We're open from eight a.m. to eight p.m. seven days a week. We provide hot lunches Mondays through Fridays and offer educational programs as often as we can." He high-fived one of the kids lounging on a couch. "This is our recreation area, where the kids can relax, shoot some pool, and stay out of the rain. Pretty much all of our clients take advantage of the meals and the recreation area, but less than half participate in our training and counseling programs. We're hoping Sam's technology program will drive that number higher."

Next up was a large conference room. Gabriel tapped on the door, then opened it. The room held a half-dozen tables, at least ten times that many folding chairs, and an ancient-looking projector. Fluorescent lights flickered and buzzed in the ceiling.

"This is our main teaching space. It's where you'll be holding your yoga sessions. Three mornings a week we offer GED classes here. We also use it for staff and other ad hoc meetings." He gestured toward a metal chair rack next to the wall. "The room's pretty big, but we'll have to move tables and stack most of the chairs to make enough floor space for yoga. I hope it will work."

"It'll be fine." I was already strategizing how to make the space feel more inviting. To be honest, the room was about as inviting as the hospital rooms I taught in. But I could bring in soft music, maybe a bouquet of fresh flowers. The windows were too small to let in much natural light, so we'd have to keep the overhead lights on. But maybe I could invest in a few strands of Christmas lights. Yoga wasn't about where you practiced, anyway. It was about how you centered your mind.

Our next stop was a large industrial kitchen, which was next to the office area. A man wearing wire-rimmed glasses, a white apron, and a serious expression was showing a mustached young man how to dice vegetables. He looked up at us, gave a slight nod, and went back to his tasks.

"This is our chef, Chuck Brown."

The mustached youth elbowed the chef and smiled. "But you can call him Charlie, like the cartoon."

The chef gave him a droll look. "Keep chopping, smart guy." He wiped his hands on the apron and approached me. "No one calls me

Charlie, by the way. I'd shake your hand, but then I'd need to wash up again. Part of what I'm teaching this joker is safe food preparation. Are you one of our donors?"

"No," I replied. "I'm going to start teaching yoga classes here."

He didn't reply, but his jaw tensed.

Gabriel continued. "Chuck manages the hot lunch program I told you about and teaches classes on nutrition and safe cooking techniques. He also mentors our more dedicated clients on commercial food preparation." He elbowed the mustached teen. "This comedian is one of them. We hope to eventually raise enough funds to open a licensed cooking school. Then we can certify students, which should make it easier for them to get jobs in the restaurant industry."

"That's impressive," I said.

"Not nearly as impressive as what Sam is doing," Gabriel replied.

Chuck gripped his apron so hard his knuckles turned white. When he spoke, his words sounded clipped. "Are you done, Gabriel? We need to get back to work."

If Gabriel noticed Chuck's irritation, he didn't show it. "Come on," he said. "Let's go upstairs."

I paused before closing the kitchen door behind me. "It was a pleasure to meet you."

Neither Chuck nor his young friend replied.

Gabriel led me up a stairway to the second floor landing. We turned right and entered a dedicated art room filled with easels, paint-stained tables, and a row of colorfully painted cloths drying on a wire rack. A forty-something woman with graying dark hair walked around the room, occasionally encouraging the three young adults seated at a table in the corner.

Gabriel introduced her as Vonnie Carlson. "Vonnie is the inspiration behind all those drawings you saw in the office hallway." His hand moved to her shoulder, where it lingered a few seconds longer than I would have expected between coworkers.

She smiled. "Gabriel's being generous. I give the kids a few pointers, that's all. The inspiration comes from inside them." She nudged him playfully. "When are you going to talk the board into letting me host an art show?"

Gabriel grinned. "One step at a time, my dear. One step at a time."

An anemic-looking young woman with curly brown hair stood and carried a wet cloth to the drying rack. Swirls of blue, purple, yellow, and orange floated among pink and red hearts.

"That's gorgeous!" I said.

"We're using them to decorate solar lanterns," Vonnie replied. She pointed to a row of cylindrical metal frames, each containing an LED light and topped with a solar panel. "Each student makes two: one for themselves and one for a friend. Everyone deserves a little beauty and light." She nodded at the young artist, who had returned to her chair without acknowledging my compliment. "Isn't that right, Echo?"

Echo. The young woman who'd created the drawing titled *My Worth*. The one Gabriel had implied was a sex worker.

"Your lantern will be beautiful, Echo," I said.

She didn't look up, but her cheeks flushed at the compliment. A puffy, bright pink coat mended with green, blue, black, and orange duct tape was draped over the back of her chair. A homeless youth's version of Joseph's coat of many colors.

Gabriel smiled and spoke to the room. "You're all doing great work here." He touched my arm. "Come on, Kate. One last stop: the computer lab."

We went back to the second floor's open area, where he took out a key ring and unlocked a conference room. This one contained eight computer workstations with large, flat-screen monitors.

"The equipment looks new," I said.

"It is. Sam donated enough money for the machines, an on-site network, and updated wiring. The network isn't fully operational yet, but we're hoping to finish it late next month. In January, we'll start our computer skills training program."

"Will you be teaching the classes?"

"No, Sam's employees will. He's giving them paid time off to volunteer here and at other Seattle-area nonprofits as part of his company's new community service initiative." Gabriel shook his head, whether in awe or disbelief, I couldn't tell. "When I approached Sam for a donation, I thought I might score a couple of mothballed laptops and maybe an old LCD screen. He came through with all of this. I'm still floored."

I grinned. "I thought you knew Sam."

"I do, or at least I did back in college. Still, not many people—especially wildly successful people like Sam—are willing to go to bat in a big way for the homeless. It's easier to toss them a couple of bucks and then villainize them. Not Sam. He took a tour of the center, wrote a check for an amount far greater than my annual salary, and joined the board. What he's doing... It will change these kids' lives."

Gabriel's words didn't surprise me. Sam, like Rene, was passionate. When he committed himself to a project, he did it with his whole heart.

We exited the computer lab and headed toward the stairwell. I gestured to a closed-off area to the right. "What's over there?"

"That's our hygiene area."

"Hygiene area?"

"Think locker room. It's hard for homeless kids to find places to clean up, so we provide them with showering and laundry facilities. I'd show it to you, but we don't allow anyone but salaried staff members inside when we're open. Board members and visiting donors can't even tour it except when we're closed. It's for the kids' protection."

"Do the kids sleep here?" Without thinking, I'd slipped into calling Teen Path HOME's clients "kids."

"No. We'd need a special license to house teens under eighteen. We're not supposed to have clients on site after eight p.m."

The phrase "not supposed to" struck me as odd, but I didn't comment on it.

Gabriel continued. "The board goes back and forth on whether we should apply for licensing to provide overnight shelter to minors, but I think it's a terrible idea. The cost would be too high."

"Financially?"

"That too. Twenty-four-hour staffing is way beyond our current budget. But that's not what concerns me. Housing kids under eighteen would hamstring us, confidentiality-wise. We would be forced to report our underage clients to the authorities."

"Report them for what?"

"For being unaccompanied minors."

"That's a crime?"

"The law is complex, but basically, no one—individual or organization—can shelter youth under eighteen without notifying the police or their parents." He paused. "Between you and me, it sucks."

34

I flashed back to life as a teenager. Dad and I had fought—a lot. But he'd always had my best interests at heart. If I'd been forced to choose between enduring his wrath and spending a night on the streets, I'd have been better off with my father. Every time.

"Isn't getting them back with their families a good thing?" I asked. "I mean, teenagers aren't safe on the streets. If they have a home to go back to … "

Gabriel swept his hand through the air. "In an ideal world, you'd be right. But we don't live in an ideal world. I had a great upbringing. From what I've seen of you so far, I suspect you did, too. The kids that come here aren't that lucky. Most of them ran for a reason."

He stared off to the side for a moment, then back at me. "I worked with a fifteen-year-old runaway once. I knew she was hiding something, but I thought it was drug use. Her parents seemed great. They certainly fooled Child Protective Services. Turned out her older brother had been molesting her since she was twelve, and she never told anyone." He closed his eyes. "She killed herself two days after she was forced to go home."

"That's awful."

"You have no idea." His eyes darkened. "The best place for these kids is a stable, supportive home. I know that. I help them reconcile with their families as soon as they're ready. But I won't force one of my clients to go home unless I'm legally obligated to. That's why we don't ask ages or last names. It's our version of a don't-ask-don't-tell policy."

"And if you *are* legally obligated to?"

"Then I have no choice. I follow the law. We'd be shut down otherwise."

I couldn't hide my disillusionment. "There's no happily ever after for these kids, is there?"

"For some of them, no. Others? Yes." He guided me down the staircase. "My dad had a saying: 'Don't let what you *can't* do stop you from doing what you *can*.' We can't fix everything for these kids, but we can still help. We counsel them. We provide a warm meal. We train them so they can get jobs in the future. If they're ready to go home, we do everything in our power to make sure reunification is successful. Believe me, that's a lot."

"It is. Don't get me wrong—I think the work you do here is amazing. But honestly, how much help can I be? I'm just a yoga teacher."

"Never use the word 'just' when describing your life's contributions. Never. A mindfulness practice like yoga can teach these kids how to manage stress. It can help them learn how to control their impulses. If nothing else, it can give them a few minutes of peace."

Deep down inside, I knew he was right, but disillusionment still dulled my initial enthusiasm.

Gabriel laid his hand on my shoulder. "Hey, don't give up before you even start. After a class or two, you'll see what I mean. Let's go to my office and fill out the new-hire paperwork. I was able to scrape seventy-five dollars a class out of the budget. It's not much, but for now it's all I've got." He grinned. "If you're lucky, it might pay for your parking."

As we continued down the stairwell, I mentally debated whether or not I should offer to donate my teaching time. Ultimately, I decided I couldn't. Seventy-five dollars was a reasonable class fee, but by the time I factored in planning, set-up time, and parking costs, I'd barely make minimum wage. If I had any hope of paying for fertility treatments, I'd need to accept income wherever I could find it.

Gabriel opened the door to his office and ushered me through it.

I glanced through the doorway at his worn metal desk and screamed.

FIVE

SOMETHING SMALL, BROWN, AND furry with a hairless tail scurried past my right ankle.

"Aack! It's a mouse!" I shrieked.

Gabriel's demeanor changed in a heartbeat. From easygoing to frustrated, with a dollop of fear thrown in for good measure. "It's not a mouse, it's a rat! Catch him!"

He had to be joking. I was frozen. Stuck between irreconcilable impulses to run for the street or leap onto the desk.

Don't get me wrong, I love animals. All animals.

Except rats.

Gabriel pushed past me, and I stumbled into the hallway.

"God dammit, Lonnie!" He yelled. "Get back here." He chased the nine-inch-long rodent as it ran out toward the kitchen.

The young men at the pool table doubled up with laughter. Gabriel paused long enough to chastise them. "Don't just stand there. Check on Ed!" A brunette tween leaped from the couch and ran into Gabriel's office.

Ed? Did that mean there was a second one?

My eyes whipped back and forth across the carpet. My feet danced. I hopped from left foot to right foot and back again, terrified that a second rodent was about to crawl up my pant leg.

The way I saw it, I had two choices: stay here and hope that Rat Boy's twin didn't chomp on my ankle or run after Gabriel to the kitchen, where hopefully one of the vermin would soon be corralled.

I chose option two.

I was ten feet away from the kitchen when a man bolted from the stairwell. He collided with me and knocked me flat on my sitz bones.

"Watch where you're going!" he snapped.

I looked up—way up—at his face. He wore a navy blue power suit, a burgundy tie, and an irritated expression, all three of which were overshadowed by his dark, overgrown beard. I tried to suppress a wave of nausea. *Naturally.* The one thing that freaked me out more than rats. A beard.

I'd been working hard to overcome my pogonophobia—the irrational fear of beards—with reasonable success. But a rat/beard one-two punch was more than my stomach could handle. I swallowed my morning coffee for the second time. "Sorry I didn't see you coming."

Burgundy Tie leaned down and yanked me to standing, causing his facial hair to brush across my forehead. Something tickled the edge of my consciousness, but I was so traumatized by the sensation of hair on my face that it flitted away before I could grasp it.

"What's all the commotion about?" he asked.

I scrambled away from him and ran to the kitchen, calling over my shoulder, "Don't worry, Gabriel's handling it." *At least I hope so.*

I pushed open the kitchen door to the metallic clank of Chuck's chef's knife slamming against granite. A brown flash of fur scurried up the side of a large compost container and disappeared under the lid. The mustached teen chewed on his lower lip, trying to suppress an attack of the giggles.

Chuck threw off his apron and marched up to Gabriel, shaking a fist. "I told you, those filthy vermin can't be in here!"

"Mellow out, Chuck," Gabriel said. "I'll have him out in a second." He kneeled next to the compost container and reached inside. Three seconds passed, then he whooped a loud "Gotcha!" His hand re-emerged, holding a squirming, scaly-tailed troublemaker who was grasping a crescent of pizza crust between two tiny jaws. Gabriel lifted the mischievous creature, grumbled words never written in the Bhagavad Gita, and opened his fist. Lonnie scurried up his sleeve and came to rest on his shoulder. I would have sworn that he—the rat, not Gabriel—was chortling.

Chuck's entire body shook. "Get that disease-carrying nuisance out of my kitchen immediately. If the health department finds rat droppings in here, we'll be shut down. I swear, if I see either of those disgusting creatures in here again, I'm putting out rat poison."

A loud sneeze came from behind us, then a stern voice. "How long have we had a rat infestation in this facility?"

Four of the five of us—Gabriel, Chuck, the mustached teen, and me—turned toward the voice of the burgundy-tied man I'd collided with earlier. Lonnie was too busy gnawing on pepperoni to look.

Chuck pointed a shaking finger at Gabriel. "Ask him."

Gabriel gave Burgundy Tie a conciliatory smile. "There's no infestation, Greg. Lonnie is a domesticated pet rat. I have two of them in my office. They're not normally in the kitchen."

Chuck grumbled under his breath, "Yeah, right."

Lonnie leaned toward Chuck and wrinkled his nose. The rat version, I assumed, of sticking out his tongue.

Gabriel continued. "Someone must have left their cage open."

"Again," Chuck added. "It's the third time this month." He moved toward the man in the suit, whose name was evidently Greg. His voice grew louder and more impassioned. "It's like I told you when you asked me to speak at the board meeting. We're losing our focus, and it's getting ridiculous."

Burgundy Tie wiped at his nose. "You made your point, Chuck. But as I told you in our meeting, determining this facility's mission isn't up to you. It's not even completely up to Gabriel. You two need to stop arguing with each other and listen to us. You are employees, and you serve at our discretion."

"Hey now," Gabriel said. "No need to get nasty. We—"

Greg didn't let him finish. "Trust me. You can *both* be replaced." His eye twitched. "You would do well to remember that."

Gabriel flushed, but he remained silent.

Chuck ignored the word "both" in Greg's not-so-subtle reprimand. "Gabriel is taking us in the wrong direction. Teen Path HOME isn't an elementary school. We have no use for goldfish and guinea pigs. We're a young adult resource center designed to teach life and employment skills." He pointed his thumb at Gabriel. "Between the rats and the 'therapy animals' this fool keeps bringing in, it's starting to feel more like a petting zoo. And it keeps getting worse. First he cut the barista training program to hire that ridiculous art therapy teacher. Now he's planning to start yoga and meditation classes. If we're not careful, he'll close the kitchen to bring in palm readers and psychics."

Gabriel's jaw clenched. "We've been over this, Chuck. These kids need skills that will help them survive physically *and* emotionally. We can talk about it again later, but now is not the time." He nodded to Greg. "If you'll excuse us, Kate and I have paperwork to do. This show is over."

Gabriel marched out of the room without looking back. Lonnie peered over his shoulder, wiggling his whiskers as if waving goodbye. I slinked toward the door after them and smiled self-consciously at Greg. "It was nice running into you."

No response. Either he didn't get my joke or—more likely—it wasn't all that funny. So much for my stand-up comedy career.

I followed Gabriel across the recreation area and back to his office. As the door closed behind us, he groaned. "What a day. Of all the times for Greg to drop by on one of his surprise inspections."

"He's one of the board members?"

"Not an ordinary member. He's the president. The worst possible person to witness that scene between Chuck and me."

"What was he inspecting? The kitchen?"

"No, he—" Gabriel stopped, as if considering how much he should say. "Never mind. It's a long story. Greg has always come to the center every week or so to hang out with the kids. I usually don't mind. It's good for them to have positive role models. He used to give us advance warning, though. Lately he seems more like an inspector than a guest. Hell, the mood he's in today, he seems more like a prison guard."

Gabriel picked Lonnie off his shoulder and eased him into a cage containing a second rodent I assumed was Ed. Lonnie expressed his displeasure with a single, high-pitched squeal, then entertained himself by chasing his brother on their exercise wheel.

I watched them warily. The two little rascals were cute, in a beady-eyed, pointy-nosed, sharp-toothed sort of way. Teeny-tiny ears, black, intelligent eyes, long whiskers. One brown, the other dusty gray. But those tails ... I shuddered. "I have to ask. Why rats?"

Gabriel shrugged. "They're a symbol."

"A symbol?"

"Of street kids."

I winced before I could stop myself.

"It's not an insult, it's a compliment. Rats are intelligent, affectionate, resourceful survivors. Did you see how fast Lonnie scrambled into that compost bin? If I hadn't known where he was headed, we wouldn't have found him until he'd finished his snack and was darned good and ready to come back to my office. Rats are also quick learners. Watch this."

He turned to the cage. "Ed, come!" The gray rat jumped off the wheel, ran to the edge of the cage, and stood on his hind legs. "Lonnie, come!" His brown bunkmate jumped off the wheel and assumed a similar position." Gabriel pulled two pieces of kibble off his desk. "Okay boys, sit." Both rats plopped their rears to the floor simultaneously. Gabriel tossed the treats into the cage. "Good job."

"They know their names?"

"That's nothing. One of the kids taught them how to play basketball."

"That's pretty amazing," I said.

"Yep. Yet despite their positive attributes, rats have a terrible reputation. The minute most people see one, their first instinct is to either run from it or kill it."

He was right. When I first saw Lonnie, I'd wanted to bolt.

"So rats learn how to become invisible, exactly like homeless teens do. They have to if they want to survive. And they're amazingly affectionate. Once they trust you, they're your friends for life."

He sat in a worn swivel chair and leaned his forearms on the utilitarian desk. "The kids respond to the analogy, and they relax more around animals of any kind. That's why I arrange for therapy dog visits as often as I can. Spending time with animals is incredibly healing."

I couldn't argue. Even being around Mouse—who would rather fillet me than save me—calmed my nervous system.

"To be honest, though," Gabriel continued, "I'm not sure buying the rats was such a great idea. They need more space, and the kids keep leaving their cage open. Lonnie is a sucker for that compost bin, so he heads straight there, and every time either of them gets anywhere near the kitchen, Chuck blows an aneurysm. I tried taking them home, but my wife loathes them." He lifted his eyes toward the ceiling. "And now we have today's incident. Chuck has one more reason the board should fire me and give him my job."

"I take it the two of you don't get along."

"It's not personal, or at least it didn't start that way. When the last site director left, everyone thought Chuck was a shoo-in for the job. He's been working at Teen Path HOME since it opened." Gabriel shrugged. "Luckily for me, the board decided my MBA was more impressive than Chuck's experience. He seethed quietly until I cut the barista training program six months ago. It was a failure, but Chuck refused to see that, and now he questions all of my decisions. He thinks diverting money to art therapy is ludicrous."

"I don't think he's a fan of yoga, either."

"He's not, which is another reason Greg's visit today was such terrible timing. Sam and I snuck your yoga classes in under the radar. If Chuck convinces Greg to bring it up at the board meeting, they might force me to cut it." He frowned. "Maybe I can sell your classes as vocational training. Can you train the participants to become yoga instructors?"

I wasn't sure teaching homeless kids a profession that guaranteed a lifetime of poverty was the best idea, but I didn't say that. "Learning to teach yoga is more complex than you think. It takes a minimum of two hundred hours of training."

"Seriously? I had no idea it was that complex."

I grinned. "It's more complicated than stretching, that's for sure."

I spent the next thirty minutes filling out new employee paperwork and listening to a heartbreaking list of dos and don'ts for interacting with teens at the facility.

"Your goal is to develop a healthy relationship with your students," Gabriel said.

"No trouble there. That's always my goal."

"It may be tougher than you think."

"Why's that?"

"These kids are like feral cats. They don't know who to trust. Believe me, they'll challenge you. You need to have thick skin and prepare for the unexpected. Grab a staff member if any physical conflicts erupt."

"Are you telling me I should expect fistfights in my yoga classes?" I grinned to let him know I was joking.

He didn't grin back. "It's entirely possible. Conflicts that start on the street sometimes end in this building. I'll attend your first few classes, just in case something happens that you're not trained to handle."

The don'ts were even more sobering.

"Many of our clients have been sex trafficked. Others have been forced to trade sex for food or shelter. You need to make them feel safe. That means no touching and no standing behind them. Avoid poses that mimic sexual positions. Otherwise you might trigger a flashback."

My heart broke at the very idea. Practicing yoga should feel, above all else, safe.

Gabriel continued. "Remember, these kids didn't end up here on purpose. They've made bad choices, but we all have. The rest is bad timing, bad luck, or bad circumstances."

For a few seconds, my mind wandered. When I was seventeen, I had a couple of beers at a party and fell asleep driving home. The car drifted right, and I woke up in a ditch. Nothing—other than Dad's Explorer and my social life for the six weeks I was grounded—had been damaged.

If the car had drifted left?

How many of these kids had simply ended up on the wrong side of that metaphor?

Gabriel's voice startled me out of my thoughts. "Any questions?"

"I'm sure I'll have hundreds, but for now, I think I've got it."

He reached out his hand, and we shook. "Awesome. I'll see you next Wednesday."

SIX

I ARRIVED HOME TO Bella's patented feed-me-now dance. "Sorry, sweetie. Lunch will be ready in twenty minutes."

Bella knew our meal preparation routine as well as I did, but that didn't stop her from trying. She suffered from Exocrine Pancreatic Insufficiency, an autoimmune disease that left her unable to digest food without special medication, but you'd never know it to look at her. Her teeth were bright white, her coat shone, and her ribs were covered with a healthy layer of fat. She barely resembled the emaciated animal I'd taken in three years ago.

I spent the next thirty minutes grinding, medicating, and incubating Bella's kibble, feeding Mouse a tin of organic salmon cat food, and nibbling a vegan protein bar. Lunchtime duties complete, I sat down to work.

I had less than three weeks until Some Like It Hot Yoga's grand opening, and I needed to decide how Serenity Yoga would respond to the new competition. I could never match their ten-classes-for-ten-dollars deal—at least not while paying my employees anything close to minimum wage—but perhaps I could offer a small discount to our current students.

I frowned. A small discount wouldn't be enough. If Some Like It Hot Yoga stole—I mean, recruited—our current students, I'd have to tweak our offerings. Hot Yoga had many benefits, but it wasn't appropriate for everyone. I could add to our therapeutic offerings and build our prenatal program. How about yoga for menopause? I didn't know from experience, but surely hot flashes and 105-degree exercise were mutually exclusive.

Before I knew it, it was almost five o'clock and time for me to head to the studio. My first class didn't start until six, but I wanted to fit in a short personal practice first. I gave Bella an extra-large ostrich tendon, rubbed catnip on Mouse's scratching post, and drove to the studio. I'd barely rolled out my mat when the front door's lock clicked open.

The smell of full-bodied caffeine wafted into the studio. Tiffany's voice called out. "It's me, Kate. I saw you drive in and thought you might like coffee."

If you'd asked me two years ago, I'd have assured you that Michael's assistant, Tiffany, would never give me anything but a migraine. When the twentyish blonde bombshell started working at Pete's Pets, she and I were rivals for Michael's affection. Forced time together, a couple of ill-conceived adventures, and a number of stern lectures from Michael had convinced us to give up our feud. Now I considered Tiffany a friend. She even worked part time for me at Serenity Yoga.

Still, dropping by unannounced, bearing my favorite guilty pleasure? The girl was sweetening me up for something.

I abandoned my mat and joined her in the lobby. Tiffany sported another new yoga outfit. Today's ensemble consisted of strappy black sandals, pink capri leggings smothered in smiling French Bulldogs, and an uncharacteristically loose black T-shirt. The words *Crazy Cat Lady* covered her breasts. To my knowledge, Tiffany had never owned a cat. Then again, why should that be surprising? She didn't practice yoga, either.

"New pet store outfit?" I asked.

Tiffany glanced down, as if she couldn't remember what she was wearing. "Um, yes. It's not my style, but it beats wearing one of those ugly Pete's Pets T-shirts." She tucked a strand of hair behind her ear, revealing an earring in the shape of a Boston terrier.

"Cute earrings," I said.

She nibbled at her lower lip, uncharacteristically quiet.

"What's up?"

"I brought you a triple soy macchiato. Enough caffeine to keep you buzzing till a week from Saturday." Her hand trembled as she handed me the cup. "I ... um ... I need to talk to you about something."

I peered at her over the cup while I sucked up foamy, full-bodied stimulants. I'd been mistaken. Tiffany wasn't here for a favor. The girl's entire body radiated pure, unadulterated guilt. What trouble had she gotten into this time? She'd matured considerably since she'd started dating Chad, her yoga-teacher boyfriend, and I'd firmly believed that her Kate-annoying, car-vandalizing, Michael-tempting days were over. Evidently I'd been wrong.

"It's about Chad," she continued. "I mean, about me and Chad. I mean ... Oh, shoot. Michael told me he should talk to you, but I wanted to do it myself. Now I'm messing it all up."

If Michael wanted to be Tiffany's and my go-between, whatever she was about to confess had to be awful. The skin on the back of my neck prickled with worry-laced annoyance. "It's okay, Tiffany. Tell me. Whatever you did, we'll figure out how to deal with the fallout later."

Tiffany looked confused. "What I did? Fallout?" Her eyes widened. "Oh, no. I didn't do anything. Not on purpose, anyway. I mean, of course I *did* something, but ..."

"Out with it already!"

Tiffany closed her eyes, then swallowed. Five full seconds ticked by before she opened them again. "I'm pregnant."

That simple, two-word sentence dropped an anvil onto my heart. I wanted to hug my friend and assure her that I was delighted at her good news. I wanted to tear the child out of her womb and implant it in my own. I wanted to drown myself in the studio's table fountain. Instead, I kept my facial expression neutral and tried not to burst into tears.

Tiffany stared at her burgundy-lacquered toenails. "It was an accident."

An accident. The most unfair phrase in the English language.

"Chad and I wanted to have kids someday, just not yet. The timing is terrible, but we'll make it work."

"I'm happy for you." I hugged her, but the embrace felt wooden.

When I pulled away, Tiffany's eyes were wet. "Kate, I know we've been stupidly competitive with each other in the past, but this time I truly didn't mean to upstage you. I know you probably can't have kids, and—"

I stumbled several steps back. "You know? How?"

Tiffany's cheeks turned as red as her toenails, but she didn't reply.

My words came out in a hiss. "Michael told you, didn't he?" Michael had sworn to me that he wouldn't tell anyone about my infertility. He'd *sworn.* Sure, I'd told Rene, but Rene was family. Tiffany was ... Tiffany.

I'll bet he would have kept his trap shut if his superhuman sperm were the issue.

"Please don't be mad at him, Kate," Tiffany begged. "He's been so gloomy lately, and I was worried. I practically dragged it out of him."

My fingernails dug into my palms, but I pasted on a fake smile. "I'm delighted for you and Chad, really." Deep down inside, it was the truth. As desolate as I felt for myself, I was truly excited for her. And frustrated. And angry. And desperately jealous.

Tiffany didn't look convinced, but she pressed forward. "I need to talk to you about something else."

What? Did she win the lottery, too?

"Michael said he'll give me three months of maternity leave, but he'll need to hire temporary help, so he can only afford to pay my salary for six weeks." She paused as if carefully considering her words. "Babies aren't cheap."

Tell me about it. Be glad you don't need to finance fertility treatments.

She continued. "Chad says he'll never make enough money teaching yoga to support a family. I knew he'd started applying for full-time jobs, but I didn't know where until this morning. I swear, Kate, if he'd told me, I never would have let him."

The slow-moving cogs in my brain finally clicked into position. Chad wasn't simply a *yoga* teacher, he taught *hot* yoga. As in Some Like It Hot Yoga. I had a feeling I knew where Tiffany was headed, but I asked anyway. "You never would have let him do what?"

She took a deep breath and held it, as if bracing herself for an explosion. "Chad's going to be the studio manager of the new Some Like It Hot Yoga." She held up her hands. "He didn't put those flyers on the cars in the parking lot. That happened before he was hired. But Kate, his boss expects him to aggressively recruit new students.

Half of his salary is based on the number of memberships he gets in the first six months."

Logical Kate knew that Tiffany wasn't to blame for my new business competition. Chad wasn't, either. If Some Like It Hot Yoga hadn't hired Chad, it would have been somebody else. Illogical Kate still felt betrayed.

"Kate, I'm sorry. Do you want me to tell him to quit?"

My plastic smile widened until my teeth hurt. "Of course not. Full-time jobs are hard to find in the yoga industry. I'm glad for him."

Tiffany's body relaxed, but her face still looked tentative. "Maybe it will be a good thing. Serenity Yoga doesn't offer Hot Yoga, so you and Chad will be going after completely different students. Maybe it's like restaurants. More on the same block increases business for everyone."

"Maybe." My fake smile remained firmly in place, but my gut wasn't fooled. Serenity Yoga was in trouble.

I taught my six o'clock All Levels and my seven-thirty Yoga for Relaxation classes on yoga teacher autopilot, cycling emotionally between worry, depression, and frustration. Part of me wanted to hurry home to confront Michael. The other part wanted to hide in the supply room and pretend my conversation with Tiffany had never happened. At ten-fifteen, I ran out of excuses and was forced to go home, where I was greeted by a spotless kitchen and the aroma of freshly baked vegan brownies, sure signs that Michael knew he was in trouble.

He waited in the living room, perched awkwardly on the edge of the sofa while pretending to read *Seattle Dog* magazine. His gorgeous blue-green eyes watched me warily. He grabbed a newly opened bottle of Chardonnay, poured an extra-large glass, and handed it to me. "Anything interesting happen at the studio today?"

"If you mean did Tiffany tell me she was pregnant, yes. If you mean did I find out that my husband was a tattletale-ing traitor, yes to that too."

"Kate, we need to talk about—"

I thunked the glass on the end table and held up both hands. "Oh, you bet we do, mister, but not now. I'm ovulating. Time for some hot, scheduled, angry sex." I stomped halfway up the staircase, then turned and growled over my shoulder, "It had better be good."

Michael looked longingly at the wine bottle, then followed meekly behind.

Twenty frustrating, no-baby-making minutes later, we skulked back downstairs. Michael avoided eye contact and sat stiffly on the couch. Bella jumped up next to him and rested her chin on his lap.

I flopped on the overstuffed chair across from them both, smiled at my calico fur child, and patted my thigh. "Here kitty, kitty."

Mouse flattened her ears and hissed. Figured.

"Sorry, Kate," Michael said. "I don't know what happened. I've never had ... performance issues before."

I picked up the still-full wine glass, downed the oaky gold tranquilizer in three long gulps, and refilled it. Good Wife Kate would have assured Michael that Mister Mopey was no problem. And of course, it wasn't. Until our fertility issues surfaced, Michael and I had enjoyed a fabulous sex life.

Good Wife Kate wasn't in the room, however. Shriveled Shrew Kate was. I couldn't assure Michael that tonight's botched lovemaking was okay, because it didn't *feel* okay. Mister Mopey was one more piece of evidence that I was no longer desirable. No longer a real woman.

I took another large swallow of wine. "Why in the hell did you have to talk about my fertility issues with Tiffany? Don't you know how stupid that makes me feel?"

Michael nudged Bella off his lap and stood. "They're not *your* fertility issues, Kate, they're *ours*. You can't seem to understand that. Frankly, you don't seem to understand much of anything anymore. I told Tiffany I should be the one to tell you about her pregnancy. I knew you wouldn't take it well."

"I'm not upset that Tiffany got pregnant. I'm upset that you blabbed to her that I can't. Michael, that information is personal. How would you like it if I ran around telling everyone that you're impotent?"

Michael shrank like a slug doused in table salt. "Tonight was one time, Kate." He shook an index finger in front of his face. "One. Performing on demand with someone who's pissed at you isn't easy, you know. And Tiffany isn't everyone." He made finger quotes around the last word. "She's my friend."

I felt like a jerk, which was appropriate, since I'd just acted like one. I abandoned the chair, grasped Michael's arm, and guided him next to me on the couch. "I'm sorry, Michael. That was uncalled for. But don't you see? That's how I feel all the time. I feel impotent. Like I'm not a real woman."

"Kate, honey, that's ridiculous. You're gorgeous, sexy, intelligent, funny, and ... " His voice trailed off.

"And?"

"And sometimes unreasonable. Lately, you're self-centered. We've always fought, but it used to feel fair. Now everything has to revolve around you and your insecurities."

My eyes burned, but I remained silent. Michael continued. "I know this is hard for you, but honey, it's hard for me, too. You're not the only one in this relationship who wants a child. I never should have promised to keep our fertility issues a secret. I need to talk about it. Tiffany may act immature sometimes, but she's surprisingly easy to talk to. She's the closest thing to a confidant that I have."

I hated to admit it, but he was right. "Michael, I'm sorry. I can be a jerk sometimes."

He didn't disagree. Then again, I didn't want him to. We were finally being honest with each other.

Fifteen more minutes of conversation, another glass of wine, and a much more successful baby-making attempt later, Michael and I went to bed. I stared at the ceiling until his soft snoring lulled me to sleep.

SEVEN

THE NEXT WEEK PASSED in a paradoxically sluggish flurry of activity. I taught yoga classes, filled out loan applications, and had more sessions of mechanical, scheduled sex with Michael. The doctor had said that our chances of conceiving naturally were slim to none, but a girl can pray for a miracle, right?

On Wednesday afternoon, I said goodbye to Bella and Mouse, grabbed my purse and a boom box I'd borrowed from the studio, and headed back to Teen Path HOME, feeling simultaneously excited and nervous. I'd pored over research on yoga for posttraumatic stress disorder and carefully designed a class that would engage teenage minds. I knew yoga could help these kids. The question was, could I get them to practice?

I spent almost a half hour looking for an affordable parking spot, then jogged to the center's entrance, arriving a scant fifteen minutes before my class was scheduled to begin. The sidewalk in front of the building was empty. No teens gathered outside the front door or chatted in groups around it. Was that a good sign or a bad one?

A brightly colored sign was taped to the front door. *Yoga class today at 1:30. Join us!* A clip-art woman in Downward Facing Dog decorated the bottom half of the sign. A naked, hand-drawn man joined her from behind in a pose straight from *The Kama Sutra.*

Fabulous.

I affected an expression of calm confidence and pushed through the door, hoping to see a large turnout. The recreation area was a ghost town. No teens traded gibes near the pool table or slouched on the couches. Scaly-tailed Lonnie didn't even make an appearance. If it weren't for the sound of banging pots in the kitchen, I'd have thought the entire building was empty.

I moved to the conference room, where I was thwarted by a closed door, lowered blinds, and a sign that read, *Therapy Visit in Progress.* Multiple voices murmured from within. I glanced at my watch and frowned. One-fifteen. Gabriel had reserved the conference room starting at one o'clock. This was officially my time.

I reached for the doorknob, then remembered what Gabriel had told me. Homeless kids didn't open up easily. If I interrupted a therapy session at the wrong time, hard-won progress could be demolished.

Crap. Crap, crap, crap, crap, crap.

I set the boom box on the floor and hustled to Gabriel's office instead. That door was closed, too. Gabriel's voice boomed from inside, punctuated by stuttering periods of silence. "I told you before…" Silence. "But…" Silence again. "Would you please listen to reason?"

Double-booked conference room or not, I couldn't interrupt Gabriel in the middle of an argument, even if it was likely one being held over the phone. So what was I supposed to do now? I considered seeing if Chuck was in the kitchen, but I wasn't in the mood to deal with his ire, so I decided to try Vonnie, the art teacher, instead.

The area at the top of the stairway was empty, except for a blonde teenage girl. *Rainbow.*

This time she wasn't smoking—or arguing with a lanky boy, for that matter. She was putting the finishing touches on a mural that spanned the wall adjoining the art room.

My mind formed a single word. *Wow.*

Like the drawing displayed in the downstairs hallway, the work-in-progress portrayed two scenes. This time the left half was a lush, park-like setting covered in thick grass, yellow wildflowers, and dark green trees. On the right, a similar landscape had been decimated by fire. All that remained were smoldering tree trunks, scorched earth, and snow-like ash dotted with yellow-orange embers. A crumbling rope bridge spanned a river separating the two sides. A terrified-looking girl with light blue eyes stood at a gap in the midpoint. Her right hand reached forward. She gaped back over her left shoulder at the devastation.

I stared at the painting, transfixed. The work was powerful. So powerful, I swore I could hear the girl's gasps. I could feel the bridge cracking around her. I wanted to warn her to turn back before the structure collapsed. I wanted to beseech her to hurry forward. Above all, I wanted to know if she'd make it.

I cleared my throat to let Rainbow know I was standing behind her. "That's amazing."

She didn't look up from her painting. "Thanks."

"What do you call it?"

"I haven't decided. *Escape,* maybe?" She laid her brush on an easel and wiped her hands on her apron. "Vonnie asked me to paint a mural that represents the words Teen Path HOME. I'm not sure this is what she had in mind." She shrugged. "I guess I'll find out when she gets back next week."

"She's not here? I wanted to ask her when I can get inside the conference room."

"The therapy dog's in there now. They were supposed to be in the recreation area, but Chuck got pissed about a dog being so close to the kitchen, so they moved to the conference room. I'd be there too, but I wanted to finish this."

"Do you know when they'll be done?"

She shrugged. "Why don't you ask them?"

Which was obviously what I should have done in the first place. I trudged downstairs and cracked open the door to the conference room. At least two dozen young adults gathered around a small, happy-looking yellow lab wearing a green vest with the words *Therapy Dog* written across the side. A dark-haired young woman kneeled on the ground next to her.

My face split into a smile. "Nicole! What are you and Hope doing here?"

Nicole jumped to her feet with the energy only an eighteen-year-old can muster. "Kate! I heard there was a yoga class today, but I had no idea you'd be teaching it." She handed Hope's leash to one of the teens. "Watch her for a second, would you? Kate and I need to catch up." She closed the space between us and gave me a huge hug. "What a wonderful surprise!"

"Do you work here?" I asked.

She gestured with her thumb to the dog. "Hope does. I'm just the dog taxi."

The small yellow lab looked nothing like the puppy mill survivor Nicole had adopted nearly two years ago. Back then, Hope had been frightened, skinny, and covered in filth. Today, her eyes sparkled, her tail wagged, and her coat was thick and lustrous. If she missed her offspring, you certainly couldn't tell. Her whole body wiggled with happiness.

Likewise, Nicole seemed transformed—from a shy, sullen teenager to a striking young adult. She was still a good twenty pounds overweight, but no traces of acne marked her face. Her smile was bright; her energy, happy.

I pointed to Hope's vest. "She's a therapy dog now?"

Nicole grinned. "I promised Mom that I'd train her, didn't I? Getting Hope's therapy dog certification was my senior year community service project. I didn't plan to keep doing site visits after graduation, but she loves it too much to stop." She winked. "I even talked my psych professor at U-dub into giving me extra credit." U-dub was the local vernacular for the University of Washington.

Nicole gestured with her chin toward her canine pal. "Look at her. She was born for this." Hope was cuddled between two young girls, so happy I would have sworn she was purring.

"She's amazing, Nicole. You saved her."

"Nope. We saved each other."

I smiled. "I'm sorry to cut this short, but I need to set up."

"No problem." Nicole gave me another quick hug, then grabbed Hope's leash. "Come on, everyone. Let's clear out."

The teens replied with a collective groan. "Hope's leaving already?"

"She can stay a few more minutes," Nicole said. "We'll hang out near the front door. If Chuck sees us again, at least we'll have an escape route."

Nicole and Hope walked in a perfect heel through the conference room door. Every single one of my potential yoga students filed out with them. They'd all come back when class started, right?

I started prepping the room by pushing the tables against the wall, which was no small feat for a 110-pound yoga teacher working by herself. Then I formed a large circle with twenty of the room's metal folding chairs. I didn't usually like teaching in a circle, but in this case it would provide several benefits: circles helped build community, no one could stand behind anyone else, and all of the students could easily see me. Gabriel said the center couldn't afford yoga equipment, but that was okay. I wanted to teach these kids a practice they could do on their own. When everything you owned had to fit into a backpack, yoga mats, blocks, straps, and bolsters were unaffordable luxuries.

A minute before class was scheduled to start, I tossed my purse under the table behind me, plugged in the boom box, and turned on my favorite Deva Premal CD. The resonant notes of Vedic chanting filled the space, calming my nervous system. I could almost feel the city's grime melt from my eardrums.

Paradise.

A teenager with a shaved head, bulging biceps, and rich brown complexion peaked through the door. He gaped at the boom box, then gestured toward the circle of chairs. "What's this?"

I flashed what I hoped was a welcoming smile. "A yoga class. Why don't you join us?"

"Yoga? Ain't that the flexibility shit?"

I smiled. "Well, yes, yoga does help with flexibility. But it's also good for the mind."

He waved his hand through the air. "Later, dude."

He was my sole visitor. Five minutes after class was scheduled to start, I still perched on the edge of a folding chair, trying not to look desperate.

Gabriel strode through the door. "Sorry I'm late. I was on the phone with my wife." He glanced at me, then at the circle of empty chairs. "Why are you sitting in here by yourself? Even the Pied Piper had to wander around to get followers, and he had a magic flute. Come on."

He led me back to the recreation area, huge smile on his face, voice booming. "Who's coming to this yoga class?"

Silence. Nothing but disinterested stares. He moved to the pool table and challenged four young men to a stretch-off. Nope. He accosted the teens still huddled around Hope. No thank you. He even hazarded a stop in the kitchen. Nada.

After ten minutes of cajoling, Gabriel had recruited a grand total of four students. Five, if you counted the therapy dog. Nicole, Rainbow, himself, and a blond male wearing a filthy gray hoodie. Hope lay at attention next to Nicole's chair.

The four humans sat equidistant from each other, empty chairs forming impermeable force fields between them. Gabriel offered a shrug. Nicole, a bright smile. Rainbow looked shyly down at her fingernails. The male leaned back in his chair, pulled the hood down over his face, and promptly began snoring. Rainbow glanced his direction and giggled. Hope cocked her head at him curiously, then flopped on her side to join him.

Disappointment hardened like wet clay in my stomach, but I turned off the music and prepared to teach. The deep thrums of hip-hop thudded from the recreation area, accompanied by good-natured gibes and the ceramic clank of pool balls. I considered turning the CD back on, but Deva Premal sounded exactly like I felt. A woo-woo interloper, intruding where she didn't belong. We were like cartoons in a child's activity book. *Which object doesn't belong?* Chimes, music, and murmured instructions were all superficial. My expectations for yoga class seemed ridiculous, too.

The goal of a yoga teacher (a good one, anyway) is to meet your students where they are and take them to a state of greater balance. Thus far, I'd attempted to meet my students where they *weren't* so I could take them somewhere they probably didn't want to go. No wonder my class was flopping.

I forged on. "Close your eyes and notice your breath."

My second mistake. Snoozing Guy slouched deeper. Rainbow glanced nervously back and forth, as if afraid someone was going to grab her.

"On second thought," I said, "keep your eyes open, but find a comfortable place to focus your gaze."

Rainbow's eyes stopped shifting. She kept them open, but stared toward the floor. Snoozing Guy kept snoring, but I could live with that. "Notice your breath and begin to make it longer."

I kept the class purposefully short and taught simple poses that connected movement and breath. When sounds intruded, as they often did, I asked my students to bring their attention back to the breath. "Yoga can help you find calmness in chaos. See if you can practice that here. Try to remain focused in spite of the sounds around us."

My students—three of them, anyway—seemed to respond. Nicole smiled and moved fluidly with her breath. Gabriel interspersed glances at the male teen with slow, smooth exhalations. Rainbow's shoulders dropped down from her ears. The tension in her body melted. For the first time that afternoon, I felt worthy.

I finished class with a three-minute Savasana (yoga's pose of quiet rest) performed seated in chairs. When I rang the chimes, all four human participants opened their eyes. Snoozing Guy surprised me by giving me two thumbs-up and saying, "That was epic. I haven't slept that well in weeks."

I assumed it was a compliment.

My tiny cohort of students filed out while Gabriel and I reassembled the conference room. When they were all gone, I spoke. "That wasn't exactly earth shattering."

Gabriel looked surprised. "What? You mean because of the low attendance? You need to have patience. For the three who came, you rocked their world."

"Two. One of them was a volunteer, and I already knew her." I wrapped the cord around the boom box and lifted it. "If this yoga pilot is going to be successful, we need to do better. Five more weeks isn't much time to build an audience."

Gabriel pushed in the last chair. "Maybe we should lightly incentivize the class."

"Incentivize it?"

"Give out gift cards for attendance."

I winked. "Ah, you mean bribe people to attend."

Gabriel grinned. "I prefer the word 'incentivize.' I have a bunch of donated gift cards in my office. We sometimes use them to build attendance in new offerings. A five-dollar grocery card or a few cell phone minutes, and … " He snapped his fingers. "Poof! Suddenly classes have waiting lists."

"Cell phone minutes? These kids don't have homes, but they can afford cell phones?"

"Fancy iPhones are rare, but pretty much everyone has at least a basic burner phone. It's their link to each other, which means it's their link to safety."

"Well, I'm all for trying anything that will—"

My words were cut off by a crash and the sound of angry yelling.

EIGHT

A MALE VOICE SHOUTED from the recreation area, "Give me my money. Now!"

Gabriel bolted out of the conference room. I grabbed my purse from under the table and ran behind him. Two young men, a redhead and a Hispanic with a close-cropped beard, were arguing in the recreation area. The redhead pinned the other against the pool table with a pool cue. Chuck, who must have come from the kitchen, was trying to get between them.

Gabriel pulled the redhead off the bearded youth's chest. Chuck grabbed his counterpart and wrestled him to the side. Both teens stopped struggling, but their bodies remained rigid. Fighting roosters prepared to jump into battle.

After a few seconds, Chuck and Gabriel made eye contact, then released the teens simultaneously.

"What's going on here?" Gabriel snapped.

The redhead spoke first. "I won the game, fair and square. Spider owes me five bucks, and now he won't pay."

"He cheated," Spider replied. "Besides, everyone knows you don't allow gambling here."

The redhead raised a fist and stepped toward him. "Then why'd you take the bet?"

Gabriel grabbed his arm and yanked it behind his back. "Knock it off, both of you. We'll work this out in my office." He nodded my direction. "I'll see you next week, Kate."

As Gabriel and Chuck marched the two young men toward Gabriel's office, I headed back to my car. Almost an hour later, I arrived home in Ballard and pulled into my bungalow's driveway. I still felt jittery, both from the fight I'd witnessed and from the forty-five minutes I'd spent battling downtown Seattle's traffic. I strode through the front door and grabbed Bella's leash. "Come on girl, we need to walk off some stress."

Green Lake Park, which contained our favorite three-mile walking trail, would do nicely. I drove fifteen minutes to the iconic lake and stopped my car near the community center's concession stand. The early November air felt brisk when I got out, so I slipped on a hat and gloves and rummaged inside my purse for my wallet. A hot cup of coffee was exactly what I needed to shake off the chill. Granted, caffeine wasn't the best choice for a stressed-out yogi, but what's an addict to do?

I couldn't locate the wallet by feel, so I started pulling items from my purse. *Studio keys, lip gloss, sunglasses, breath mints…*

Thirty seconds later, my purse was empty. I searched the entire car. On the floor, between both front seats, underneath them. I found an old plastic water bottle, three quarters, and at least two shedding seasons' worth of dog hair, but no wallet. I'd had it when I paid for parking before my yoga class, and I remembered putting it back inside my purse on the way to Teen Path HOME. Could it have fallen out when I tossed the purse under the conference room table? I shifted the car into reverse and headed back to the center.

A truck was parked in the loading zone, but I got lucky for once and found a spot on the street two blocks away. In fifty-degree weather, Bella would probably be safe inside the car for fifteen or twenty minutes, but it was parked in full sun, so I couldn't risk it. I clipped on her leash. "Guess you're coming with me." I plugged the three quarters I'd found into the meter. Eight minutes. "No time to waste, sweetie. Let's go!"

Bella, always excited to explore regardless of the location, leaped out of the Honda and trotted happily beside me, pausing only to mark her new territory. Unlike earlier, the sidewalk in front of Teen Path HOME's entrance was bustling. I recognized a number of teens, but my eyes locked on three. Rainbow and Jace loitered half a block away, near the loading zone again. This time they were accompanied by another young woman. I recognized her pink, duct-tape-covered coat instantly. Echo.

The three were locked in a bizarre triangle that didn't seem at all amorous. Rainbow sulked, arms crossed, glaring at Jace and grumbling under her breath. Jace ignored Rainbow and spoke sternly to Echo. Echo stared at the ground. Her fingers were twitchy; her eyes, desperate. She rubbed her hands up and down her arms, as if she were freezing inside her thick winter jacket in spite of the fifty-degree sun.

She leaned toward Jace, clearly pleading. He shook his head as if disgusted, then reached into his pocket. I wasn't close enough to hear, but his lips formed the words "last time" before he pulled out a small plastic bag. Echo snatched it and cuddled it close to her belly. Rainbow threw up her hands and marched away from them both.

We arrived at the entrance to Teen Path HOME at the same time. "Everything okay over there?" I asked.

"Yeah, fine." The disgust in her voice contradicted her words. "I hate it when he does that."

"Does what?"

"Nothing. Never mind." She glanced down at Bella and her face brightened. "What's your dog's name?"

"Bella. Be careful, she's not always—"

Before I could finish warning her that Bella wasn't always friendly with strangers, the teenager had already kneeled down and wrapped her arms around my German shepherd's neck. She rubbed her nose against Bella's, a dangerous move likely to result in a nose-ectomy.

"Aren't you a big, beautiful, sweetheart?" she said.

Bella replied by planting her paws on Rainbow's shoulders and bathing her face in saliva.

"Wow!" I said. "She loves you!"

"Animals always love me."

Rainbow rubbed her face back and forth in Bella's scruff, as if the dog were a furry black bath towel. Each time she pulled away, Bella licked her face wet again. I wasn't sure whether teen or beast enjoyed the game more, but Bella was clearly winning.

I could have watched the two new friends bond for hours, but my watch told me I had five minutes left on the meter. "Sorry, Rainbow, I'm in a hurry. Did you see a wallet in the conference room? I might have left mine there."

She ignored my question and reached into her backpack. When her hand reemerged, it held a cell phone. "Bella and I need a selfie."

Tick, tick, tick. One more minute gone.

She wrapped her right arm around Bella's neck again, pulled their faces together, and held out her phone. "Say cheese." An electronic click later, she glanced at the screen. "Perfect." She turned the device around to show me. Rainbow's lips were puckered in a sultry kiss. Bella's long, black-spotted tongue reached for her cheek.

The teen ruffled Bella's ears, then tossed the phone back inside her pack. "Think we'll go viral on Instagram, baby?" She turned back toward me. "I wasn't looking for a wallet, sorry. Bella and I will hang out here while you go look for it."

"Thanks for the offer, but I'd better take her inside with me. I'll only be a minute."

She pointed to a small sign on the door: *Only Service Animals Allowed.* "Chuck's head will explode if he sees her inside the building."

I flashed on Chuck's enraged face when Lonnie invaded the kitchen. Bella trusted most clean-shaven men, but not all of them, and she protected me instinctively. If Chuck saw her and yelled, the result might be a Bella-Chuck face-off. Literally. Still, leaving Bella alone with a relative stranger? That invited a whole different kind of catastrophe.

Rainbow scowled. "I'm not going to steal her or anything."

"It's not that. She doesn't like other dogs, and she's not reliable with strangers."

Bella leaned into Rainbow's thigh, her way of simultaneously demonstrating affection and making me look like a moron.

Rainbow pointed to the opposite end of the block. "I'll keep her over there away from people."

Tick, tick, tick. Two minutes left on the meter.

I thrust Bella's leash into her hand. "Fine. But don't let anyone—especially another dog—near her. If she gets stressed, have someone come get me. I'll be back in a minute."

I was gone fifteen.

I retraced my steps starting with Gabriel, who dug through the lost-and-found box. No wallet there. I searched the recreation area and the conference room. I crawled underneath tables and checked under the pool table. I rummaged through trash cans. I even glanced around upstairs near Rainbow's mural. Nothing.

I never carried more than fifty dollars in cash, but replacing my driver's license and credit cards would be—as Aunt Rita used to say—a pain in the patootie. The biggest loss, though, was a snapshot of Dad, Dharma, and me that was taken when I was an infant. That photo was the only evidence I had of us as a family. Why hadn't I made a copy?

By the time I trudged back to the street, Rainbow was seated on the curb. My hundred-pound monster dog was flopped across her lap, staring at her with pure German shepherd adoration. Neither teen nor beast seemed to have missed me in the slightest.

"Bella says she wants to live with me now," Rainbow said.

I smiled in spite of my frustration. "Too bad. She's stuck with me."

When Bella and I got back to my Honda, a seventy-five-dollar parking ticket was stuck on my windshield. That's when I realized Rainbow had never asked me if I'd found my wallet.

NINE

ANOTHER WEEK PASSED, AND with it, seven more days of my waning fertility. Still, I was hopeful. My period was officially overdue. My cycle wasn't always regular, so being a day or two late didn't guarantee successful conception, but no bleeding meant no disappointment, at least not yet.

A well-aimed stream of urine on a plastic stick could have given a definitive answer in three minutes or less, but Michael and I agreed that we didn't want to know. We wanted to hope. If I wasn't pregnant, my cycle would tell us soon enough. Besides, not knowing would give us the perfect excuse not to bring up our fertility challenges at dinner with Dharma and Dale the next night. Why ruin a fun evening with my mother and her partner when the whole thing might be a non-issue?

I double checked to make sure I had enough cash in my replacement wallet to pay for parking, then I headed back to Teen Path HOME for my second Wednesday afternoon yoga class. Now that Gabriel was planning to bribe—oops, I mean *incentivize*—the teens to attend, I hoped class would be bigger. I was doing my part to make yoga more attractive to the kids, too. I'd ditched the Deva Premal CD for a Hip Hop meditation MP3 I'd found on the Internet. The music wasn't as soothing as I was used to, but maybe upbeat energy would entice a few more students to pop their heads in the door.

Meet them where they are, right?

It seemed to work. Two minutes before class time, my circle of twenty chairs was half filled.

Snoozing Guy walked up to Gabriel and held out his palm. "Pay up, man."

"After class. And only if you stay awake."

"Ah man, that blows." He shrugged at me. "At least the music doesn't suck this time." He fist-bumped another teen and slid into the chair next to him.

I allowed my new students to settle in and gave them a short spiel. "Gabriel brought a few towels in case some of you want to rest on the floor at the end of class. Yoga is typically done in bare feet—"

Snoozing Guy's friend interrupted. "Crank's going to take off his shoes?" He waved his hand across his face. "Rank!"

Snoozing Guy, whose nickname was obviously Crank, slugged him in the arm.

I grinned. "As I was saying, yoga is *typically* done in bare feet, but you can keep your shoes on if you want." Everyone did, so I slipped mine back on as well.

As I guided the class to start lengthening their breath, I surveyed my students. Directly across the circle, Gabriel gave me a thumbs-up and a wink. Two empty chairs away, Snoozing Guy and his friend continued to trade barbs.

The rest of the occupied chairs contained, among others, three Latina teens dressed in matching Teen Path HOME T-shirts, an overweight girl with stringy dark hair, and a transgender youth wearing a tight red crop top, a curly blonde wig, and four-inch black stilettos. I smiled. A six-foot-two version of Tiffany. All she needed was neon-pink yoga pants and a pair of Boston terrier earrings to complete the outfit.

My attention kept drifting back to a single student, however: Rainbow. Something was obviously upsetting her. She'd slipped in mere seconds before class started and refused to make eye contact. Her lips trembled as if she were holding back tears. I vowed to connect with her after class, or at least make sure that Gabriel did.

What seemed like five, but was actually sixty, minutes later, I ended class with a smile and the words "Thank you." I normally ended by touching my palms together in the Anjali mudra and saying Namaste, the Sanskrit word loosely translated as "The spirit in me honors the spirit in you," but that ritual seemed as out of place as my Deva Premal music had been.

The transgender teen called the class 'the GOAT.' Sleeping Guy's friend replied, "Yeah, that was dope."

I'd never felt so old.

Or so satisfied.

Gabriel handed out the gift cards while I said goodbye to the students. Rainbow loitered in the back of the room until everyone but Gabriel and I had left, then approached me.

"I wanted to say thank you. You're amazing. I can't believe how much you're helping me. I feel safe when I'm with you."

She didn't *look* like she felt safe. She looked grief-stricken. Barely able to keep from sobbing.

"I'm glad you're finding the class useful," I replied. "But honestly, there's nothing special about me. You're the one doing the work."

For a moment, the shadows behind her eyes lifted. "I hope you keep coming after the six-week series is over. I miss yoga. I used to take classes in high school."

I almost asked her which high school, but I realized that doing so might violate Gabriel's don't-ask-don't-tell policy. "I hope I get to teach more classes here, too."

Rainbow stared down at her knees, as if gathering courage. "Um ... I heard that you own a yoga studio."

"Yes, Serenity Yoga in Greenwood." I reached into my pocket and handed her a business card. Gabriel gave me a dark look.

"Do you ever need help?" Rainbow asked. "I'd work for cheap. Like mega cheap. I'd be your slave for free yoga classes."

Gabriel dropped a chair into the metal holder, clanging it loud enough to make me glance in his direction. He vigorously shook his head no.

Even I couldn't miss a hint that obvious. "Sorry, I don't have any openings right now."

Rainbow's face shifted, from hopeful anticipation to practiced indifference. "Whatever." The nonchalance in her voice sounded forced.

"Don't take it personally, Rainbow," Gabriel said. "Kate already has lots of employees. Besides, I can't risk losing you as a student here. How else will I get the board to authorize adding more classes?"

She rolled her eyes.

Gabriel gestured with his chin toward the door. "Why don't you see if Chuck needs help with the lunch dishes? Kate and I have a few things to discuss."

The teen shuffled out the door. "Fine. I didn't want to hang out here anyway."

Gabriel waited until the door closed behind her before speaking. "You were about to slide down a very slippery slope there, Kate."

"How? I mean, you're right, I have plenty of help. Still, I could have made up a job for her. We have space in our classes."

"Bad idea. If you want to work here, you'll have to learn to keep clear boundaries, especially with kids like Rainbow."

"Kids like Rainbow?"

"She's almost certainly a minor. The board has been very clear. We have a zero-tolerance policy when it comes to fraternizing with the kids."

"I wasn't planning to take her out clubbing. I was going to let her post a few flyers in exchange for yoga classes. What's so bad about that?"

Gabriel's jaw firmed. "I'm sorry, Kate. *Any* off-site activity with one of our underage clients is out of the question."

"Even if—"

He held up his palm. "No exceptions. We're under intense scrutiny right now. If the board catches wind that you're doing something even slightly suspicious, we could *both* lose our jobs."

I was about to press further, but our conversation was interrupted by a high-pitched scream: "Get your hands off me!"

This time, the ruckus was next to the kitchen.

A six-foot-tall, stocky man with a graying crew cut and a vicious expression held Rainbow's tiny wrist in one hand, her backpack in the other. She struggled, clearly trying to escape. A small crowd of murmuring onlookers gathered nearby. Chuck wasn't among them.

Gabriel's voice boomed. "What's going on here?"

As the stranger whipped toward Gabriel, Rainbow jerked her arm from his grasp and yanked back the backpack. She hugged the pack to her chest and stumbled several steps back. Crew Cut stomped the same number of steps toward her.

"Your little road trip has come to an end, young lady. You're coming with me."

Gabriel stepped between them, face locked in a dangerous expression. "She's not going anywhere until I know who you are and what you're doing in my facility. Step away from her or I'll call the police."

Crew Cut sneered. "Be my guest. The cops can shackle the little delinquent and drag her ass home that way. She's a sixteen-year-old runaway, and I'm her stepfather. Police or no police, she's coming with me."

Gabriel's voice softened but he didn't yield. "Rainbow, is that true?"

"Rainbow?" The stranger snorted. "That's what she's calling herself now? Rainbow? What other sunshine has she blown up your ass?"

"Sir, I wasn't talking to you." Gabriel spit out the word "sir" like a swear word. His voice softened again. "Rainbow, who is this man?"

"No one. Just the pile of trash that married my mother."

The stranger raised his right hand as if preparing to strike her. "Watch your mouth, you little—"

In one fluid motion, Gabriel grabbed the stranger's wrist and twisted his arm behind his back. "That's it. You're out of here."

The stranger kept snarling, this time at Gabriel. "Fine. March me out like some bum. You'll regret it. I'll be back, and next time I'm bringing the cops. We'll see how tough you are when they arrest you for harboring a runaway."

He struggled out of Gabriel's grip and pointed at Rainbow. "Don't let that innocent face fool you. Give her an inch and she'll shoot you in the back. Tell them, *Rainbow*," he sneered. "Tell them what an ungrateful little wretch you are. I let you live in my house and eat my food, and how did you repay me? You swiped my cash and stole my gun."

Rainbow involuntarily glanced at her backpack.

Gabriel's voice softened, but it held a dangerous intensity. "Rainbow, do you have a gun?"

She gaped at him with wide, frightened eyes. "I ... I ... "

That's all she got out before she choked back a sob and darted out the front door.

TEN

I spent the rest of the afternoon working on payroll and trying not to obsess about Rainbow. I'd spent twenty minutes combing the streets for her after I left Teen Path HOME, to no avail. She'd blended back into the cityscape as if she'd never existed.

I knew Gabriel wouldn't approve of my search, but that didn't stop me. Rainbow was in trouble, and not just because of her stepfather or the gun she likely carried on her person. She'd been upset about something in class, long before her stepfather arrived.

By the time I left my home office at five o'clock to head for the studio, the day's overcast skies had darkened to charcoal. Some Like It Hot Yoga's *Ten Classes for Ten Dollars!* sign turned my mood the same color. If I didn't come up with a brilliant new marketing strategy, ten dollars would soon be my bank account balance.

When I arrived at the studio, Tiffany was watering the plants in the lobby. She wore leopard-print yoga pants and a form-fitting T-shirt with the words *Three Months Down, Six to Go* written across her lower belly. She noticed my gaze and ran her fingertips along the words. "Chad bought me this. I'm actually only at ten weeks, so it's a little early for me to start wearing my pregnancy like a billboard. But it makes Chad happy, so I figured what the hell. I'm young. What are the chances that something will go wrong?" Her face turned bright red. "I mean, not that you're old ... "

I placed my hand on hers. "I get it. I'm happy for you, remember?"

She furrowed her brow. "Well you certainly don't *look* happy. Is everything okay?"

"Honestly? No." I shared what had happened earlier at Teen Path HOME.

"That crew cut guy sounds like a real jerk," Tiffany said. "If he finds her again, will she seriously have to go home with him?"

"Gabriel and I talked about it afterwards. If he's really her stepfather, she probably will."

"You're kidding."

I shrugged. "It's the law. Gabriel was upset, but he said there wasn't anything he could do about it."

"But you said that guy was going to hit her!"

"It sure looked that way, but he never actually touched her. If he does hit her, or if Rainbow says that he has in the past, Gabriel will arrange for the police to take her to a foster home, at least temporarily."

Tiffany shuddered. "From what I hear, that may be worse."

I'd heard the same thing, but I didn't want to think about it. Ignorance is bliss, right?

Four hours and two drop-in classes later, I ushered my final students out the front door. The clouds had stopped threatening, choosing instead to douse the sidewalks in icy sheets of rain. Thunder rumbled in the distance.

That was my cue to hurry home. Bella, for all her bravado, was terrified of thunder. Mouse was great for separation anxiety, but thunder phobia required human comfort.

I was halfway out the back door when I heard a tentative knock at the front. Selfish Kate urged me to keep going. *Ignore it. You closed five minutes ago.*

But how could I? What if one of my students had forgotten something important, like her house keys? "Hang on, Bella," I muttered to the empty space.

I hurried back through the lobby and glanced out the window. A waterlogged teenager waved at me. What was Rainbow doing here? Wet hair was plastered against her scalp like a blonde helmet. Water poured in rivulets down her face.

She knocked again. "Kate, I can see you standing there. Let me in. I'm freezing."

Three reproachful voices vied for dominance in my head. Dad led off with a stern admonition: *Don't let her in. If you give shelter to a known runaway without calling the police, you're guilty of harboring a minor.* Gabriel added, *You have to keep strict boundaries. All off-site contact with minors is strictly prohibited.* Dharma used Gabriel's own words against him: *Don't let what you can't do stop you from doing what you can.*

Like Dad always said, I was my mother's daughter. Prohibitions notwithstanding, someone needed to help Rainbow. Why shouldn't that someone be me? I couldn't fundamentally change the teen's plight, but I could at least get her out of that storm. As for calling the police? They'd either ship her back home or slap her in foster care. Rainbow had risked reaching out to me, but her trust was fragile. If I blew it tonight, there would be no second chances.

Okay, Dharma. You win.

I unlocked the deadbolt and ushered her inside. Rain dripped from her jacket, forming dark blue splotches on the carpet.

"Wait here a second," I said. "Let's get you dried off, then we'll talk." I snatched a roll of paper towels from the restroom and tossed them to her. "I'm glad to see you. I was worried about you. But how did you know where to find me?"

Her teeth chattered. "You gave me your business card. I know it's lame to show up like this, but I didn't know where else to go. Jace took off with the tent, and I can't stay with any of my friends near the center. My stepfather might find me again."

"Would that be so terrible?"

She flinched. "I can't go back to him. I won't. I'll kill myself first."

My stomach lurched. "Don't say things like that, Rainbow. Don't even think them." I paused. "Your boyfriend took off with your belongings?"

"The tent isn't mine, it's his. Jace isn't my boyfriend anymore, either. He won't pick up my calls, and he's blocked me on social media."

"What happened?"

She balled up the wet paper towels and tossed them into the garbage can. "Does it matter? He's gone, and our camping supplies are gone with him. Now I really am homeless." She shivered. "Tonight, of all nights."

"Can you stay at a shelter?"

"I can't risk it. I look too young. If they figure out I'm under eighteen, they'll call the police." Thunder clapped in the distance. Rainbow buried her face in her hands. "I'm so totally hosed."

I poured a cup of hot water from the dispenser, added a bag of chamomile tea and two packets of sugar, and handed it to her. Rainbow held the cup in both hands, inhaling its sweet, floral steam. Her hands trembled.

"Honestly," I said. "I don't know what you should do either."

There had to be a solution, but damned if I could come up with one at the moment. I couldn't leave a homeless teen alone overnight at the studio, not without getting an earful from the teacher who opened at six the next morning. Perhaps Rainbow could spend the night in the covered garage. It would be cold, but at least she'd be dry. Dharma's voice chastised me. *Come on, Kate. You know the security guards will toss her out before midnight. You can do better than that.*

She was right. November in Seattle wasn't Juneau in January, but it was cold outside tonight. Wet, bone-chillingly cold. The city council might be turning a benevolent blind eye to the area's homeless encampments, but private security forces were not. Rainbow would be forced back onto the streets long before dawn.

I couldn't leave her on the studio's property, and I couldn't send her back out into the storm. Which left me with one final idea. An idea that would likely mean losing my job at Teen Path HOME

So be it.

I sighed. "Okay, you can come home with me and sleep on my couch."

She smiled. "Thanks, Kate, I—"

I held up my second and third fingers, stopping her. "On two conditions. One: You can't tell anyone I did this, and two: it's only for tonight. We'll come up with another plan in the morning. I have a friend who might help." By "friend," I meant my mother's boyfriend, Dale Evans.

"Your friend's not a cop, is he? If you call the cops, they'll make me go home."

"Not a cop. An attorney." Calling Dale a mere attorney was a vast understatement, although these days Dale spent most of his time running Dale's Goats and Dharma's Asses, an animal rescue on Orcas Island. But prior to moving to Orcas, Dale had been a legal legend. Suffice it to say that anyone who convinced Dale to represent them usually got off, even if they were guilty. I had no idea whether or not Dale had ever represented a runaway, but he had plenty of local contacts. If he couldn't personally help Rainbow, he could connect her with someone who could. Tomorrow night's dinner would give me the perfect opportunity to quiz him. For once, the universe was on my side.

I glanced at Rainbow's backpack. "Actually, there's a third condition. Before I take you anywhere, I need to know something. Was your stepfather telling the truth? Do you have a gun?"

She tightened her grip on the pack. "Scary stuff happens out there. I need to protect myself."

"Do you even know how to use it?"

The teen looked affronted. "Of course! If I didn't know how to use it, I never would have taken it. My mom's husband is a creepy ghoul, but he's ex-Marine. Glock is his middle name. His version of stepfather-stepdaughter bonding happened at the shooting range."

"Is the gun loaded?

"It's not much good to me if it isn't."

She had a point.

"You won't need to protect yourself in my home," I replied. "Take the gun out of your pack and unload it."

Rainbow shook her head. "No way I'm going to—"

"This is *not* up for discussion." The sternness in my voice wasn't faked. "I will not allow you to bring a loaded gun into my home." I pointed at the rain cascading down the glass door. "If you don't like it, you can sleep out there." I paused for a count of three, then softened my tone. "You came to me, remember? You have to trust me."

She reluctantly unzipped her pack and pulled out a black, semi-automatic handgun. She pressed a button. The clip dropped into her palm. "There, happy?"

I'd never carried, but Dad had taught me plenty about handguns. "Now the one in the chamber."

Rainbow frowned, but she racked the slide twice. A bullet fell to the ground.

"Pick that up," I ordered. I reached out my hand. "Give me the gun. I'll keep it tonight."

"How do I know you won't shoot me with it?"

"You've got the ammunition."

She hesitated, then handed me the revolver. I slid it inside my purse.

"You're going to give it back to me, right?"

I didn't speak, but the answer was probably not. I couldn't let a sixteen-year-old teenager carry a stolen gun. But before I admitted that, I needed to speak with Dale. "We'll talk about it tomorrow. For now, my only goal is to keep both of us safe."

Rainbow's doubts notwithstanding, my intentions were honorable. Just like the ones paving the road straight to hell.

———

I coached Rainbow on the drive back to Ballard. "My husband's a good guy, but he doesn't like surprises, especially if he thinks I'm getting involved in something that's none of my business. Let me do the talking and don't tell him about the gun, okay?"

She nodded.

"You got along pretty well with my German shepherd last week, so I think you'll be fine. But since you're coming onto her territory, I can't be sure. If she barks or lunges at you, stand completely still and I'll grab her."

"Don't worry about Bella," Rainbow replied. "She and I are buddies. She won't bark at me, and even if she does, I won't care. I already told you. I'm good with animals. I was going to be a veterinarian."

"Was?"

Her expression remained carefully neutral, but her voice quavered. "High school dropouts don't get into vet school, even if they ace the GED."

"Don't give up on your future so quickly."

"I don't have a future. Not anymore." She turned away and stared out the passenger-side window, firmly closing the door on our conversation. We rode the rest of the way in silence.

I parked in the driveway behind Michael's SUV and said a quick prayer, asking for my husband to be in a good mood. Rainbow and I entered the living room to the tangy smell of homemade marinara and Michael's off-key rendition of ABBA's "Dancing Queen." Cooking and singing. A good sign.

I tossed my purse and the car keys onto the sofa and called, "Hey sweetie, I'm home!"

Michael's voice came from the kitchen. "You're late. I decided to cook us a late-night dinner, but I expected you home half an hour ago. The pasta is mush."

Bella slinked into the living room, ears plastered down on her head, obviously stressed about the thunder. But then she spied Rainbow and her body language transformed. Her ears lifted; her rear wiggled. She planted her paws on Rainbow's shoulders and swept her black-spotted tongue across the teen's cheeks.

Rainbow grinned and scratched Bella's ribs. "Told you she likes me," she whispered.

Michael continued belting out lyrics in an off-key contralto. I motioned for Rainbow to follow me to the kitchen.

She glanced inside the room and stifled a giggle. "Chuck would have a heart attack at this mess."

Diced red onions, green peppers, and fragrant fresh basil covered the floor. Homemade tomato sauce dotted the walls and dripped from the light above the stove. Spaghetti noodles adhered to the wall like stranded earthworms drying on pavement. Almost two years of living together and I still couldn't believe Michael could create such delicious food out of so much chaos. An unopened bottle of red wine sat on the table: his low-key way of asking if I still might be pregnant. He bent over the oven and pulled out a loaf of home-baked garlic bread.

I picked up the bottle and slid it back into the wine rack. "No wine for me tonight."

"Really?" He turned toward me, face split in a huge grin. Then his gaze landed on Rainbow. He took in her worn clothes, her wet hair. The dirt trapped underneath her fingernails. The grin flattened, landing somewhere between a smile and a grimace. "I see you brought company." His eyes clearly telegraphed the question, *Who is this and what is she doing here?*

I smiled and mouthed the word *later*.

Out loud, I said, "Michael, this is Rainbow. I invited her to stay overnight with us tonight."

Michael's smile remained frozen in place, but the small muscles next to his jaw quivered. He pointed to the cupboard. "Welcome, Rainbow. Grab a plate. Silverware is in the drawer underneath the cutting board. Iced tea's in the fridge." When Rainbow's back was turned, he gave me a dark look and mouthed, *Later indeed.*

"Can you keep dinner warm for a couple more minutes?" I asked. "We need to get Rainbow out of these wet clothes and into something warm." I moved next to him, gave him a peck on the cheek, and whispered, "Be nice. She's had a tough day."

I led Rainbow upstairs to Michael's and my bedroom, where I tossed her jeans, a warm sweatshirt, and a pair of bright green Seahawks slipper socks. "Put these on in the bathroom and bring your wet clothes back out. I'll wait here."

She wrinkled her eyebrows. "Afraid to leave me alone?"

"Not at all." Truthfully, I was afraid to face Michael, but I chose not to share that information.

When she reemerged, her face was clean; her fingernails, less grimy. My jeans hung low on her thin hips, but the hems still ended two inches above her ankles. The slipper socks bulged unfashionably up her calves, but at least she looked warm.

"Let's go throw your outfit into the laundry," I said.

That task complete, we joined Michael in the kitchen, where Rainbow downed three large helpings of overcooked pasta while Michael and I picked at our plates in awkward silence. When she stood and carried her plate to the sink, I turned to my husband. "Rainbow and I will do the dishes, Michael. Why don't you relax with Bella in the living room?" My words were polite, but we both knew what I was actually saying. *Get out of here and leave us alone to talk.* Michael gave me a you'll-pay-for-this-later look, but he acquiesced.

I filled the sink with sudsy water, washed the first plate, and handed it to Rainbow to dry. According to Gabriel, teens at the center opened up when their hands were busy creating artwork. I hoped drying dishes would have a similar effect.

"Rainbow's not your real name, is it?" I asked.

"No. I figured it would be harder to track me down if I made up something new. I like Rainbow better than my real name, though. It sounds like my life still has hope."

"There's always hope."

She rolled her eyes and put the plate in the cupboard.

"So, are you going to tell me your real name?" I asked.

She shrugged. "No reason not to. The drill sergeant's already found me. It's Rain. Rain Roads."

"By drill sergeant, I assume you mean your stepfather," I said.

"Who else?"

"What's going on between you two, anyway?"

"He's a sleazy slimebag, that's what's going on."

I frowned. "Can you be more specific?"

"He can't hold down a job, and he's got a terrible temper."

I thought of my own history of anger management issues. "Lots of people get angry."

"Not like Dean does. He's a mean drunk, and he drinks a lot."

"That's his name? Dean?"

Rainbow shuddered, as if hearing the name gave her the willies. "Yes, and he's a bloodsucking leach. He drank Mom's money and drained what was left of her self-confidence. I never understood why she put up with his crap. I guess she figured he was the best she could do."

She shrugged with an indifference that seemed affected. "I'm no better. I settled with Jace, though I actually believed he might love me. I never would have left Tacoma with him otherwise." She scoffed. "I won't make that mistake again. How could anyone love me? I'm too broken."

I considered placing my hand on her shoulder, but I wasn't sure how she'd receive my touch. "You're not broken, Rainbow. Not even close. Bruised, maybe, but not broken."

I meant it. Rainbow's energy didn't have the hard edge of someone beyond help. At least part of her was still reachable.

"How long have Dean and your mom been married?" I asked.

"Two years, three months, and eleven days. Not that I'm counting."

"That's a long time for you to live with someone you don't like."

"It wasn't always this bad. When Mom and Dean were both just drunks, she shielded me from the worst of it. But since she's graduated to heroin, she's hardly ever home."

"Your mom's a heroin addict?"

Rainbow flashed a tough smile, but she couldn't disguise the vulnerability in her voice. "You didn't think I grew up with the Bradys, did you?"

I ignored the comment and handed her a serving spoon. "Does your stepfather use heroin too?"

"G. I. Joe? Use drugs? No way. He's Jim Beam and Budweiser all the way. It was the one thing Dean and I could agree on. We both hate heroin." Rainbow opened the silverware drawer and slid the dried spoon inside. We continued cleaning silverware, piece by piece.

"You've had to deal with a lot for someone so young."

"I suppose so. Mom's boyfriends always knocked her around some, but Dean's by far the worst, especially when she's using."

"He hits her?"

Rainbow shrugged. "Like I said, he's a mean drunk. That's why she takes off. So she can shoot up in peace."

"If she's gone so much, how does she hold down a job?"

"She doesn't."

"But if Dean doesn't work..."

"They live off Mom's allowance."

"Allowance?"

"That's what she calls it. It's my grandparents' money. They died in a car accident when I was five."

"I'm sorry."

"Thanks. I still miss them."

I considered my own childhood memories with Dharma. More specifically, my lack of childhood memories. Dharma left when I was a toddler, and I had no recollection of our brief time together. "You were only five when your grandparents died. You remember them?"

"Definitely. I practically lived with them."

I gave her a questioning look.

"Mom's always liked to party, so she dumped me with them a lot. According to her, they were judgmental jerks, but I loved them, and they did right by us. They left Mom the house and their life savings."

"Why does she call it an allowance?"

"Because they tied everything up in a trust. Mom gets monthly deposits for our living expenses, but if she wants anything extra, she has to ask the trustee, and he usually says no. She hates Grandma and Grandpa for that, but I think they were smart. If she'd gotten the money all at once, she'd have shot it up her veins by now."

I calculated eleven years of living expenses in my head. "That must be quite the trust fund."

"What you mean?"

"It's supported both of you since you were five."

She shrugged. "Mom's not rich or anything, but it puts food on the table. When it's not enough, Mom does tricks or the drill sergeant takes on odd jobs. I wanted to get a job, too, but Mom wouldn't let me. She says my contribution is keeping my grades up."

For the first time, I wondered if Rainbow might be deceiving me. The mother she described didn't seem like the type to care about grades. Then again, what family wasn't eccentric?

"Your home life seems tough," I said. "I'm sorry about that. But living on the streets can't be much easier. Why did you run?"

Rainbow closed the silverware drawer and reached for a sauce pan. "Mom was gone too long this time. She's been on benders before, but only for a day or two. Three at the most. By the time I left, she was gone over two weeks. I tried to find her, but she wasn't in any of her normal places. That was almost three months ago. I was planning to go back when she did."

"How do you know she's not back already?"

"When she isn't strung out, she's not a terrible mother. If she'd come home and I wasn't there, she would have messaged me on Instagram, especially now that school's in session."

"She wouldn't call you?"

"My cell phone stopped working shortly after I ran. The one I have now is a burner. Mom doesn't have the number." There was a long pause. When the teen spoke again, her voice was so soft, I could barely hear it. "I'm afraid she's so far gone now that she'll never come back. I can't live with Dean if she's not there."

"Living with your stepfather is that hard?" I asked.

"It's unbearable."

I lowered my voice. "Rainbow, does he hit you?"

"Sometimes, but I can handle that."

I consciously kept my expression neutral, but my entire body vibrated. "What *can't* you handle?"

She didn't answer, at least not directly. "I used to sneak out to see Jace sometimes. Dean caught me, and he took the lock off my room. He claimed he did it because he needed to keep an eye on me." She finished drying the pan and set it on the stove. "I woke up the next night, and he was standing over my bed, staring at me."

"Did he … " I was afraid to finish the question.

Rainbow twisted the dish towel between her hands. "No. I screamed, and he left. But I wasn't about to give him a second chance. Jace and I took off the next day."

I stared into her eyes, trying to discern whether or not she was telling the truth. The shadows behind them indicated that she wasn't, at least not completely. I suspected, however, that any lies were ones of omission. Her real story might be worse.

"Rainbow, you have rights. If your stepfather hurt you, we can call Child Protective Services. You won't have to go back to him."

"So I can get stuck in the foster system? I'm better off on the street."

I wasn't so sure. "What about your biological father?"

"What about him? Mom got pregnant at sixteen, and she wasn't exactly the Virgin Mary. She has no idea who my bio dad is. For most of my life, it was just Mom and me. Then it was Mom, me, and Master Sergeant Sicko. Now it's just me."

She tossed the towel on the counter. "I'm tired of talking. Are we done here?"

The answer, of course, was no. We weren't even close to finished. But I'd already pushed Rainbow pretty hard. One more nudge and I might lose her. "Sure. Let's grab some sheets, and I'll make up the sofa bed for you. It's actually pretty comfortable."

It was a great plan. Or it would have been, if Michael hadn't been pacing the living room like a caged mountain lion. Bella lay near the fireplace, eyes worriedly tracking him.

"Michael, would you please grab a set of clean sheets? Rainbow's ready for bed." Her real name, Rain, still felt foreign to me.

90

Michael stopped pacing and glared. "Kate, I need to talk to you." He paused for emphasis. "Alone." Another pause. "Now."

Rainbow tensed. I smiled, hoping to reassure her. "Your clothes are probably done washing. Why don't you toss them in the dryer? There are fresh sheets in the linen closet upstairs." I pointed to the sofa. "Pull this out and make it up. Michael and I will chat in the office. We'll only be a few minutes."

She glanced at the front door, as if mentally planning an escape route.

"You're safe here," I assured her. "I promise."

Michael marched into the office. Mouse awoke from her nap on the desk, growled at Michael, hiss-spat at me, then tore into the living room. "Don't try to touch the cat, Rainbow!" I called. "She's not as nice as Bella."

I turned to close the door, then reconsidered and left it halfway open. If Rainbow decided to bolt, I wanted to hear it.

Michael lowered his voice, but his tone was decidedly cranky. "Who is that kid and why is she staying at our house?"

I told Michael everything that I knew so far. That I'd met Rainbow at Teen Path HOME, that she was a sixteen-year-old runaway from Tacoma, that her boyfriend had taken off with their camping supplies, that her mother was missing, and that she'd had an altercation with her abusive stepfather today.

"How do you know anything she told you is true?" he asked.

"I guess I don't. But what was I supposed to do? She was soaked, and it's freezing outside. Would you seriously want me to leave her out there alone?" Michael didn't answer. "Besides, Bella likes her. I trust Bella."

"Are you insane? Bella's a dog! She hates Sam, for god's sake. Sam's one of the nicest people we know."

"That's different. Sam has a mustache." My words sounded ridiculous, but I believed them. Bella had her share of quirks. She sometimes hated perfectly nice people for no discernible reason. But the reverse had never been true. Put simply, Bella wasn't fond of everyone, but when she *did* like someone, they deserved to be liked. Period.

"Didn't your billfold get stolen at that teen center?" Michael asked. "Are you positive this Rainbow kid didn't take it?"

"You're right, Michael. Rainbow might have stolen my wallet. Or someone else might have taken it. Or I might have lost it. Or it might be in my car somewhere. What does it matter? What do we have in this house that's worth taking? Food? The thirty bucks or so we have in cash?" I pointed to my ancient computer. "She won't get any money hocking this, and it's worth twice as much as our television. Do you have a hidden stash of gold somewhere you haven't told me about?" Three silent seconds passed. "Look, I'm not saying that we should keep Rainbow here permanently. Just a few days until I—"

"A few days!" Michael exclaimed. "Kate, listen to yourself. That girl is a teenage runaway. Keeping her here is illegal. We could get charged for harboring a minor and lord knows what else. If she won't go back to her family, you have to call the police."

I shook my head. "No. I promised to help her."

"And you will. By connecting her with the authorities."

I didn't reply, but the look I gave him spoke volumes.

"Kate, be reasonable. Say we keep her here for a day, a week, even a month. How does that help her? She'll end up back on the streets. You know that."

Unfortunately, I did.

Michael grasped my shoulders in both hands. "We have to be the adults here. If Rainbow's being abused at home, Child Protective

Services will get involved. They deal with these kinds of situations every day. We don't. You need to leave it to the professionals."

I hated what Michael was saying, mainly because I knew he was right. I stared at the carpet, willing myself to come up with a different solution. I couldn't.

"Okay," I said.

"Okay what?"

I met his eyes, frustrated. "Okay, I'll call the police, but—"

A sound halfway between a sob and a squeak came from the doorway. A betrayed-looking Rainbow stood behind the partially closed door, clutching my feral calico tightly against her chest.

My first reaction was astonishment. How did she manage to pick up Mouse without needing stitches?

My second was horror. How much of Michael's and my conversation had Rainbow overheard? How much had she misunderstood?

I'd been about to tell Michael that I'd call the police, but not until tomorrow, after Dale and Dharma arrived, and *only* if Rainbow agreed. I'd hoped that together, we could come up with a plan that was truly in Rainbow's best interests.

Rainbow's voice shook. "You lied. You promised me, no cops." She set the cat on the floor and backed two steps away. Mouse hissed at me, then bolted.

I took a cautious step toward her. "You didn't let me finish."

"Don't come near me," she yelled. "You lied to me, just like Jace!" She reached for the doorknob and pulled. The door slammed between us.

Michael and I stared at each other, mouths open in surprised guilt.

"Well, that went well," I said drolly. "Any other great ideas?" A second door slammed, and I jumped. "The front door! She's running."

By the time we got to the living room, Rainbow—and her back-pack—were gone. Bella stood on her hind legs, scratching at the front door and whining. Rain flooded the windows.

"Michael, she doesn't have a coat." Rainbow's clothes, including her coat, were still whirling around in my dryer.

"We'll find her," he said.

We grabbed our jackets, clipped on Bella's leash, and jogged out to the sidewalk. I kneeled next to my canine buddy, soaking my knees in icy rainwater. "Which way did she go, girl?"

Bella cocked her head and stared at me, bewildered.

Out of sheer desperation, I tried a different command. "Find it!"

As trained, Bella dropped her nose to the ground and searched for a cookie.

"She doesn't know what you want, Kate."

"We have to do something."

Michael pointed at my Honda. "Rainbow can't have gotten far. Get your keys and we'll drive around and look for her."

Michael and Bella searched our neighbors' yards while I ran inside to grab my car keys. My purse sat on the floor, next to the opened sofa bed. I rummaged through it, pulling out items one at a time. *Lip gloss, chewing gum, wallet, keys.* "Yes!" I examined them more carefully and groaned. *Damn. The studio keys.* I continued searching. *Hairbrush, wallet, pens ...*

I froze.

Wallet?

I laid the second wallet next to the first. The first one was new, almost empty. This one was worn. It bulged with business cards, credit cards, and miscellaneous grocery receipts. Everything except the cash was still there. I pulled out the beloved photo of Dad, Dharma, and me, and held it to my lips.

Rainbow *had* stolen my wallet. She must have had it in her pack all along. Why had she kept it? Better yet, why had she gone inside my purse to put it back?

I realized the answer to the second question, and my stomach dropped to my knees. *Oh no. The gun.* I'd been so concerned about my keys that I hadn't noticed Rainbow's gun was missing. She must have snagged it while Michael and I were arguing in the office. How could I have been stupid enough to leave her alone with my purse?

Michael opened the door. "Kate! Are you coming?"

My husband was a strict gun control advocate. Now wasn't the time to admit that I'd brought a semiautomatic into our house. Especially a semiautomatic that was now missing. "I can't find my keys."

He pointed to my left. "Isn't that them on the end table?"

Damn. They'd been there all along. Rainbow must have tossed them on the end table when she pulled out the sofa bed. I scooped them up and joined Michael at the door. "Let's go."

Michael, Bella, and I drove around Ballard for over an hour, but we didn't find Rainbow. I shouldn't have been surprised. A few-block walk any direction would have taken her to a bus stop. A couple of bucks or the flash of a Metro pass, and she could be anywhere.

But would it be somewhere dry?

My conscience plagued me. Rainbow wasn't dressed to spend the night outside in this deluge. With no coat and no shelter, would she even survive?

We finally gave up and went home. I gathered Rainbow's now-dry clothes, my stash of vegan protein bars, and the fifty-seven dollars in cash Michael and I had between us and placed it all inside a plastic container. I set the container on the doorstep and taped a sign with the word *Rainbow* on top, like a frightened pet parent trying to lure home a runaway kitten. I deluded myself that she'd find it. Maybe she hadn't gone far. Maybe she was hiding nearby, watching Michael and me.

When I got up at seven the next morning, the prior night's rain had moved on, replaced by dense, eerie fog. The plastic container still sat, unopened, on my doorstep.

Michael placed his hand on my shoulder. "Maybe she had another coat in her backpack."

"Maybe." I doubted it, though. A second coat would have taken up too much room. I hoped she still had the money she'd stolen from me. If she had money, she could at least get a hot meal.

Michael left for Pete's Pet's at seven-thirty. He promised to drive around the neighborhood to look for Rainbow, then gave me a sheepish look. "I know you'll probably spend most of the day searching for her. I want to find her, too. But don't forget that Dale and Dharma are coming in from Orcas Island tonight. They'll be here by five."

I promised to be home by four-thirty. I ground and incubated Bella's kibble, fed a tin of organic tuna cat food to Mouse, and checked that damned container at least five hundred times. At nine, I opened it up again, took out the cash, and returned the rest of my offering to the doorstep. If Rainbow came back, she'd at least get the clothes and the food. I needed the money for parking.

Bella danced near her leash as I shrugged on my coat, clearly hoping to come with me.

I ruffled her ears. "Sorry, Bella. You'll have to let Mouse entertain you. Only service dogs are allowed." I left my disappointed canine buddy behind and headed for Teen Path HOME.

ELEVEN

I MANEUVERED THROUGH RUSH hour traffic to Teen Path HOME knowing three things for certain. One: Rainbow wouldn't be there. She wouldn't risk going anywhere near Teen Path HOME while her stepfather was looking for her. Two: Once I told Gabriel that I'd ignored his edict and taken Rainbow home with me, I likely wouldn't be invited back either. Three: Neither of the above mattered.

I was desperate to find Rainbow, and Teen Path HOME seemed like the most logical place to start. The staff must know where to look for runaway teens. If not, the youth at the center definitely did. I sprang for an expensive parking spot two blocks away and rushed to the center. Half a block into my journey, I turned right and froze. Something was wrong. Terribly wrong.

Police cruisers pulsed red and white warnings into the mist and blocked Teen Path HOME's street from both ends. Yellow crime scene tape cordoned off the center's entrance. A crowd of people loitered around it. Near the loading zone, a group of about fifteen teens huddled around something on the ground that I couldn't see.

Chuck stood outside the crime scene tape, arguing with a police officer. Vonnie, the art teacher, stood nearby, sobbing. A frustrated-looking officer appeared to be questioning her. I didn't see Gabriel, but that wasn't surprising. As the facility's director, he was likely inside with the police.

The group of teens parted, exposing a yellow lab wearing a green vest. It was Hope. Nicole kneeled on the ground next to her. She saw me, waved, and handed Hope's leash to one of the teens. As she maneuvered toward me, Nicole wore a somber expression.

"I'm surprised to see you here," I said. "I thought you and Hope came on Wednesdays."

"We don't keep a set schedule. I try to mix it up so Hope can interact with more people." She pointed to the gathered crowd. "As you can see, mornings are busy."

"What's going on?"

"I don't know, at least not for sure. The police had already blocked off the entrance when I got here. They're not letting anybody inside, and they aren't saying why."

"You say you don't know for sure. Does that mean you have an idea?"

She frowned. "People are talking, but you know how rumors are. It's like that telephone game. They're usually wildly inaccurate."

"Tell me anyway. What are people saying?"

She glanced at the entrance, then at her shoes. "That someone found a body when they opened up this morning."

Concern about Rainbow sparked to alarm. "A body? Whose?"

"I have no idea. Like I said, the police aren't talking. I almost left, but I figured if the rumors are right and someone was murdered, people will need a therapy dog today more than ever." As if proving her point, a ponytailed girl, no older than fourteen, kneeled, wrapped her arms around Hope, and murmured into her fur.

"Murdered?" I asked.

Nicole frowned. "I assume so. The police wouldn't barricade the block for a heart attack, would they?" Her expression turned pensive. "I guess it could be a suicide."

The word "suicide" yanked my mind back to Rainbow. She'd told me she'd rather kill herself than go back to her stepfather. That was just teenage melodrama, right?

I frowned at the cordoned-off entrance. Whatever had happened here—suicide, murder, accident, or spontaneous combustion—I damned sure was going to find out. I pointed at Chuck, who was still browbeating a patrol officer. "Let me see if they'll tell me anything."

I pushed my way through the crowd and sidled up to the crime scene tape. The officer left Chuck mid-complaint and blocked me. "I'm sorry, ma'am. You'll have to stand back."

"I work here."

"As I told this gentleman, no one can enter the building until—"

A familiar voice cut off the rest of his sentence. "Kate? Is that you?"

A petite and pretty woman with long, dark hair strode up to me. Detective Martinez. I'd met Martinez the night of my friend George's murder. She'd also investigated the stabbing death of Nicole's stepfather. Nicole's instincts had been right. If Martinez was on site, the police suspected murder.

"I should probably say I'm surprised to see you," Martinez said, "but I'm not. I'm beginning to think you're a murder scene groupie. I catch myself looking for you sometimes."

"So it *is* a murder," I replied.

She nodded.

Martinez and I were closer to acquaintances than friends, but I'd helped her solve the two previous cases, and I'd grown to respect her. I hoped the reverse was true.

"What are you doing downtown?" Martinez asked. "Did you open another business?"

"No, one yoga studio's plenty for me." I pointed at Teen Path HOME's brightly colored exterior. "But I teach here sometimes, too." I didn't volunteer that so far I'd taught a grand total of two classes. "I know the scene's off-limits to the public, but if you let me inside, I might notice something relevant."

Martinez hesitated, but only for a second. She nodded to the patrol officer. "Let her through. She's with me."

"Are you kidding me?" Chuck growled. "She's just a freakin' yoga teacher. If she's going in, I'm going in too."

The patrol officer gestured me through. His stern voice echoed behind me. "Sir, I warned you to stand back."

I had thousands of questions for Martinez as I entered the recreation area, but one was by far the most important. "Who was killed?"

"I'll tell you in a few minutes," Martinez replied. "I'd rather you not know until I get your unfiltered impressions." She handed me booties and gloves. "Put these on. Don't touch anything, and don't go anywhere without me. You're not a cop, but you've got good intuition. Tell me anything you notice, even if you think it's irrelevant."

My first thought? Everything seemed perfectly normal. That was the peculiar thing about violence. The world around it somehow kept spinning. If there'd been a life-or-death struggle in this room, I couldn't see it. No chairs overturned; no tables upended. A triangle of racked billiard balls lay carefully positioned on the pool table.

My second thought was significantly more sobering. Where was Gabriel? From what I could tell so far, the police weren't interviewing anyone inside. My stomach felt hollow. "Have you spoken to the other staff members?" I asked.

"A couple of them," Martinez replied. "Right now we're focused on processing the scene."

She led me to the conference room next. The tables were all neatly in rows; the chairs, stacked in their holding racks. The blinds were partially open, allowing in tiny slivers of light.

"Nothing out of the ordinary so far," I said.

Martinez nodded. "Let's go to the kitchen."

I filled the silence as we walked back across the recreation area. "I don't go looking for murder, you know. Somehow it manages to find me."

"Uh huh." Martinez pressed open the door to the kitchen.

"Seriously. My mother says it's my dhar—"

That's when the chaos erupted.

A flash of brown fur zoomed over Martinez's boot and into the kitchen. She jumped and yelped, "What the hell?"

Male voices rang from inside.

"There's a rat in here!"

"Christ, it touched me!"

"Watch out, it might have rabies!"

"Don't hurt them!" I cried. "They're pets!"

Martinez slammed the kitchen door shut, trapping Lonnie on the other side. Her face contorted in horror. "Them? You mean there's more than one?"

"There are two. Ed and Lonnie. They belong to the site manager."

She cracked open the door and yelled through it, "It's the victim's. Catch it and keep your eye out for a second one."

My throat tightened. "Gabriel's dead?"

Martinez groaned and buried her face in her hands. "Dammit! I didn't mean to say that."

A new voice joined the chorus, this time coming from Gabriel's office. "Get that animal away from my body!"

"That must be Ed!" I bolted toward the sound.

"Kate, stop! Don't go in there!"

Martinez's warning came two seconds too late.

I froze in the doorway to Gabriel's office, sickened. Gabriel's body sprawled face-up on the floor, lips frozen in a permanent grimace. Crimson liquid covered his chest and soaked the carpet beneath him. The smell of blood made me woozy, but my psyche could have handled that. Gabriel's eyes, on the other hand, would haunt my nightmares forever. Wide open. Unblinking. Dead.

A man I assumed was the medical examiner crouched over the body. A second man—who I recognized as Martinez's partner, Henderson—crawled under the desk, trying to capture a nine-inch gray rodent.

I swallowed—hard—and said the first two words that came to my mind. "Ed, come!" As trained, the oversized rat scurried out from underneath the desk and stood on his hind legs near my ankles. I reached down, picked him up, and allowed him to crawl to my shoulder. When he burrowed his head in my curls, I would have sworn he was crying.

The medical examiner glared at me sternly. "Get that rodent out of here."

Henderson backed out from under the desk. "What in the holy hell are you doing here?" I opened my mouth to answer, but he held up his palm. "Never mind. I don't want to know. Get out, and don't come back in here again."

No problem there. If I could hit rewind, I wouldn't have gone in the first time. I retreated from the office to the hallway and sagged against the wall. Saliva flooded my mouth. *Please God, please don't let me vomit. Not like the night I found George's body. I need to stay upright. I need to talk to Martinez.*

I closed my eyes and took a steadying breath. Then a second. Then a third.

Martinez's voice came from a great distance. "Geez, Kate. I'm sorry. I shouldn't have let you come inside the building. You didn't need to see that." A pause. "Kate, are you okay?" Another. "Kate?"

I held my hands up, eyes still firmly squeezed shut. "I'm fine. Just give me a minute."

Two more deliberate breaths later, I slowly opened them.

I immediately wished they were still closed.

A drawing of a teenage skeleton stared back at me. An empty white rectangle occupied space next to it. The card underneath the blank space read, *Another Life.*

Rainbow's drawing was missing.

Should I tell Martinez? The missing drawing might not be relevant. Gabriel had mentioned that he wanted to use *Another Life* in Teen Path HOME's promotional materials. Maybe he had taken it down to make copies.

Or maybe Rainbow...

A disgusted-looking officer interrupted my thoughts. He carried an unhappy brown rodent in a large Tupperware container. Lonnie scratched desperately against the side, trying to escape.

The man I would forever think of as Officer Tupperware spoke. "What do you want me to do with this..." He shuddered. "This *vermin* now, Detective?"

I pointed to the container. "His name is Lonnie, and you need to let him out of that. Now."

Ed crawled halfway down my arm and sniffed at his brother's plastic prison.

Martinez flashed me a you're-obviously-nuts look and gestured with her chin to Officer Tupperware. "What do you expect him to do? Carry that rat around on his shoulder like you're doing?"

The officer's face turned green. "Uh uh. No way. I'd rather be shot."

"I'm serious," I said. "You can't keep an animal in a sealed plastic container. He'll suffocate."

Martinez took the container from the officer and handed it to me. "Fine. You take it then."

I opened the lid. Lonnie raced up my shirt and hid in the back of my hair. I could have imagined it, but I thought Ed gave Officer Tupperware a dirty look before scrambling up my arm to join him. I handed the container back to Martinez, who snapped the lid back on and handed it to the officer.

She frowned. "You say the rodents belonged to the victim?"

"To Gabriel, yes."

She nodded to the officer. "Better call Animal Control."

I ignored the electric objections pulsing down my spine. Ed and Lonnie already lived in a cage. How much worse could one in an animal shelter be?

"Do they have facilities for rats?" I asked.

"Not my problem," Martinez replied.

It wasn't mine either. So why did I feel so guilty? Ed gently tugged my earlobe, as if whispering, *Take us home, Kate.* I ignored him. Lonnie upped the ante by chewing on my hair. I considered handing them back to Officer Tupperware, but I couldn't. Gabriel had cared for these creatures. Frankly, I was growing a little fond of them myself.

"Fine," I mumbled. "You win. But you're going to the pet store."

Martinez looked at me quizzically. "Who are you talking to?"

"Sorry, I was thinking out loud. They can stay at my husband's pet supply store until you find out if Gabriel's family wants them."

The right side of Martinez's mouth twitched upward. "Isn't this how you ended up with that dog?"

I ignored her. She was right. But unlike Bella, Ed and Lonnie might be adoptable. "I need their cage," I said. I pointed at Gabriel's office. "It's in there, on the table next to the desk."

As if reading my thoughts, Detective Henderson emerged from the room. His beard sported significantly more gray than the last time I'd seen him, but his ample beer belly had shrunk several inches. Henderson had always played the "bad cop" role in the Martinez-Henderson duo, at least when they were interrogating me. If his facial expression was any indication, not much had changed. He gave a dark look to Martinez, then spoke drolly to me. "Kate Davidson. Why am I not surprised?"

Martinez pointed to Gabriel's office. "Learn anything interesting in there?"

"Not much. The ME said the body's not in full rigor yet, so he estimates the victim died between six and eight hours ago."

I did the math in my head. "That means Gabriel was killed between one and three this morning. What was he doing here at that time of night? The center would have been closed for hours."

Henderson shrugged. "He might have been working late."

"Or meeting someone," Martinez added. "He obviously wasn't alone."

Lonnie crawled down my arm, readying for a high dive attempt to the floor. Ed wasn't far behind him. I needed to get these two locked up before they took off for the kitchen again. "I know I can't go inside Gabriel's office, but I need to contain these guys. Can you please get me their cage?"

"Sorry, Kate," Martinez replied. "I don't care if you take the animals until we figure out where they belong, but nothing else leaves that office until we finish processing the crime scene."

"How am I supposed to get them home? They can't run loose in my car."

She pointed at Officer Tupperware's container. "We can poke a couple of holes in the lid."

I would have sworn that I heard both rodents gasp. "Absolutely not," I said. "It's way too small. Did you see how panicked Lonnie was inside there?"

"Oh, for god's sake," Henderson grumbled. "Where's a good cat when you need one?" He spoke to the officer. "Go find a cardboard box somewhere and punch holes in it."

The six of us went in separate directions. Officer Tupperware left in search of a box. Henderson ambled back into Gabriel's office. Martinez and I moved to a couch in the recreation area. Lonnie and Ed hunkered down on my shoulders, as if using my hair for camouflage.

Before that morning, if anyone had asked me to wear a stole made of live rats, I would have assured them I'd rather do Hot Yoga in Hades. The mere thought would have made me want to run, gagging, for the nearest restroom. Now I felt exactly the opposite. The tiny creatures' warmth settled my stomach. Comforted me. Made the scene in Gabriel's office less horrible somehow.

Such is the power of animals.

Even animals people think of as vermin.

"Notice anything significant so far?" Martinez asked.

"You mean besides the hole in Gabriel's chest?"

Admittedly, now wasn't the best moment for sarcasm, but I was stalling. Trying to figure out what I should tell Martinez about Rainbow's missing drawing. I didn't know when it had been removed, but its absence was certainly suspicious. If, as I assumed, the drawing had been stolen, Rainbow was the most likely thief, which made her the most likely suspect in Gabriel's murder. Means and opportunity were no-brainers. She'd had plenty of time to get to Teen Path HOME before Gabriel was killed, and she'd carried a handgun and ammunition. What I couldn't figure out was motive. Why would Rainbow have come back to Teen Path HOME? And if she did, why would she have killed Gabriel?

Martinez gently nudged my arm. "There's something you don't want to tell me, isn't there?"

Guilt gnawed at my stomach, but I told her anyway. "There's a drawing missing from a display in the hallway."

Martinez pulled out a notebook. "We noticed it too. The witness who found the body teaches art here. She's pretty upset, so it's hard to get much out of her, but she says nothing was missing from the display when they closed up last night. Evidently the missing piece was done by a kid named … " She consulted her notes. "A kid named Rainbow. Does that ring any bells?"

"I've met her a couple of times." Which was true, if incomplete.

Martinez continued. "She also said there was some hullabaloo here yesterday with the kid's father. Evidently he claimed that she'd stolen a gun?"

"I was here when that happened. But it was her stepfather, not her father, and no one actually saw a gun." *At least no one but me, and then not until eight hours later.* I avoided eye contact by plucking Lonnie off my shoulder and stroking his back.

Martinez narrowed her eyes. "You're hiding something." She stared me down silently for ten interminable seconds, making my discomfort grow with each tick of the clock. On tick number eleven,

Officer Tupperware returned, carrying a large cardboard box and two clear plastic evidence bags.

"The evidence techs said we could use this box for the rats. I've also got a couple of other items I think you should look at."

The first bag contained a metal cash box. A large dent near the lock hinted that the lid had been forced open. The second held a handgun that looked an awful lot like the one I'd temporarily taken from Rainbow.

"Where were these?" Martinez asked.

"Behind a dumpster in the alley," Officer Tupperware replied.

"Together?"

"The gun was inside the box."

"Good work," Martinez said. "Have the lab dust them for prints."

I envisioned my bare hands taking the gun from Rainbow and placing it inside my purse. Color drained from my face.

"Kate?" Martinez asked. "Are you sure you're okay? You look like you're about to pass out."

"I need to tell you something." I swallowed, but the knot in my throat tightened anyway. "You might find my prints on that gun."

Martinez suddenly got a lot less friendly. She tossed Ed and Lonnie into their new cardboard prison and sequestered me in the conference room for forty-five minutes. After an evidence tech took my fingerprints, I told her everything. That Rainbow was one of my yoga students, that she'd shown up at the studio asking for my help, that she had, indeed, stolen her stepfather's handgun, and that I'd taken it from her before driving her to my house.

"She swiped it from my purse again before she bolted. But honestly, I don't think she has anything to do with Gabriel's murder. I don't even know for sure that it's her gun."

"We'll figure that part out easily enough. Ballistics can confirm it's the murder weapon, and I'll check the serial number to see if it belongs to the stepfather. Fingerprint analysis will tell us the rest. But Kate, what the hell? Why didn't you lead with this information?"

"I hoped it wouldn't be relevant." The answer, though honest, sounded completely lame, even to my own ears.

"Enough stonewalling," Martinez said. "I need you to be honest with me. Where is Rainbow now?"

"I have no idea."

Martinez's glare would have fried onions.

"Honestly, I don't know. I came here today because I was trying to find her. Detective Martinez, I don't think she did this. She had no motive."

"I can see plenty of motive. We found a mess in the kitchen. Looks like your friend broke in here to swipe supplies and got caught by the victim."

"Gabriel," I said. "His name was Gabriel."

Her expression softened. "Gabriel. You told me yourself that this Rainbow kid was adamant about not going back to her stepfather, and that if Gabriel saw her, he'd have been forced to turn her in. She might have panicked. People have killed for less."

I ignored the comment, mainly because I knew it was true. "You mentioned that someone broke in. Did you see signs of forced entry?" I asked.

"Depends on what you mean by forced," Martinez said. "We found an open window in the kitchen. It doesn't appear to have been jimmied, but the lock doesn't fully engage, either. The art teacher didn't know anything about the broken lock, but she told us this Rainbow kid volunteered in the kitchen."

"So do a lot of other kids."

"Fair enough. But you have to admit, your friend looks suspicious."

Something still felt off about the theory. "If the burglar—and I'm not saying it's Rainbow—got interrupted in the kitchen, why did the shooting take place in Gabriel's office?"

"I don't know, but there are lots of possibilities. Maybe she *didn't* get caught in the kitchen. Maybe she got caught swiping the drawing. Maybe Gabriel brought her into his office to talk. Hell, maybe he called her into the office for some nefarious reason and she shot him in self-defense. For all we know, he wasn't the Mr. Nice Guy we've all been led to believe."

"Why dump the gun?"

"What do you mean?"

"It was found in the alley, right?"

"Yes. What's your point?"

"Whoever left it there had to have known someone would find it. The cash box, I can see. Most of these kids carry everything they own in a backpack, and a cash box that size would be too big to take with them. But why not keep the gun or dump it somewhere far away?"

"Criminals don't always behave logically, Kate. From what you've told me about Rainbow, I doubt she came here intending to kill anyone. The victim surprised her, and the unthinkable happened. She was probably afraid she'd be caught with the evidence." She sighed. "Hell, she's just a kid. She likely planned to come back and pick it up later. She may have assumed that no one would look behind the dumpster."

"But we don't know for sure that Rainbow—"

"You're right. We don't know anything for sure. That's why we're collecting evidence." Martinez stood. "I'm not rushing to judgment here, Kate. We're still processing the scene. Even if we don't find anything else relevant—and we almost always do—the gun will likely tell us all that we need. Until then, we wait."

I'd never been a fan of waiting, but in this case, time might be on my side. I picked up the box containing Michael's and my new foster pets. "If it's okay, I should probably go and get these two guys settled. You know where to find me."

"I do." She pointed her index finger at me and said sternly, "Don't forget that. And, Kate?"

"Yes?"

"I need to talk to that kid. You'll let me know if she contacts you, right?"

"Absolutely." *Right after I convince Dale to represent her.*

TWELVE

I LEFT THE BUILDING almost two hours after I'd gone inside. Not surprisingly, Nicole and Hope were gone. A dozen of the center's teens still huddled around the crime scene tape. They seemed lost. Unsure where to go now that their daytime shelter was off limits. I tried asking them about Rainbow, without much success. Most of them claimed they didn't know her. All of them said they had no idea where she might be staying.

I didn't believe them, or at least not all of them. Rainbow had spent too much time at the center to have made no connections. But these kids didn't know me, and in their world, trust had to be earned. If I wanted any of the Team Path HOME clients to help me find Rainbow, I'd need to figure out how to make it worth their while.

Dharma's voice whispered in my subconscious, *Are you sure Rainbow's the one you're supposed to be helping?*

It was an excellent question. My mother believed that solving murders was my dharma—my lifework. She claimed I was meant to bring justice to those who couldn't find it for themselves. Which begged the question: Who needed justice in this case, Rainbow or Gabriel? Admittedly, I hadn't known Gabriel well, but he'd seemed like a good man. A good man who'd died a violent death, perhaps at the hands of a youth he was trying to help. Rainbow seemed like a basically good kid, too. But I'd cared about basically good kids who'd committed horrendous crimes before. If Rainbow *had* killed Gabriel, she'd need to atone for her crime. It was the only way she could heal. If she hadn't, however ...

Either way, I had to find out, which meant that Michael and I would have two topics to argue about in the near future: his fostering Ed and Lonnie at the pet store and my getting involved in another murder investigation.

I figured I might as well tackle the easiest one first. Pete's Pets only carried dog and cat supplies, so I stopped at a big box pet store and purchased a cage like the one in Gabriel's office. I hoped that having familiar surroundings would make the little fellows feel more secure. I added an exercise wheel, a bag of bedding, and a box of generic rat kibble. My replacement Visa card hadn't arrived yet, so I paid for the supplies with a check from my rapidly dwindling checking account. I considered stopping at the drug store for a pregnancy test, but I couldn't handle any more disappointment. Not today.

I finished shopping and hurried to the studio, hoping to get Ed and Lonnie settled in at Pete's Pets before my three o'clock private client. Luckily—or unluckily, depending on your viewpoint—Michael wasn't there. He'd left Tiffany in charge and gone home to start dinner preparations.

I'd been looking forward to spending the evening with Dharma and Dale chatting about goats, yoga, and Michael's and my married life. Now I had a different agenda: convince Dale to represent Rainbow. Dale had helped my loved ones out multiple times in the past.

This time my request felt different, though. This time I was asking him to represent a relative stranger. A relative stranger who was also indigent. Even for Dale, it was asking a lot.

I helped Tiffany clear out a space for Lonnie and Ed's cage, so busy strategizing the evening to come that I barely noticed her *And Baby Makes Three* T-shirt. "I don't know, Tiffany. Are you sure this is the best place for them?" I gestured at the display of cat kibble, litter, and mouse-shaped toys. "Ed and Lonnie will think they're next on the menu."

"It's like that Alanis Morissette song."

I gave her a droll look.

"You know, 'Ironic.' Jeez, Kate, how old are you anyway? I thought for sure you'd get that reference. That song was decades ago."

I ignored her and kept talking. "Do me a favor. If Michael calls, don't let him know about Ed and Lonnie. I'd rather tell him about them myself."

Tiffany swiped her hand through the air. "Pshaw. You're making a cavern out of a rat hole." She nudged my ribs with her elbow. "Get it?"

"Yeah, yeah. You're a big comedian." But I smiled in spite of myself.

"Seriously, Kate, it'll be fine. Michael's a big softy, and he adores animals. He'll love having the little dudes here." She leaned forward and poked a long, burgundy-painted nail through the wires. Ed nudged it with his nose, then chomped on it.

Tiffany jumped back, squealing. "He bit me!"

"It wasn't a bite; it was a love nibble." I surreptitiously massaged my earlobe where Ed had chewed on it earlier.

Tiffany examined her nail. "Do you think he has rabies?"

"Of course not. He probably thought your fingernail was food."

"I don't know, that bite was pretty hard." She held her index finger a foot from my eyelids. The nail was missing a rat-bite-sized chunk of paint. "He ruined my manicure." She chewed on her lower lip. "Maybe it's not such a good idea to leave them here after all. Michael will have a stroke if a kid gets bitten."

She wasn't wrong.

"Why don't you take them to your place?" she asked.

"I have a cat, remember? They wouldn't survive the night. How about your apartment?"

"My landlord doesn't allow pets. Besides, Chad would have a fit. He's already convinced I'm going to get that toxo-whatever disease from handling cat litter here at the store."

"Toxoplasmosis?"

She nodded.

"You know you can't get toxoplasmosis from clean litter, right?"

"Of course I do. But try telling that to Chad."

We negotiated for a while longer, but ultimately I prevailed. When I left, Tiffany was gingerly hand-feeding rat kibble between the cage's metal bars. The fat little guys snatched each piece from her, then sat on their haunches to consume it. I had a feeling that the next time I saw Tiffany, she'd be sporting a *Crazy Rat Lady* outfit and Mighty Mouse earrings.

I taught my private client while firmly set on yoga teacher auto pilot. The instructions I gave her were adequate, but my mind never entered the space. It wandered between Ballard and Teen Path HOME, seeking solutions to unanswered questions. Where was Rainbow? Were Gabriel's murder and her disappearance connected? Who had taken Rainbow's drawing and why? What was Gabriel doing at Teen Path HOME in the middle of the night? How did Rainbow's gun—it had to be her gun, didn't it?—end up hidden behind the dumpster?

By the time I said goodbye to my frustrated-looking student, my energy felt tense; my back, achy. Almost as achy as it did when I started my—

115

Oh no. Please God, please let this be a normal backache. Please, this one time, give Michael and me a break.

The red stain I discovered on my underwear felt almost as lethal as the one I'd seen spread across Gabriel's chest. No need to spring for a pregnancy test after all. Mighty Katie had struck out.

I spent the drive home trying to figure out what to tell Michael. A lifetime had passed since we'd said goodbye this morning, and I'd have less than half an hour to fill him in before Dharma and Dale arrived. What was I supposed to say?

Hi, honey. You'll never believe the day I had. Remember that guy Gabriel I told you about? Well, he's sporting a brand spanking new hole in his chest, courtesy of a gun that's probably covered in my finger-prints. I left you a present—two of them, actually—at the pet store. Oh, and that little bundle of joy we hoped I was carrying? It was all a big joke. One big guffaw from the universe.

I wiped the backs of my hands across my cheeks. *Get it together, Kate. You can't let Dharma and Dale see you like this.*

I wasn't sure why I was crying, anyway. I was upset about getting my period, sure, but more than that, I was pissed. I was no Mother Teresa, but I tried to be a good person. I'd always believed that the universe was essentially benevolent. That in the end, life was fair. Yet instead of carrying the baby Michael and I so desperately wanted, I was bleeding into a tampon. Again. Nothing about that seemed fair.

I wished Dharma and Dale weren't coming over. I hadn't seen them in almost six months, and fifteen minutes earlier, I'd been looking forward to their short visit. Now I couldn't stand the thought of being around anyone, including myself.

I bathed in my pity party the entire drive home, grateful that at least I'd have a few minutes alone with Michael before they arrived. But damned if that trickster universe didn't have one more practical joke up its sleeve. When I pulled into the driveway, Dale's rattletrap orange Plymouth pickup was parked on the street. They were early.

I put on my game face and snuck in through the door to the kitchen, hoping I could catch Michael alone there. The kitchen was empty, but Michael had obviously been busy. Red lentil beans dotted the floor, interspersed with a snow-like dusting of dried oregano and basil. Papery garlic skins decorated the counter. I ignored the sink overflowing with pots, pans, knives, and cutting boards and took a deep inhale. Freshly baked sourdough.

Laughter and light conversation floated from the living room. I steeled myself to join the party but stopped, nailed to the floor by a white business envelope Michael had conspicuously left on the table. The reply to our IVF loan application. I slid the folded page out of the envelope.

Denied.

Why was I surprised? I wouldn't have loaned that much money to us either. I grabbed the last clean wine glass, filled it to the top from an open bottle of Cabernet, and joined Dale, Dharma, and Michael in the living room. Michael glanced up from the couch and looked pointedly at my wine glass. His smile didn't go past his lips.

"Trying the new red?" His code for *no baby again?*

I pasted on an equally rehearsed smile and said, "I figured red would go better with your lentil stew than white." A pause. "Was that today's mail on the table?"

"Yes."

"Hmmm."

We were dancing our new dance. The pretend-nothing's-wrong waltz. If only we'd stop stepping on each other's toes.

Dharma glanced quizzically between us, long gray braid swishing across her shoulders. I wrapped her in a huge hug and said, "It's wonderful to see you."

"You look tired," she replied.

"Dharma, you have no idea."

Dale leaned forward in the guest chair. "Missy Kate, come give this old boy some sugar, too." He gestured toward his feet. "I'd come over there and hug you myself, but as you can see, I'm otherwise indisposed."

He was referring to Bella, who had draped herself across his work boots. Mouse surveyed us all from the top level of her cat tree. I kissed him on the least hairy part of his cheek. "It's great to see you, too. It's been too long." I glanced around the room, looking for their black-and-white fur child. "Where's Bandit?" Dale's precocious Jack Russell Terrier usually went everywhere with him.

"I left him at the rescue with a dog sitter. I love the little monster, but he's a troublemaker. Dharma and I are going to be busy this weekend with the farm animal festival. We won't have time to chase after him."

By "farm animal festival," Dale meant a Friday-through-Sunday fundraising event organized by four of Washington State's most prominent farm animal rescues, Dale's Goats and Dharma's Asses included. This year's festivities were going to take place in Olympia, Washington's capital, which was about two hours south of Seattle. The activities ranged from adoption events to goat agility competitions to in-depth classes on farm animal husbandry.

I appreciated Dale's subterfuge, but I knew he was lying. Dale hated being away from Bandit as much as I hated being separated

118

from Bella. He'd left him on Orcas because it was safer than trying to keep Bandit and Bella separated. Our two dogs had a love/hate relationship. Meaning that Bandit loved to torture Bella, and Bella hated every hair on his black-spotted body. Bandit might start their inevitable fight, but with their size difference, Bella would certainly win it. I'd been worried about how we could keep the two warring animals safe overnight. Dale must have shared my concern.

I buried my day's traumas and dove right into my concerns about Rainbow. "I'm glad we're all four together tonight. I could use some advice about a friend of mine."

A single chime came from the kitchen.

"That's the oven timer," Michael said. "Let's talk over dinner."

When we got to the kitchen, Michael surreptitiously slid the denied loan application under a pile of magazines, then pulled the bread from the oven and cut it into thick, steaming pieces while I told Dharma and Dale about how I'd met Rainbow, her status as a runaway, and Michael's and my failed attempt to give her shelter the night before. I decided to avoid mentioning Gabriel's murder, at least to start. Talking about murder would be easier after everyone had downed a couple glasses of wine.

Michael covered the bread and set it on the table. "I feel terrible about it now, but I told Kate to call the police. I was afraid we'd get in trouble for harboring a runaway."

"Your instincts were good," Dale said. "Anyone who provides shelter to an unaccompanied minor is legally required to contact either the parents or the police within eight hours. Keeping her longer than that would have been a mistake."

Michael sighed. "I know. I looked it up online this morning. Still, it was after ten at night when she got here. Would it have killed me to wait until morning? If I'd given that kid a little more time to settle in and trust us, she might be safe right now instead of hiding out on the streets, cold and frightened."

"The thing is, she's in more trouble than you realize." I took a deep breath. "There's been a murder."

I'm not sure what reaction I expected, but if it was surprise that I'd stumbled into another murder investigation, that's not what I got. Dale stared at me, expression neutral but interested. Dharma nodded her head approvingly. Michael's shoulders slumped in a combination of guilt, depression, and defeat. On the plus side, he didn't chastise me this time.

I told them about my morning's expedition to Teen Path HOME. The scene outside, Gabriel's body, the missing drawing.

Michael's eyes grew wide. "The murder victim was Gabriel? As in, Sam's college roommate Gabriel? Is Sam okay?"

Dull achiness throbbed behind my eyes. I stared at the table and rubbed the crease between my eyebrows. It was a good question. One I should have been able to answer. "Honestly, I don't know. I'm not sure he knows yet."

"You didn't call him?"

"I've been so worried about Rainbow, it never occurred to me." I mentally promised to remedy that after dinner.

"I wouldn't be too worried about the teen," Dale said. "At least not yet. The missing drawing is hardly conclusive evidence."

"The police have more than the drawing, though." I continued my story, ending with the gun the police discovered and why I suspected it belonged to Rainbow.

Michael's eyes flashed with anger. "You brought a loaded gun into our house?"

"It wasn't loaded, at least not at the time. Besides, I didn't know what else to do."

"There wasn't anything else *to* do," Dharma assured me. "The child needed help."

"The police are looking for her?" Dale asked

"Yes. As far as I know, they don't have an arrest warrant for her yet, but she's definitely a person of interest." I hesitated, trying to broach my true intention carefully. "What would you say to her, if you were her attorney?"

Dale frowned and raked his fingers through his beard. "The first thing I'd tell her is that running makes her look guilty. I'd encourage her to talk to the police as soon as possible. With counsel present, of course."

"Could that counsel be you?"

Dale pretended to misunderstand my question. "Representing a minor isn't all that complicated. Any lawyer who's passed the Washington State Bar Exam could do it."

Dharma scowled. "That's not what Kate means, and you know it. If the girl ends up arrested, will you represent her?" The tone of her voice clearly implied that the only acceptable answer was yes.

"Don't you think the child's parents should be the ones to find her representation?" Dale asked.

"I don't think they will," I replied. "Rainbow's mother disappeared on a heroin binge three months ago and her stepfather's a ghoul. As far as I know, she doesn't have anyone else. She'll end up with a public defender."

"Assuming she's arrested," Dale countered.

"Even if she doesn't get implicated in that man's death, someone obviously needs to look out for her interests," Dharma said. "Her home life sounds atrocious."

Dale frowned. "You know, you ladies are putting an awful lot of stock in that young woman's story. Teenagers have been known to stretch the truth on occasion. Her mother may be sitting by the phone in a panic, waiting for someone to call saying her daughter's been killed—or worse. And the stepfather may not be perfect, but he also may not be the ogre you've been led to believe. Not every kid that runs away from home has nowhere to go, and not every man who yells at his kid is an abuser. Sometimes the family simply needs help figuring out how to resolve conflict."

"I don't think that's the case here." In fact, I felt certain it wasn't. As certain as Bella was that psycho killers drove UPS trucks.

"You may be right," Dale replied. "Then again, you may also be wrong. Either way, your young friend has options. If she truly doesn't have anywhere to go, Child Protective Services will intervene."

I vehemently shook my head. "Rainbow doesn't want to end up in foster care."

"Can you blame her?" Dharma said. "A troubled teen in the foster system won't have it easy."

Dale turned to Michael. "Are you going to sit there and let them gang up on me?"

"Sorry, Dale," Michael replied. "I'm with them on this one."

Dale sighed. "Of course you are. You know, some kids in the system turn out fine. She might be one of the lucky ones."

Dharma leaned back and crossed her arms. "Do you really believe that?"

The expression on Dale's face told me he didn't. I didn't either. More importantly, Rainbow didn't believe it. I couldn't let her end up back on the streets, tossed aside like a bag of trash. "Dale, I'm afraid for her. She's not safe on the streets. If they put her in the system, she'll run again. I know she will."

Dale didn't speak for several seconds. When he did, his entire white beard seemed to frown. "You know, Kate, it was a heck of a lot more convenient for me when you got into trouble on Orcas. At least then I didn't have to abandon the farm to help."

"I'm not the one in trouble this time. It's a kid who has no one else. Dale, she's sixteen."

Dale peered over his wine glass at Dharma, as if looking for moral support. Dharma lifted her eyebrows and shrugged.

He moved on to Michael, who shook his head. "I'm still kicking myself for not helping her last night."

"Fine. You win." Dale gestured around the table. "You all win. Find me the kid and I'll talk to her. No promises after that."

"Thank you, Dale. I'll make it up to you someday, I promise."

Now all I had to do was find her. My mood should have been lightened, and honestly it was, a little. But my heart was still weighted by Gabriel's death and the unborn child I might never conceive.

Michael made a pretense of normalcy by mopping up the dregs of two large bowls of hearty tomato, artichoke, and lentil stew with chunks of whole-grain sourdough. An unlikely concoction that I usually found irresistible. Tonight, I could barely force myself to touch it.

Still, I tried. I took small sips of wine and moved food around on my plate in a desperate attempt to make it seem like I'd eaten. Dharma's concerned gaze burned a hole through my forehead.

I'd become sensitive to energy in my late twenties. I'd originally thought reading energy was a skill I'd acquired teaching yoga. But during those long, uncomfortable minutes avoiding Dharma's gaze, I realized it was genetic. Dharma examined me, brow creased in concern. She noted the dark circles under my eyes; the unspoken sadness between Michael and me. As she watched my food move in circles, her expression grew quizzical. Something was wrong, but what?

"Are you okay, Kate?" She asked. "You look a little peaked to me."

I tried to smile, but my lips refused to obey. "I'm not feeling all that well tonight. It's probably the stress about Rainbow." I picked up my wine glass, but even the earthy scent of Cabernet made my stomach churn.

Dale glanced at my plate, then at my wine glass, then back at my plate again. "Dharma's right. You've seemed off all night, and you look positively green. You remind me of that friend of yours, Rene, back on Orcas when—" He stopped speaking. The right side of his mouth lifted. "You've barely taken a sip of that wine. That glass is a big fat pretense, isn't it?"

Michael gestured wildly beside me, trying to get Dale's attention.

"Why Miss Kate, you've been playing us. You're pregnant!" He reached across the table for my hands, beaming. "It's about time you two made me a grandpa!"

We all reacted to Dale's words. Michael squeezed his eyes shut, as if willing himself to disappear. Dharma gave Dale a look that would have soured milk. I . . .

Well, I lost it.

To my horror, my throat spasmed. My eyes started burning. I couldn't cry. Not here. Not in front of Dharma and Dale. I pulled away from Dale's grasp, tossed my napkin on the table, and pushed back my chair. It caught against my heel and crashed to the floor, almost taking me with it.

My words came out in garbled half gasps. "I'm sorry . . . I . . . I need to use the restroom." I stumbled out of the kitchen, bolted across the living room, and took the stairs two at a time.

Dharma's stern admonition echoed from the kitchen. "Dale Evans, you're a big-mouthed old fool."

I slammed the door to the bathroom and locked it behind me. Solid wood muffled Dale's plaintive reply. "Dharma, why are you mad? What did I do?"

Tears streamed down my face in spite of my best efforts to contain them. I sat on the edge of Dad's jetted tub and tried to catch my breath. *Please, God. Please don't let anyone follow me up here. Not even Michael. Please give me a few minutes alone to get myself back together.*

God wasn't listening, or—more likely—not even an all-powerful deity could stop Dharma once she'd made up her mind. I heard three soft taps on the door, then Dharma's concerned voice. "Kate? Are you okay?"

"I'm fine. The lentils must have upset my stomach." The tremor in my voice betrayed me.

I imagined Dharma placing her palm against the door's cool, smooth surface. "Can I come in?"

I didn't reply. Instead, I waited through one long breath, then another.

Dharma spoke again. "Kate?"

I wiped smudged mascara from under my eyes, then stood and unlocked the door. Bella nosed through it first and nudged my hands, whining. Dharma locked the door, took my prior place on the jetted tub and patted the space beside her. "Not the most comfortable room in the house, but it'll do. At least the men won't follow us here. Sit. Let's talk."

I sat. I avoided making eye contact with Dharma by staring into the mirror above the sink. A stranger with hollow, red-rimmed eyes stared back at me.

"Kate honey, what's going on? And please don't say it's an upset stomach. If it's none of my business, fine. Tell me that. But don't lie to me."

I stared at my hands and kept breathing.

"Dale's a good man. He's usually a smart one, too. But he really stepped in it tonight."

"It's okay."

"No, it's not, but it's nice of you to say so. Do you want to talk about it?"

I opened my mouth to say no, then closed it again. The true answer, which surprised me, was yes. Words that had come so hard with Rene poured out of me sitting on cold porcelain next to Dharma. Maybe it was because I'd already told someone other than Michael. Maybe it was because I'd been forced to deal with Tiffany's pregnancy. Then again, maybe Dharma was becoming more like a true mother to me than I'd ever imagined.

"I'm not pregnant, but it's not for lack of trying. Michael and I can't have children."

"Can't?"

"No, at least not without help. And maybe not even then."

For the next twenty minutes, I told Dharma everything. About rising FSH levels, scarred fallopian tubes, missed opportunities. "Having a child naturally isn't out of the question, but it's pretty darned unlikely. We want to try IVF, but it's expensive." I met her eyes. "I mean *really* expensive. The doctor says that given my test results, the chances of a single cycle being successful are less than ten percent. We've applied for a couple of loans, but so far we've been denied. I shouldn't have gotten upset when Dale assumed I was pregnant, but I'm touchy right now, and I can't seem to control my emotions. I'm sorry."

"Don't be ridiculous, Kate. I only wish you'd told us sooner. Then Dale wouldn't have stepped in that big pile of goat dung." She gave me a squeeze, then turned me to face her. "I know I missed the first thirty-two years of your life, but I hope that's behind us now."

I smiled. "We're certainly working on it, aren't we?"

"Yes, and you know what that means, don't you?"

I shook my head.

"It means you have family." She paused, as if thinking. "I spent most of my life trying to save mountain gorillas, which didn't exactly leave me rich."

"I know, Dharma. Animal activism may be the one career that pays worse than teaching yoga."

"I could talk to Dale, though. He—"

I held up my palms, stopping her. "No, Dharma. Michael and I already owe Dale a pregnancy's worth of legal fees. We can't accept any more from him. It's too much."

The least attractive part of me hoped that my words weren't convincing. I wanted Dharma to browbeat me into taking Dale's money. She was right. History notwithstanding, she was my mother. The universe had given her a child, and she hadn't even wanted one. I needed that same miracle, more than I needed anything else, including my pride.

She didn't let me down. "Dale should be the one to decide what's too much, don't you think? He's smart about money, and he made a lot of it when he was a full-time attorney."

"I know. But it's not about whether or not he can afford it, at least not completely. Rene's wealthy, and she offered to lend me the money too. But how can I take money from a friend to finance my family, especially when I may never be able to pay it back?"

Dharma gave me a stern look. "Kate, don't you ever call Dale a 'friend' where he can hear you. Not unless you want to hurt his feelings. Dale thinks of you as his daughter."

A new wave of tears threatened my eyes.

Her expression softened. "Did you know that Dale gave up practicing law for several years?"

"Yes. I was his first client—at least his first criminal client—afterwards."

"Did he tell you why?"

I nodded. Dale had worked his legal magic and gotten a domestic abuser off with a fine. Three days later, that same client killed the woman he'd been abusing.

"Then you know that since the day that woman died, Dale has been trying to atone."

"Her death wasn't Dale's fault. He was just doing his job."

"I've told him the same thing hundreds of times. He refuses to believe it." Dharma grasped my hands and squeezed. "Don't you see, Kate? You might be doing Dale a favor. Helping to bring a new life into the world might make him feel like he's evened things out."

The tears threatening my eyes spilled down my cheeks. "Even if we get the money, the whole process seems so hard. How many months can I wait, peeing on plastic sticks and dreading my period? The tests showed that my egg reserves are low, so our chances of success aren't all that great. It would probably take multiple tries. I'm unstable enough on a good day. Can you imagine me dosed up on hormones for the next year?"

"Get used to it. Pregnancy hormones won't be much better." Dharma grinned. "I have a feeling we'll all survive. Will you let me talk to Dale?"

My reply came out as a choked whisper. "Yes. But please don't ask him tonight. I need to talk it over with Michael first."

"I won't say a word until after we've hit the road for Olympia. Kate, I promise, everything's going to be all right."

For the moment, at least, I believed her.

THIRTEEN

I WAVED GOODBYE TO Dharma and Dale at seven the next morning, wishing they could have stayed longer. We'd spent the rest of the night hanging out, catching up, and trying—unsuccessfully—to convince Mouse to allow one of us to pet her. By unspoken agreement, the four of us didn't talk about my retreat to the bathroom or what Dharma and I had discussed while we were sequestered inside it. If Dale's questioning look was any indication, Michael hadn't clued him in about what was wrong with me. I didn't think it was possible, but his discretion made me love him even more.

After we all went to bed, Michael and I discussed Dharma's offer. To my surprise, he readily agreed to take out a loan from Dale should Dale be willing to give it. Neither of us liked the idea of taking money from him, but if the banks continued to reject our loan applications, it was the best option available to us. As long as Dale agreed, of course.

In the meantime, I distracted myself by making a plan to help Rainbow. The morning yoga teachers would staff the studio until eleven-thirty, so when Michael left to open Pete's Pets, I rubbed catnip all over Mouse's living room cat tree, gave Bella an ostrich tendon, and pulled out a notebook. Two long sips of fragrant caramel-hazelnut coffee later, I started brainstorming.

Action item number one. Find her. Which led to the first problem: How? I'd spent limited time with her. Certainly not enough to know who—other than her boyfriend, Jace—she'd hung out with. I planned to confront Jace the next time I saw him, but now that he'd dumped Rainbow, I doubted he'd know where she'd gone.

Jace couldn't be her only friend though, could he?

Rainbow had been active at Teen Path HOME. She'd taken part in the art and kitchen programs, which meant she'd spent time with Vonnie and Chuck. She might have spoken with them about her life outside the center. At the very least, they might know which of the other teens she'd befriended.

Underneath the words *Find Rainbow*, I added a bullet point: *Talk to Vonnie, Chuck, and Jace*. Below that, I added, *Interview other youth at the center*. If the teens I'd spoken with yesterday were any indication, most of them would stonewall me, but I couldn't know that for sure until I tried.

I tapped my pen against the notebook. What if I sweetened the deal? Money was tight, but my childbearing future wouldn't be significantly altered by a fifty-dollar finder's fee. I added *Go to bank machine* to my growing to-do list.

Bella's tail thumped on the carpet beside me. "Don't worry, sweetie. Michael and I may starve, but we'll always feed you."

I turned back to the notebook. What else did I know about Rainbow? I wrote down the word *Tacoma*. Rainbow mentioned that she'd lived in Tacoma before she ran away. Now that she was in trouble, would she go back there? I doubted it. The risk of running into her stepfather would be too high. But I couldn't eliminate the possibility, either.

How did knowing that Rainbow was from Tacoma help me, though? Tacoma had over two hundred thousand residents, and I had no idea which part of the city Rainbow used to call home. Was I supposed to drive up and down every street on the off-chance that I'd see her?

Bella finished her tendon and hopped up on the couch beside me. Mouse glared at me from the top of her cat tree.

There had to be a way to narrow it down. Rainbow's home address would be a great start. Detective Martinez undoubtedly knew it, especially if the serial number on the gun had been traced back to Dean. The question was, would she give it to me? I wrote down another note: *Call Detective Martinez.*

How could I find the address if Martinez refused to tell me? Rainbow's last name was Roads, or a version of that name with a different spelling. Since no one knew who Rainbow's biological father was, she and her mother probably shared the same last name, or at least they had at one time. Unfortunately, Rainbow hadn't told me her mother's first name. And while I knew her stepfather's first name, I didn't know his last.

Ugh.

Directory assistance would probably be a dead end, but I added searching it to the list anyway.

Bella sighed and placed her chin on my thigh. Her way of saying that watching humans write in notebooks was boring. I rubbed the bridge of her nose, and she licked my fingers with her black-spotted tongue. I sat up straighter. *Bella's tongue! The photo!* Rainbow had posted the selfie she'd taken with Bella on Instagram. If her Instagram profile was public, I might be able to find it. She might have left some clues there.

I pushed Bella off my lap. "Come on, sweetie. We're going to the office."

I pulled up a browser and started typing. I knew Rainbow's real name was Rain Roads, but I had no idea how she spelled it. I did a quick Google search and jotted down the options I found. For her first name there were six: Raine, Rain, Rainn, Rayne, Reine, or Reign. Seven, if you counted Rainbow. For her last, six more: Rhoades, Rhoads, Rhodes, Roads, Roades, and Rodes.

If my math was correct, that left me with forty-two possible combinations. If Rainbow used an unknown middle name or a different name entirely, I could be scouring social media until Rene's twins graduated from college. Still, it was worth a try. I'd never used Instagram before, but how complicated could it be? I added *Search for Rainbow on Instagram* to my growing to-do list. Below it, I added all of the different spellings I'd found.

Ten more minutes of brainstorming later, I put planning aside and began ticking off items.

I started by calling Teen Path HOME in hopes of connecting with Vonnie and Chuck. After three rings I got a short but to-the-point voicemail. "Thank you for calling Teen Path HOME. Due to unforeseen circumstances, we will be closed until further notice. For immediate assistance, please call the Seattle/King County twenty-four-hour crisis line at—" I hung up before listening to the rest of the message.

Closed until further notice? Had the police closed Teen Path HOME for the foreseeable future? It wasn't impossible, I supposed, but in my all-too-frequent experience, crime scenes were processed and released pretty quickly.

I tried Martinez next. Another voicemail. I left a message asking her to call me.

Two options down, two to go. Directory assistance seemed like a long shot, so I pulled up Instagram instead. I created an account and played around with it for a few minutes. Fortunately, the interface was easy to figure out, even for a relative technophobe like me. I flipped to a blank page on my notebook and prepared to search in earnest.

I created a seven-by-six matrix with potential first names on the vertical axis, last names on the horizontal. I spoke out loud to no one in particular. "Please let Rainbow's account be public." Bella padded into the room and cocked her head at me curiously.

"Sorry, sweetie. I was talking to myself. Go back to sleep."

Bella complied.

I picked up my pen and prepared to check off each possibility one at a time. I typed each name into the search bar and scanned through dozens upon dozens of teeny tiny profile pictures, clicking on every one that wasn't an obvious mismatch. Fifteen minutes later, my efforts had netted me a cramped index finger and significant eyestrain. None of the accounts so far were Rainbow's.

On minute sixteen, I struck pay dirt.

I recognized the smile in her profile photo immediately. *Rayne Rhodes. Lover of animals, creator of art.* She'd posted hundreds of photos, most of which were of animals. Ed and Lonnie, dogs, cats, even a few chickens. Interspersed with the animal shots were photographs of food, much of which I assumed she'd helped prepare at Teen Path HOME.

The images that drew me in the most, however, were her melancholy tributes to life on the streets. Photos of drug paraphernalia, people lined up outside food banks, tired-looking teenagers smoking in doorways, sleeping bags scattered along sidewalks.

I continued scrolling until I came across Rainbow's selfie with Bella. My breath caught.

So that's how her stepfather found her.

The photograph of the two new friends was adorable. Bella's long, black-spotted tongue reached toward Rainbow's cheek. Rainbow leaned toward it, as if hoping Bella would give her a dog-saliva facial. Above Rainbow's head, slightly to the right, a sign read *Teen Path H*. The only letters missing were the O, the M, and the E. Anyone with access to a browser could have found her. *Ah, sweetie*, I thought. *So young. So naïve.*

The last post had been created two hours before the altercation with her stepfather. Either she'd smartened up since then or she'd been too busy hiding to take adorable snapshots. I scanned her 347 followers, looking for people I recognized. Number ten was Jace Foster. I clicked on his picture. His profile was private.

Number thirty-eight stopped me cold. *April Rhodes.*

The woman smiling at me shared Rainbow's blonde hair and stunning gray-blue eyes, but she was significantly older. Unless this was a long-lost aunt that Rainbow had failed to disclose, April had to be Rainbow's mother.

Her profile was public, but it didn't tell me much. April rarely posted, and she hadn't at all in over four months. I typed *April Rhodes* into an Internet white pages site. A Tacoma address and phone number were listed. I was about to check for Facebook accounts when the phone rang.

Michael didn't bother saying hello. "What the hell, Kate. You dumped two rats off at the pet store without even bothering to ask me?"

Ah, crap. Ed and Lonnie. I'd forgotten to tell Michael about Ed and Lonnie.

"I'm sorry, Michael. With everything that happened last night, it slipped my mind. They were Gabriel's. I offered to foster them until Martinez can find someone to take them. How are they doing?"

"How are *they* doing? They're doing great, thank you very much. My store, on the other hand, is a disaster. The two scaly-tailed jerks got loose overnight and threw themselves a rat welcoming party. The droppings they left everywhere were bad enough, but evidently they were hungry. They chewed open eight bags of cat food. Rabbit is their favorite, in case you were wondering."

"I'm sorry, Michael. I didn't think they'd be able to get out again."

His voice rose half an octave. "Again? What do you mean, again?"

"They got loose the first time I went to Teen Path HOME. Gabriel told me that the kids sometimes left the cage open, so I didn't think much about it."

Only, in retrospect, the kids hadn't done anything of the sort. Gabriel had been simultaneously right and dreadfully wrong. Ed and Lonnie were, as he'd asserted, smart. Remarkably so. That's where he'd been right. He'd been wrong about their means of escape. No one at the center had left the cage open. The little monsters had found an escape route all on their own.

"Martinez wouldn't let me take Ed and Lonnie's cage, but I bought one exactly like it," I continued. "They've obviously figured out how to open it from inside. You should probably figure out a better way to secure the door."

"I should probably take them to a rescue," Michael countered.

"No," I said automatically. "They've already been traumatized by Gabriel's death."

As insane as the words sounded, I knew they were true. Ed and Lonnie might be tiny; they might be so-called vermin. But they were sentient beings, and they mourned Gabriel the same way Bella had mourned George. I wouldn't add to their suffering.

My shoulders tensed. "I won't let you shuffle them around like a couple of—"

"Like a couple of rats?"

I sighed. "I was going to say like a couple of pieces of unwanted property. Michael, animals—even rats—suffer from stress. They grieve. They hurt. They deserve better than being relegated to the animal equivalent of a detention center."

A long pause, then Michael's voice. "You're right. Of course you're right." He sounded guilty, which reminded me why I was so crazy about him. "But if we're not taking them to a rescue, I'm bringing them home. We can lock them in the office."

"The same office that our semi-feral cat lives in? Ten minutes with Mouse and all we'll have left are their tails."

As if in reply, my calico fur child slinked into the office. Bella followed her to the dog bed where the two best friends curled up together, happily ignoring me.

"Not all cats are hunters, you know," Michael said. "Besides, these rats are huge. They're almost as big as Mouse is."

"And if you're wrong?"

Silence. Exactly like I'd expected. My animal-loving husband would never let Ed and Lonnie come to harm. He simply needed time to realize it.

Five seconds later, he replied. "Fine. But they can't stay at the store much longer. It's not safe. One of my customers stepped on the brown one this morning."

"Is Lonnie okay?"

"He's fine, but Mrs. Krapinski had a conniption fit. I doubt she'll ever be back."

"I know the situation isn't ideal, Michael, but it's also not permanent. Martinez is checking with Gabriel's relatives. One of them will probably want the two little guys."

"Maybe." Michael didn't sound convinced. "I'll give you a week to find someone to take them, Kate. After that, they have to go. Period."

I hung up the phone with Michael, picked it back up, and tried Martinez again. I'd found the Rhodes family address on my own, but I hoped Martinez would have other useful information. If I was really lucky, she'd inform me that she'd found someone who wanted Ed and Lonnie.

She answered on the second ring. "Kate. I was about to return your call. Have you heard from Rainbow?"

"Sorry, not yet. I'm actually calling about something else."

"What's that?"

"My husband's a little cranky about the rats. Have you found anyone that wants them?"

"They're not my highest priority, Kate. Not even close. I mentioned them when I spoke to Cherie Cousins, the widow, and she wasn't interested."

"You spoke to Gabriel's wife? How's she doing?"

Martinez hesitated. "Honestly, she strikes me as off. Henderson did the death notification with a patrol officer, so I didn't see her initial reaction. But when she stopped by the station this morning, she seemed more pissed off than grief-stricken."

I leaned forward in my desk chair, fully alert. This might be good news, at least for Rainbow. "I never officially met her, but I saw her with Gabriel once. I got the feeling their marriage was troubled."

"It was. Cherie freely admits it. She hated his work. She claims that she warned him that—and I'm quoting here—"hobnobbing with freeloading teenage criminals" was dangerous, but he refused to listen. She practically blames him for his own murder."

"Is she a suspect?"

"The spouse is always a suspect. Frankly, I'm surprised no one's told her to lawyer up yet. Any lawyer worth his salt would tell her to keep her mouth shut. She admitted to Henderson that she and Gabriel fought on Wednesday night. That's why he was at the center so late. He was planning to sleep there."

"Was he leaving her?"

"Not that she's admitted, at least not yet."

"You said she stopped by the station. Why?"

"She wanted to make sure Gabriel's body would be released to the funeral home this afternoon. Not my decision, but she's been hounding everyone she can think of. She's determined to have the memorial service on Sunday."

"Already? That seems fast."

"A little, but it's not as unusual as you might think. People grieve differently. For some, burying the dead is the first step to moving on with their lives."

I envisioned Gabriel's body as I'd last seen it—sprawled on the floor, crimson stain spreading around it. "So the autopsy's complete, then?"

"Yes. I have the report here on my desk."

"Any surprises?"

"None. The victim died of a gunshot wound to the chest, but that was obvious at the scene. I suppose something weird could show up in the tox screen, but I doubt it."

"What about the gun? Did you find out who it belonged to?"

"If you're asking if we can implicate the teen, the answer is yes." She paused. "Or at least probably."

"Probably?"

"The serial number matched a gun registered to the stepfather. The guy's name is Dean Boothe. He and I had a nice long chat last night."

"Does he know how to find Rainbow?"

"He claims he doesn't have a clue. Frankly, given his lack of concern for the girl, I'm inclined to believe him."

"What about fingerprints? If it was Rainbow's gun, mine should be on it."

"The outside of the gun was wiped clean, but we pulled some off the magazine. They don't match yours or any prints in the system so far, but I'd bet my pension that they'll match the teen's when we find her. *If* we find her."

"If?"

"She could be anywhere by now, including out of state. Runaways are good at staying under the radar. It's a miracle her stepfather found her the first time."

"Not really."

"What do you mean?"

I told Martinez about Rainbow's Instagram account and the photo she'd posted showing Teen Path HOME's sign. "I'm betting that's how Dean ended up at the center."

"He mentioned that he found her via a social media account. I assumed she'd checked in on Facebook or something."

"She took the photo she posted with a cell phone. Can you trace her phone?"

"In theory, if we knew the number. I asked the stepfather about a cell phone. He canceled the kid's account the day after she left home. She's probably using a burner."

"If Dean was trying to find her, why did he cancel her phone?"

"Mister Wonderful said he wasn't willing to spend his hard-earned money supporting a thief." I heard the telltale squeak of flesh sinking into a desk chair. "He's not exactly parent-of-the-year material."

"What about Rainbow's mother?"

"The husband says she's still MIA, but I'm following up on that. Henderson's been interviewing homeless youth in the area, but so far, they all claim not to know Rainbow. Big surprise there. These kids almost never open up to the police. Has anyone told you anything?"

"Not yet, but I'm working on it. I was planning to go to Teen Path HOME but it's closed. Is it still an active crime scene?"

"No. We released it yesterday."

I wrapped the phone cord around my index finger, making teeny tiny tourniquets until the tip of my finger turned purple. "I'd like to chat with the kids. They don't know me well, but a few of them took my classes. They might tell me more than they did Henderson."

Silence.

I stopped hinting and asked the question directly. "Any idea where I can find them?"

More silence. Nothing but the static hum of the phone line. Finally, Martinez spoke. "You're not a police officer. I can't encourage you to interview potential witnesses."

"But?" I asked, hopefully.

"This is hypothetical, of course, but since you knew Gabriel, I wouldn't be surprised if you attend that memorial service on Sunday. If the kids are there, no one could stop you from talking with them."

"Great idea. Where is it and what time?"

"I don't know the time, but the body's being released to Queen Anne Memorial."

I leaned back in my chair and smiled. "Thank you."

"For what?" Martinez replied. "Like I said, I'm talking hypotheticals." She paused. "And, Kate?"

"Yes?"

"If for some weird reason you see Henderson at Gabriel's memorial, don't tell him we had this conversation. I wouldn't want him to get the wrong idea."

My smile thinned to a smirk. "Definitely not."

Martinez's voice turned serious. "Kate, hypotheticals or not, you know I'm breaking protocol here, right? Please don't make me regret it."

"I won't." I paused, curiosity warring with common sense. Curiosity won. "I appreciate your help, and believe me I'm not complaining. But why are you telling me all of this?" Martinez had always been kind to me, but until Gabriel's death, she'd never treated me as anything other than a witness.

"I didn't take you seriously before, and people almost died. Twice. I won't make that mistake again. You'll let me know if you find the kid, right?"

"I will. I promise." For the first time in our tenuous friendship, I meant it.

FOURTEEN

As soon as I hung up the phone with Martinez, I pulled up the website for Queen Anne Memorial. I barely recognized the man in the photo labeled Gabriel Cousins. Photograph Gabriel sported a wide but rehearsed-looking smile, a close-cropped head of curly black hair, and a midnight blue power suit. I saw no trace of the shaved-headed, kind, passionate man I'd met at Teen Path HOME.

His obituary read more like a resume than a tribute. The first paragraph indicated that Gabriel had graduated magna cum laude from the University of Washington with a bachelor's degree in international studies, followed two years later by a master of business administration. He had married college sweetheart Cherie Harris immediately after receiving his masters degree.

The second paragraph listed a variety of professional positions Gabriel had held, awards he had won, and honors he'd received. The accolades ended by stating that four years after obtaining his MBA, Gabriel had become the youngest employee to be promoted to the position of regional vice president at a consulting firm whose name

I recognized but couldn't place. A single sentence, almost an afterthought, mentioned that he'd spent the last several years of his life helping displaced youth. Neither Teen Path HOME nor Gabriel's role there were mentioned.

The final paragraph said that he was preceded in death by his parents and sister and was survived by his wife, Cherie Cousins, and in-laws, Dara and Andre Harris. A private ceremony would be held at Queen Anne Memorial at ten in the morning on Sunday, November 13.

I frowned at the word "private," but it didn't deter me. My phone call with Martinez had provided no definitive answers, but it had given me a starting place, and I wasn't about to waste it. Time to scour my closet for a black dress. On Sunday, I was going to crash a funeral.

But that was two days away. Rainbow was still out there somewhere, alone. Maybe frightened. Maybe in danger. I tucked the Tacoma address for April Rhodes inside my purse. As soon as I finished teaching my noon All Levels Yoga class, I was going on a field trip.

I performed the plethora of duties required of a pet owner planning to be gone for the day. I ground and incubated Bella's organic, grain-free, medicated kibble, tossed a can of tuna cat food into Mouse's food bowl, and filled the water dishes I'd placed in every room with fresh water. After both creatures had snarfed down their breakfasts, I took Bella on a quick walk to take care of her biological duties. She pinned me with sad brown eyes when she realized I was leaving her behind.

"Sorry, sweetie. You can't come with me today. My afternoon's going to be crazy. Michael should be home no later than six, and if you're a good girl, I'll take you on an extra-long walk tonight."

Bella's stare chastised me all the way to the door. Mouse observed my departure with feline indifference. Somehow I managed to feel guilty about both.

I pulled into my studio parking spot two minutes before noon, which was twenty-eight minutes later than I should have arrived. A line of disgruntled students huddled outside in the rain. I gifted them with lame apologies and an autopilot sequence of Sun Salutations, twists, and other poses designed to build energy and stimulate digestion.

I wish I could say that I made up for my tardiness by teaching a fabulous class, but honestly, I have no idea if class that afternoon was good, bad, or indifferent. My body was in the room with my students, but my mind was thirty-five miles south in Tacoma, grilling Rainbow's stepfather. I held no illusions that Dean would lead me directly to Rainbow. If he knew where his stepdaughter was hiding, he'd have her sequestered at home already. But I *did* think that talking with Dean might help me understand the teenage enigma. Who was Rainbow before she left home? Why had she run? Was she capable of violence? If her stepfather wasn't willing (or able) to answer, perhaps being inside her house would give me the information I needed. Rainbow must have left traces of herself there, if only energetically. Would I be able to sense them?

I said Namaste at one-fifteen on the dot and started hustling students out the door precisely one minute later. A first-time student lagged behind, pretending to browse the books in my tiny retail area. I plastered on my best impersonation of a patient smile and moved next to her. "Did you have a question?"

"Yes," she said. "Classes here are pretty expensive. Do you offer any new student deals?"

I bit back an unwelcome (and atypical) feeling of irritation. It was a relevant question, but I knew where this was going. "Your first class was free. I can't make it much cheaper than that." I winked to let her know I was kidding. Sort of.

"That's great, but what about after that?" She pulled out a cell phone and pointed at Some Like It Hot Yoga's website. "Fifteen dollars seems pretty outrageous when I'll be able to take the same class for a dollar across the street."

In spite of my best efforts, my smile wavered. "It's not the same class. Serenity Yoga's classes are smaller and more intimate." At least I assumed so. The windows across the street were still covered with newsprint, and I suspected they would remain covered until the grand opening on Tuesday. "We provide individualized instruction. Our maximum class size is twenty, but most of our classes have between eight and fifteen students. Some are smaller." I was telling the truth, but I had a hidden agenda. I was hoping she'd do the math. If we charged a dollar a class, each class would bring in less than Seattle's minimum wage to teach it.

The twenty-something yogini frowned. "So basically, you're telling me that you won't match their price."

If I didn't end this conversation soon, I'd say something I'd deeply regret when I read myself quoted in her one-star Yelp review. I reached across my desk and pulled out two guest passes. "Tell you what. Try two more classes here as my guest. Hopefully you'll decide we're worth the investment."

As a revenue-generating tactic, my multiple-free-class strategy would be an epic fail, and I knew it. My new friend would attend classes with me precisely two more times before she defected to Some Like It Hot Yoga. If I wanted to stay in business, I'd have to come up with a better strategy.

But not today. Today, I needed to get her out of the studio so I could hit the road to Tacoma. Mission accomplished. The instant my temporarily satisfied student headed toward the parking lot, I locked the studio's front door and jogged next door to Infant Gratification.

For once, I had a sleuthing plan that would satisfy me without making Michael's head explode. Michael would be furious if I went to Rainbow's house alone, and honestly, I didn't want to. My questions were too amorphous; my plan, too fractured. I needed someone to go with me. I needed a sidekick.

I needed Rene.

She sat behind the checkout desk, looking bored. My eyes swept past the new red-soled infant stilettos she had on display and landed on a black T-shirt that was folded in half on her desk. The words *Some Like It Hot Yoga* arched over a nubile woman posing in Warrior Two. I had a feeling the phrase *Ten Classes for Ten Dollars!* decorated the back.

"Seriously, Rene? You too?"

"I didn't buy it or anything. Chad's giving out free T-shirts to all the neighborhood businesses. He's trying to get people excited about the grand opening. Plus, anyone who refers students to them gets a free week of yoga classes. It's actually a pretty good marketing idea. You didn't get a shirt?"

I felt my jaw clench. "I'm not his target audience."

She unfolded the shirt and held it up. "It's kind of tacky but cute. I was going to give it to the twins' nanny, but if it bugs you too much, I'll throw it out."

I sighed. "It's fine. I'm just in a bad mood. Is the nanny on twin duty today?"

"Yes, though I wish I had the girls with me. Business is dead on Fridays. Everyone who doesn't shop earlier in the week puts it off until the weekend. I thought Friday afternoons would be the perfect time to work on new designs. But as it turns out, you can't schedule inspiration. It comes when it comes." She frowned. "Which obviously isn't today. I don't suppose you're up for a coffee break?"

"I'll do you one better. How about a road trip?" I quickly told Rene everything that had transpired the day before.

"Geez, Kate, I'm sorry. Sam and the rest of the board had a conference call to talk about Gabriel's murder last night, but I don't think he knows that you accidently saw the body. If he did, he would have told me. That must have been awful. You okay?"

I flinched. Sam. I'd been so wrapped up in visiting with Dharma and Dale and then trying to find Rainbow, I'd forgotten to call him. Again.

"Other than being a terrible friend, I'm fine. Sam probably doesn't even know I was at the center yesterday. I meant to call, but my day got so crazy ... " My words trailed off. The excuse sounded too lame to continue. The past twenty-four hours had been crazy. I'd stumbled upon another murder, gotten my period, temporarily re-homed two rats, and spent a heart-wrenching evening confessing my fertility issues to Dharma. But none of that truly explained why I hadn't picked up the phone. I'd avoided my two closest friends for so long, it had become second nature. That had to change.

"How is Sam?" I asked.

"Honestly? He's horrified. Everyone at Teen Path HOME is. According to Chuck, the police have a suspect. Hopefully they'll arrest the killer soon."

"Actually, that's why I'm here."

I filled Rene in on the rest of the story. That I had befriended Rainbow, that the police suspected she was the shooter, and that I was trying to prove her innocence.

"All of that happened in the last two weeks?" Rene exclaimed. "Good Lord, Kate. We have to get together more often. I'm completely out of the loop."

"I agree, and I think we should start today. I'm going to talk to Rainbow's stepfather, but I don't want to go alone. Will you come with me?"

Rene perked up like a poodle who'd been offered a cookie. "You're playing Sherlock again? Count me in!" She looped her Coach bag over her shoulder. "I'll text the nanny and tell her to hang with the twins until Sam comes home, but we'd better get going. Traffic in Tacoma can be awful. We can strategize on the way."

I used the one-hour drive to fill her in on everything I knew about Rainbow, what I'd learned during my conversations with Martinez, and the ideas I'd written in my notebook.

"I'd like to talk to the youth at Teen Path HOME, too."

"It's a good idea, but they won't be there," Rene answered. "The board closed the center, at least for now."

"I heard that on the answering machine. Why?"

"Everyone's going all wonky about the murder. The board members are executive types—super nervous about anything that would give their businesses bad publicity. The donors are worse. Sam said that the board is considering closing the facility permanently. For now, they've decided to suspend all programs until they have time to hold an emergency in-person meeting. Sam thinks it's a huge mistake, but he's only one vote out of seven."

"I get why people would be nervous, but the kids rely on the center's services. Closing seems extreme."

"Honestly? It is. Something weird is going on, and it has been for a while. Sam has been stressed for weeks, but he refuses to talk to me about it."

"Sam's keeping a secret from you?"

"Yes, and it's not at all like him. Honestly, Kate, I don't know whether to be insulted or worried."

We spent the rest of the drive discussing twin toddler antics, recently started periods, and Dharma's offer to see if Dale would pay for my IVF treatments. I thought Rene might be upset that I was willing to take money from Dale since I'd refused a similar offer from her, but in fact she was exactly the opposite.

"What a brilliant solution, Kate! It simultaneously helps you, Dale, and Dharma."

"Well it obviously helps me. The benefit to Dale is a stretch. But how would it help Dharma?"

"She still feels guilty for leaving you when you were an infant."

"Guilty? Why? I mean, when we first reconciled, sure, I could see that. But we've put all of that behind us now."

"You're too close to see it, Kate. I know you've forgiven Dharma. You know it, too. But after over thirty years of separation, the bridge you've built must feel terribly tenuous to her. She has a lot of skinned knees and missed birthday parties to make up for. Helping you have a child of your own is a pretty good start."

I hadn't thought about it that way, but Rene had a point. Dharma *did* have a lot of missing time to make up for. She wasn't the only one. Guilt weighed down my shoulders. The circumstances were different, of course, and the time period was shorter. But I'd abandoned Rene exactly like Dharma had me.

I stared at the car in front of me, grateful that I wouldn't have to meet Rene's eyes when I spoke. "I know we talked about this already, but I'm truly sorry for ditching you for so long."

"It's okay, Kate, I—"

"Please let me finish. At the time, avoiding you seemed like the only way I could protect my sanity, but I was wrong. And selfish. It won't happen again."

I hazarded a glance in Rene's direction. She raised her eyebrows in mock consternation. "It'd better not." Her expression turned serious. "You hurt me, Kate. I won't lie. But it's over."

"You deserved better."

Rene stared out the passenger window for several seconds. "Do you remember that line from the movie *Love Story*?"

"What line?"

She turned and made direct eye contact. "Love means never having to say you're sorry."

I nodded.

"Well, it's a load of crap. Love means never holding a grudge." She took my hand and squeezed it. "We're good, I promise."

We drove ten more miles in companionable conversation. "We're making super good time today," Rene said. "When is this guy expecting us?"

"His name's Dean Boothe, and he's not. I didn't tell him that we were coming."

"You didn't call first?"

"No. I was afraid he'd refuse to see us. That'll be harder to do if we're standing on his doorstep."

"But Kate, it's a Friday afternoon. He's probably at work. We might be driving all this way for nothing."

"Not for nothing. If Dean's not home, we can talk to the neighbors. But I'm betting he'll be there. Rainbow described him as an alcoholic, and not a high-functioning one. She flat-out said he wasn't able to hold down a job. If he's not camped on a barstool somewhere, he'll be home." I hoped.

I exited off the freeway and navigated through the side streets of South Tacoma. Rene rummaged through her bag and pulled out a makeup mirror. She touched up her lipstick and blush, then slid off her wedding ring and zipped it inside her coin purse. Rene's version of going undercover.

"You do realize that Dean's married, right?" I asked.

"Sweetheart, you'd be surprised how seldom that makes a difference."

Actually, I wouldn't.

Rene had some magical hold over men. As her best friend, I used to resent the cloak of invisibility I wore in her presence. As an amateur sleuth, I relished it. Male suspects were much more likely to say something foolish when Rene was in the room. I couldn't explain it. Rene was gorgeous, but there were millions of gorgeous women in the world. Rene's magic was deeper. More primal. She exuded some intoxicating pheromone that anesthetized the male brain. Rene was the queen bee, men were her workers.

She pointed to a small, single-story rambler. "This is it."

I'm not sure what I'd expected. A crumbling-down crack house? A muddy, weed-infested yard scattered with used condoms and hypodermic needles? Maybe a condemned wreck with boarded up-windows.

Rainbow's home was none of that. It wasn't glorious, either. Just a small gray-blue house that could have used a good landscaper. The rose bushes along the sidewalk were overgrown, and the weed-choked grass hadn't seen a lawn mower in months. But from the outside, at least, the house looked like an average lower-middle-class home. Rainbow may not have liked her stepfather, but he and her mother had kept their lives together, at least on some level.

"Okay, Kate," Rene said. "What's our plan?"

"To be honest, I don't have one. My primary goal is to find Rainbow. I hope her stepfather—or her mother, if she's back—can connect us with her friends or tell us places that she used to hang out. If not, maybe they'll let us look through her room."

Rene wrinkled her lips, unimpressed.

I shrugged. "It's a start."

"Do you at least have a cover story?"

I probably should have had one, but history had proven that I was a terrible liar. An admirable quality in a yoga teacher; not so handy as a budding detective. "I'm going to stick to the truth, at least as much as possible."

"So what's my role?" Rene asked.

"The day I saw Rainbow's stepfather at Teen Path HOME, he wasn't exactly friendly. I don't know if he'll remember me, but if he does, the association won't be pleasant. I'm hoping you can sweeten him up and convince him that my finding Rainbow is in his best interests."

"His, not hers?"

"Both, if possible. I don't know how much he cares about Rainbow, but if what she told me is true, he certainly cares about himself."

"Sounds like a real charmer."

"Maybe, but I don't know what to believe, at least not yet. Martinez doesn't think Dean was parent-of-the-year material, but Dale warned me not to make too many assumptions, and he's right. I've only heard Rainbow's side of the story. Who knows how much she's embellished? Dean could be anything from an abusing jackass to an overbearing man who, in spite of appearances, loves his stepdaughter. We should go in assuming either could be true."

"In other words, we're winging it."

"Pretty much."

As we walked up the sidewalk, I examined Rainbow's home. It seemed perfectly harmonious and yet oddly out of place with its neighbors. The single-story structure was small, about the same size as my Ballard bungalow. The roof, shingles, and paint were in good condition, indicating that until recently, the house had been well cared for. The windows, however, were filthy. Garbage overflowed the outside trash can and spilled onto the driveway. I glanced around to make sure no one was looking, then took a peek under the lid. Beer bottles. Lots of them. I led Rene up the single step to the doorway, rang the doorbell, and waited.

Nothing. No barking dogs, no nosy neighbors, no footfalls on the other side. Only a stern-looking *No Solicitors* sign to keep Rene and me company.

"Told you we should have called first," Rene said.

I pressed the doorbell again. No response. "I was convinced he'd be home."

"Well then, let's make sure that he isn't." Rene lifted a French-manicured finger and pressed the doorbell over and over and over again.

"Rene, stop that. It's annoying."

She kept pushing. "That's the point."

After the twelfth repetition, a sluggish male voice came from inside. "Oh for Christsakes. I'm coming. Can't you read?"

The corners of Rene's mouth lifted. She turned to me and winked.

The door cracked open and a single bloodshot eye peered through it. "Read the sign. No solicitors. Or bill collectors. Or religious freaks. Basically, get the hell off my doorstep."

I gave Rene a let-me-handle-this look and reached out my hand. "Hello. You're Dean Boothe, correct?"

"Who's asking?"

My name's Kate Davidson. I'm a staff member at Teen Path HOME, and I'm here about your stepdaughter." It was close to the truth, anyway. I *did* work at the center, even if it was as a contract yoga teacher.

"She ain't here. She's a runaway." He wrinkled his face at me, as if attempting to focus. "Have I met you before?"

"Not officially, no. But I was on site the day you came to pick up Rainbow." I almost slipped and said *the day you tried to abduct Rainbow*, but I checked myself. "She hasn't been at the center since then, and I'm trying to find her. She's in trouble."

"Yeah, I know all about it. The cops told me. And like I told them, so what else is new? That kid's been trouble since the day I hooked up with her mom. Rest assured, when she gets back I'll kick some sense into her."

Rene's body stiffened, but her facial expression remained friendly. "Teenagers can be challenging, that's for sure."

Dean's liquidy eyes washed over Rene, but they showed zero attraction. The cloud of Budweiser-laced body odor surrounding him must have dampened the effect of her pheromones. "Who are you?"

"I'm connected with Teen Path HOME, too," Rene said. "My husband and I founded the technology program. I'm here to evaluate whether or not your stepdaughter still meets our scholarship requirements."

"Scholarship? You mean you're giving the little tart money?"

"We're considering it. Rainbow has shown promise, but I understand she's had some trouble recently. None of the youth we work with are completely free of challenges, of course, but this seems to be of a more serious nature." Rene pulled a hundred-dollar bill out of her wallet and held it up where Dean could see it. "We'd be willing to pay for your time."

Dean nudged the door open and stepped through it. "The house is a mess. I'll answer your questions out here."

"We'd rather come inside where the conversation will be more private," Rene replied. "We'd also like to speak with the child's mother."

"My wife's not here."

"We can wait." Rene's eyes widened in coquettish innocence, but the smile she flashed was predatory. The lashes of a kitten, the fangs of an alley cat.

Dean's knuckles whitened on the doorknob. "You'll be waiting a very long time."

We stood on the doorstep in silence, Rene and I staring at Dean, Dean at the C-note. After several seconds, Rene pulled out her billfold and opened it. She slowly slid the money back inside.

Dean released his hold on the door and backed away. "Fine. You win. We'll talk inside."

He led us to a small, threadbare living room cluttered with pizza boxes, beer bottles, and a thick layer of dust. The scent of his body odor diminished, replaced by cigarette smoke and mildew. "Excuse the mess. My wife hasn't been home to clean for a while."

He picked up a pile of mail stacked on the couch and tossed it onto an end table. He gestured for us to sit, then crossed his arms and leaned against a worn leather recliner. "So tell me again. Exactly why are the two of you here?"

"Before we launch into all of that, would you mind getting me a glass of water?" Rene asked. "I'm parched."

"My dishes are all dirty."

Rene stared at him, expression deadpan. "Well then, I guess you'll have to wash some."

Dean scowled at me. "I suppose you're thirsty, too."

"Yes, water for both of us, please," Rene replied. "And ice would be lovely." I halfway expected her to add a lemon slice to the order, but she simply flashed that predatory grin again.

As Dean disappeared into the kitchen, I leaned toward her and whispered, "What are you up to?"

"Snooping," she whispered back. "Are you going to sit there like a doofus or join me?"

I chose option two. While Rene thumbed through the mail on the end table, I wandered around the living room and tried to absorb the space's energy. I was surprised, and not completely in a bad way. The room hadn't seen a dust rag in months, but before that, someone had lightened it with personal touches. Colorful throw pillows decorated the threadbare couch, and half-burned candles sat inside the nonfunctioning fireplace. Photographs of Rainbow and her mother in younger, happier days dotted the walls. The two played in parks, posed with Santa Claus, and visited the Point Defiance Zoo. In spite of her mother's addictions, Rainbow had been loved, at least at one time. But as the years passed, the photos grew less frequent, and the mother aged at three times the rate of her child. Her hair grew coarser; her skin more sallow, her smiles less frequent. Rainbow was about ten in the most recent photo, which meant that April must have been in her mid to late twenties. Crow's feet and sagging skin made her look at least forty. After that, the photos stopped. Either no one took them anymore, or they were too dismal to display.

I heard the telltale sound of ice plunking in water and scooted back to the couch. Rene opened her bag and dropped something inside it. Had she found something in the mail pile? Before I could ask her, Dean returned, balancing two opaque, lime-green glasses and a bottle of beer.

He handed one of the glasses to Rene. "Here's your water." He pointed with his chin toward her purse, and she tensed. "If you don't want to bathe in it, that hundred dollars you promised me had better start finding its way from your wallet to mine."

Rene's tension melted into a placid smile, but she didn't reply. She took a tiny sip of water, then set her glass on the end table. I abstained, dreading the inevitable aftertaste of cheap plastic.

"And while you're at it," Dean continued, "it's time you told me why you're really here. And drop the scholarship nonsense. A real school wouldn't bribe me to get information."

"Like I told you outside," I said, "I want to find Rainbow."

He took a deep pull from the bottle. "Join the party. So do the police. She's gotten herself into real trouble this time." He ran his fingers through his crew cut. Large dandruff flakes snowed to the carpet. "Rayne's a runaway. What makes you think I know where she is?"

"You found her once."

"You mean the other day at that soup kitchen? That was a fluke. I found a photo she posted online. Rayne's a devious little trouble-maker, but she's smart. She won't make that mistake again. You still haven't told me why you want to find her."

"Like you said, the police are looking for her," I replied. "I have a friend—an attorney—who might be able to help her, but we have to find her first."

Dean gestured around the small, dingy living room. "Take a look at this place. Do I look like I can afford some fancy attorney?"

"My friend sometimes takes pro bono cases."

"Well, la de da for him. Some of us have bills to pay." He whisked his hand through the air. "Doesn't matter. I already told you: I have no idea where the little she-devil's gone off to this time. Stumbling across that photo was a fluke. I'd been looking for her for over a week before I found that."

My indignation went up several notches, taking my vocal volume with it. "You'd only been looking for Rainbow for a week? She's sixteen and she ran away months ago! Why on earth did you wait so long?"

Dean's fists clenched. "Is that a question or an accusation?"

Rene leaned forward, expression locked in one-hundred-percent charm mode. "Sorry, Kate can be a little abrupt sometimes. What she means is, did something happen that made finding your stepdaughter more urgent?"

Dean's fists relaxed, but his jaw remained tense. "My wife came home, that's what happened. April showed up here on Halloween, finally sober, and she was pissed as hell that the little brat wasn't here waiting for her." His eyes flicked toward the ceiling. "I'll tell you the same thing I told her: If she'd stayed home for a change, she could have taken care of her own progeny. I didn't sign up for this shit."

"Wait a minute," I said. "Your wife was home on Halloween? I thought she'd been gone for months."

"Except for that one day, she has been."

I frowned.

"Look, April's a partier. I knew that when we got married, but it's gotten worse. A few drinks, I can understand. A joint or two, fine. I don't like it, but fine. But she moved on to coke. Then it was heroin.

I told her loud and clear: I will not allow that poison in my house. If I find it, it goes straight down the toilet. So when she wants to shoot up, she takes off."

"You don't stop her?" Rene asked.

"How am I supposed to do that? April's not my prisoner. Neither is Rayne, for that matter. You can judge me all you want, but I'm not a bad guy. When the kid took off, I thought she'd gone to stay with her mom. When April finally sobered up and came back alone, I realized I was wrong, so I started looking for her. I found her at that soup kitchen." He shrugged. "Not that anyone appreciated it. April took off again before I even found Rayne, and the brat refused to come home."

"Can't you report her missing?" I asked.

"Who?" he snorted. "The kid or her mother?"

"Both, actually."

"What good would it do? The police already know about Rayne. As for my wife, I called the cops the first time she took off, and they didn't do crap. Evidently it's not against the law for an adult to leave home. And what would they do if they found her? Throw her in the drunk tank? Try to force her into rehab? Been there, done that. It always ends the same." He pantomimed shooting up in the crook of his elbow. "Believe me, April will come crawling back when she runs out of money. She always does."

I didn't buy Dean's story, at least not all of it. He was hiding something. Rene's expression told me that she thought so, too.

"I'm not so sure I believe you," I said. "If I came home and found out that my daughter was gone, I'd sure as heck try to find her. Addiction or not, I wouldn't disappear again. Not if I had any choice in the matter."

Dean smirked. "I don't give a rat's ass what you believe. And if you think heroin addicts care about anyone but themselves, you haven't spent any time with one."

"You're right. I haven't. But I've met a few battered women."

Dean flinched as if he'd been slapped. "Battered? What are you talking about?" He paused, then his eyes widened. "Oh, I get it. The little troublemaker told you that I slapped her mother around."

"Did you?" I asked.

"Of course not. Rayne's pulling your chain. She's a blue-eyed, angel-faced con artist, almost as good at manipulating people as her mother."

He thunked his beer bottle next to Rene's glass on the end table. "You want the truth about why Rayne took off? Fine. Here's the truth. That girl's nothing but trouble. Always has been. Sneaks out every night doing god knows what. After April took off this last time, I put my foot down. I told Rayne that her partying days were over. She had to be home no later than eleven on school nights and stop sneaking out after I went to bed. I even took the lock off her door and started checking her room every few hours to make sure she was home."

Unease churned deep in my belly. Rainbow said she'd caught her stepfather staring at her while she was sleeping. She'd hinted that physical abuse was about to turn sexual. Was that the truth or a terrible misunderstanding … or was it a lie told to deliberately deceive? Dean claimed that Rainbow was a master manipulator. Had she manipulated me?

"The night before she took off, we had an argument." Dean's voice grew firm. "I finally told her, if you live in my house, you play by my rules. If you don't like it, you can leave." He shook his head, almost sadly. "I honestly didn't think she'd call my bluff."

He stood and took the glass from my hands. "It doesn't matter anymore. Rayne chose her path. Now she has to walk it." He turned to Rene. "I've already given you more time than I wanted to. Give me my money and get on your way."

"We will," I replied. "But before we go, I'd like to look around in Rainbow's room."

"Why?"

"In case there's something inside that will help us find her."

"There's nothing there. I already looked."

Rene lowered her eyes to her purse, then lifted them back to Dean's face. She arched her eyebrows, implicitly asking, *Do you want it or not?*

Dean sighed. "Fine. It's a waste of your time, but fine." He strode down the hall and gestured to a closed door on the right. "Have a party." He marched back toward the living room without following us inside.

"What a sweetheart," Rene whispered.

"You were right. He's a real charmer." I pushed open the door, flipped on the light, and froze.

Rene almost collided with my back. "Kate, what's wrong?"

I squeezed my eyes shut, then opened them again. "Nothing. Sorry. It's just, I know this room."

This was the bedroom depicted on the right side of Rainbow's missing drawing, *Another Life*. The baby blue curtains had faded to gray, and the princess bedspread had been replaced with a solid blue comforter, but everything else was unmistakably familiar.

I wandered around the small space, searching for traces of the violence Rainbow had portrayed on the left side of her drawing. There were none. No beheaded teddy bears, no bloodstained bedspreads, no signs of decay. The only hints of trauma were the drawings taped to the walls—desolate, photograph-quality charcoals of cocaine addicts, discarded needles, and shredded, blood-soaked toys. Each work had Rainbow's unique style but was signed with overlapping capital R's. For Rayne Rhodes, I assumed.

"Did Rainbow draw these?" Rene asked.

"Yes. I recognize the style."

"I'm impressed. And terrified. She's got talent, but … "

"I know. It's pretty dark stuff."

Rene pointed to a sketch taped above the bed. "What's up with that one?"

Honestly, I couldn't answer. The drawing was of a house, or at least what was left of it. The two-story structure was half submerged in an ocean of quicksand. The top half of a *For Sale* sign peeked above the surface. The windows were boarded over. The dark green siding was cracked and covered with mildew. The drawing was titled *Refuge.*

"That's not this place, is it?" Rene asked.

"Wrong color. The architecture is wrong, too. A friend's house, maybe?"

Rene stared over my shoulder, then stepped away. "She probably made it up."

I continued staring at the drawing. I couldn't know for sure, but I suspected this was a place Rainbow knew well. She clearly borrowed from her life when she drew. From where had she borrowed this? And why?

Rene interrupted my thoughts. "I'll say this for the kid, she's smart." She gestured to a collection of books piled on the room's wooden desk. College-level texts on biology and calculus, an ancient copy of *Merck's Veterinary Manual*, a hardcover book titled *Canine Rehabilitation and Physical Therapy*. No angst-filled dystopian novels. No teenage romances with bare-chested men on the covers either. No high school yearbook. No diary. No address book. Nothing that could lead us to Rainbow or anyone who knew her.

We searched her closet, rummaged through drawers, sorted through papers in the garbage can, and slid our hands between the bed's mattress and box spring. If Rainbow had left any clues in this room, she'd either hidden them thoroughly or her stepfather had already confiscated them.

Dean's voice came from the hallway. "Told you there wasn't anything interesting in there. Happy?"

"No," I said honestly. "I'm not happy at all." The more I learned about my new teenage friend, the more confused I became. I pointed at the drawing of the house. "Does that mean anything to you?"

He hesitated. "No. Should it?"

"She titled it 'Refuge.' I thought it might be a friend's house or a place from her past. Some place she might go if she was in trouble."

"I don't think so, Kate," Rene said. "It doesn't look like a place you'd go to feel safe."

"You never know with this kid." Dean tapped an index finger against his temple. "She's not right in the head. I told April that Rayne needed help, but she refused to see it." He gestured at the rest of the artwork. "Does that look like the work of a well-adjusted teenager?"

"Probably not," I admitted.

He leaned against the door jamb. "I told you, there's nothing here. No matter what lies Rayne told you, I'm not a monster. If there was an easy way to find the kid, I'd have done it already."

Rene placed her palm on my arm. "Come on, Kate. Let's go. There's nothing here that can help us." She handed Dean the money she'd promised him. "Before we go, can I use your restroom?"

He shrugged. "It's down the hall to your left."

Dean and I loitered by the front door while Rene powdered her nose. When she re-emerged from the restroom, she had a surprisingly triumphant look on her face. "We'll get out of your hair now. Let me grab that water glass and put it back in the kitchen."

"I'll take care of it," Dean said.

"Thanks, but I'm thirsty." She picked up the glass and, in an uncharacteristic moment of clumsiness, dropped it. Water splashed across the mail and poured onto the carpet.

"Oh my gosh!" Rene exclaimed. "I'm so sorry. Get me a towel, quick!"

Dean jogged to the kitchen. Rene pulled an envelope out of her bag, presumably the one she'd swiped earlier. She slid it in the middle of the mail pile and winked at me. "I can be such a klutz sometimes."

Dean arrived back at the table and handed Rene a worn terry towel. She blotted the wet carpet and papers, tossed several half-melted ice cubes into the glass, and handed it to Dean. The towel came away gray. "I'm sorry about the mess."

She pulled a business card out of her billfold. "We'll get out of your hair now. That has my business number. If Rainbow or her mother show up again, call it. There's another hundred dollars in it for you."

Dean took the card from Rene but he spoke to me. "Can you really get Rayne a good attorney for free?"

"Yes."

"Then if I learn anything, I'll call. I meant what I said before. I'm not the monster Rayne made me out to be."

164

Halfway down the sidewalk, Rene whispered, "Drive a few blocks then find someplace inconspicuous to park. I have something to show you."

She pulled a bottle of hand sanitizer out of her purse and rubbed her palms vigorously together, removing all germs and the top layer of skin in the process. "If I didn't get hepatitis from that water glass, I for sure got MRSA in the bathroom. No one's cleaned that toilet in months."

"What was the water-spilling charade about?"

"I'll show you once we're parked."

I pulled into a convenience store lot and turned off the engine. "Okay, Rene, talk."

"While you were walking down memory lane with Rainbow's family photographs, I was sorting through the mail."

"I saw you. I take it you found something interesting."

"You could say that. April Rhodes is Rainbow's mother, right?"

"Yes."

"I found an open envelope addressed to her."

"That's hardly surprising. She lives there." I paused. "Or at least she does part time. If her husband's telling the truth, she's been gone more lately than she's been home."

"Yes, but this wasn't junk mail or a credit card statement. It was a certified letter from a law firm."

That got my attention. "Is Rainbow's mother in legal trouble?"

"That's what I thought at first, or that maybe she was filing for divorce. I didn't have time to look at it before Dean came back from the kitchen, so I borrowed it."

"Borrowed?"

She swished her hand through the air. "Borrowed, stole … potayto, potahto. I put it back while Dean got the towel. He didn't have a clue." She looked insanely, justifiably proud of herself.

"Well, don't keep me guessing here. What did the letter say?"

She pulled out her cell phone, pressed a few random-looking places on the screen, and handed it to me. "I took a picture of it. See for yourself."

The letter on her screen was dated October 27.

From: The Law Offices of Johnson, Meek, and Fredrickson
To: Ms. April A. Rhodes

We received your request for a one-time payment of ten thousand dollars ($10,000) from the trust fund of Rayne Rhodes. This request has been denied. As outlined in Ms. Rhodes' trust documents, fund disbursements are conditional on her maintaining a grade point average of three point five or higher. Ms. Rhodes' first monthly scholastic report for the 2016–2017 school year was due on October 10. Until we receive this documentation, we are unable to release the requested funds or deposit future monthly stipends for living expenses. We will reconsider this request upon receipt of the required documentation.

Sincerely,
Fred Fredrickson, Attorney at Law

I swiped across the screen, but there were no additional pages. "Interesting, huh?" Rene asked.

I handed the phone back to her. "Email this to me, would you?" I drummed my fingers against the steering wheel and stared out the windshield. Rainbow had told me about a trust fund, but she'd said it was her mother's. Did she know it actually belonged to her?

Rainbow's mother could have easily deceived her. Her grandparents died when she was five, and the payments had likely been electronic. Periodic grade reports would have been trickier for April to get without a teen's knowledge, but she could have asked Rainbow's teachers directly. I bit back a rising sense of anger. Did this poor kid have *any* adults in her life who didn't take advantage of her?

"Earth to Kate," Rene said. "What are you thinking?"

"That I'm glad I didn't grow up in Rainbow's family."

Rene tapped the top of her phone screen. "Did you notice the date on the letterhead?"

"Yes. October 27."

"It would have arrived right around the time April came home. Isn't that when Dean started looking for Rainbow?"

I felt my jaw clench. "Yes."

"You see what that means, don't you? That jerk wasn't looking for Rainbow because he cared about her. Her mother probably doesn't care all that much either. They both needed her to get back in school so they so they could pick a few more dollars off the money tree."

I mumbled words so foul, they might be illegal.

Rene continued. "The letter is addressed to Rainbow's mother. Do you think she asked for the ten thousand dollars?"

"No. The timing's off. The request would have been sent not too long before the denial letter was written, and Dean said April was gone until Halloween. I think Dean asked for the money, pretending to be his wife. He probably didn't know about the grade requirement. When the letter arrived and Mommy Dearest returned home, they both realized they were screwed."

"Unless they found Rainbow and got her back in school," Rene added.

"Exactly."

"Where do you think Rainbow's mother is now?"

"I have no idea. Stoned in a crack house somewhere? Off selling her body for drugs? Trying to track down her daughter herself?" I pointed to the phone. "That letter tells us one thing for sure. Dean definitely doesn't know where Rainbow is. If he did, he'd have brought her home by now."

Rene dropped the phone back inside her purse. "Maybe, maybe not. He certainly won't get more money out of the trust fund if Rainbow's in prison. Maybe he's trying to figure out a new end game."

"It's possible, I suppose." I turned the key in the ignition. The Honda's engine rumbled to life.

"Does any of this help solve Gabriel's murder?" Rene asked.

"Honestly, I don't see how it would. I'll call that trust fund lawyer, Fred Fredrickson, after we get back to Seattle, but if he's anything like Dale, he won't tell me anything."

"So where does that leave us?"

"Exactly where we were before. Trying to find Rainbow."

FIFTEEN

THE SEATTLE AREA TRAFFIC gods extracted their revenge on the drive home. Interstate 5's infamous Tacoma traffic netted us almost sixty minutes of stop-and-go driving. The downtown Seattle corridor added another half hour. I dropped Rene off at Infant Gratification and asked her to give Sam my condolences. By the time I got to the studio, the Slow Flow teacher was already checking in students for her seven o'clock class.

"Hey Kate," she said. "I don't know who taught the noon class today, but they left the place in a shambles. The garbage cans were all full, and there were more leaves on the carpet than outside on the trees. I'm pretty sure the yoga room floor hadn't been swept either. I got here early for my five-thirty class, so I cleaned everything myself, but you might want to remind whoever it is that this is a shared space. Students notice when the studio is dirty, and it's not my job to clean up after everyone else."

I felt blood rush to my cheeks. "I'll talk to them." Informing her that the inconsiderate boob was yours truly would have served no purpose other than to make us both feel uncomfortable. Instead, I thanked her for the extra effort and made a mental note to add a small bonus to her next paycheck.

The moment my butt hit the driver's seat, I pulled out my cell phone and closely examined the photograph Rene had sent me. White parchment, black print, blue-and-gold letterhead. The twist about Rainbow's trust was certainly interesting, but how did it help me? The letter said nothing about the teen's current whereabouts. Could there be a connection to Gabriel's murder? A shadowy motive was taking shape in my mind, but I wasn't sure I believed it.

The letter gave me more questions than answers, but it had also introduced me to someone who might be able to answer them: Fred Fredrickson, Attorney at Law.

I pulled up a browser and clicked on the website for Johnson, Meek, and Fredrickson. The office had closed for the weekend almost two hours ago, but I dialed the phone number just in case. The voicemail message encouraged me to call back on Monday.

I pulled up an Internet white pages site. Fred Fredrickson's home address and phone number weren't listed. There wasn't even an F. Fredrickson to give me false hope. I was disappointed, but only a little. Even if I'd managed to track down the administrator of Rainbow's trust after-hours on a Friday, chances were pretty much zero that he'd have divulged information to Rainbow's yoga teacher, no matter how good her intentions.

If he was contacted by the police, however ...

I pulled out Martinez's card. She answered on the second ring.

I dispensed with the pleasantries and jumped right in. "I promised I'd call you if I learned anything about Rainbow."

Her voice sharpened with interest. "You found her?"

"No, but I have new information. Turns out, Rainbow's a trust fund kid. Her mother and stepfather have been living off her inheritance for years. I strongly suspect that's why her stepfather came looking for her. He needed his golden gosling to come back home."

"Reeeeally." She drew out the word, making three distinct syllables. "I've spoken to that man three times now, and he never once mentioned a trust fund. How did you find this out?"

I hesitated. "Umm ... let's say a friend told me." I didn't think "borrowing" and photographing mail was a federal offense, but I wasn't willing to take any chances.

Martinez sighed. "In other words, it might not have been strictly legal."

I hoped Martinez heard the grin in my voice. "I'm exercising my right to remain silent. But I know who the trust administrator is." I gave her Fred Fredrickson's contact information. "The office is closed for the weekend, but maybe you can use your police magic to locate him."

"If I had any magic, I'd have found Rainbow already." She paused. "Then again, maybe the trust is why I haven't."

"What do you mean?"

"I've been assuming Rainbow has a few hundred dollars on her at most. That limits where she can hide. If she has thousands, she has options I haven't considered."

"There's no way she has that kind of money. At least she didn't. I don't think she even knows the trust is hers and not her mother's. But I do think her trust might be connected to Gabriel's murder."

"How?"

"The trust fund gives her parents thousands of reasons—maybe millions, depending on how large the fund is—to want Rainbow home." I fleshed out my theory by saying it out loud. "The trust has strings attached. Stepdaddy dearest won't get a red cent unless Rainbow gets back in school and maintains a high GPA."

"How would killing Gabriel accomplish that?" Martinez asked.

"Stick with me for a second, because the rest of this might be a stretch. Gabriel wasn't happy when Rainbow's stepfather showed up at the center. Their argument got physical, and Gabriel threatened to call the cops. There's no way he would have sent Rainbow back to that jerk without a fight. He once had a case like hers that went bad on him. The kid committed suicide."

"That's terrible."

"Yes, and Gabriel wanted no part in a repeat performance. What if Dean came back to the center that night looking for Rainbow and found Gabriel instead? Heck, he might have found Rainbow and Gabriel both. The two men could have gotten into a fight. Dean could be the shooter."

"So basically you're saying that the stepfather came to Seattle in the middle of the night, found Rainbow and Gabriel at the center, took the gun away from the kid, and shot Gabriel with it?"

"It's a theory."

"I don't buy it."

"I said it might be a stretch, but it's the best idea I've got."

"I have a better one. The kid was at the center, exactly like you said. *She* and Gabriel fought. *She* shot him."

"I don't think—"

"Kate, you're not being rational. The physical evidence points to the kid. All of it." I imagined Martinez ticking off points on her fingers. "First, we have the missing drawing. Who would have wanted it except for the teen?"

"A fan of her work?" The idea sounded ludicrous, even to me.

"Second, the gun. Ballistics confirmed that the handgun found at the scene is the murder weapon." She paused, as if considering whether or not to continue. "Third, we got a match on the fingerprints. We're ninety-nine percent sure they're the kid's."

"I thought you hadn't found any fingerprint matches in the system."

"We didn't. I sent a patrol officer out to the kid's house this morning."

Dean had admitted that he'd spoken with the police, but he'd conveniently neglected to mention that they'd been at his house. Then again, why would he? The only reason he'd spoken to us at all was to score Rene's money.

Martinez continued. "The guy's a jerk, but he's a cooperative jerk. The officer got prints off the kid's bedroom door knob and a water glass on her nightstand. We'll double check when we catch Rainbow, but the prints from the bedroom match the ones on the magazine. She's our shooter. The judge issued an arrest warrant this afternoon."

Martinez's words sucked the oxygen out of my Honda. The space felt cramped. My lungs, empty. I opened the door to let in some air. "It doesn't make any sense. Why would Rainbow kill Gabriel? He was on her side."

"I don't know, Kate. We still need to talk to the kid. But it makes a lot more sense than the story you came up with. Remember that cash box we found the gun in?"

"Yes."

"It was wiped clean too, but the chef—Chuck, I think his name is?—said it's a petty cash box that he keeps in the pantry. Rainbow volunteered in the kitchen a couple of days a week, so she would have known about it. According to Chuck, there was over three hundred dollars inside when he left that night. When we found it, the box was empty except for the gun."

I groaned. "That's why you said Rainbow had a few hundred dollars. You think she stole that money." The Rainbow I knew wasn't capable of premeditated murder, but swiping petty cash? Absolutely. I knew that firsthand.

"It certainly seems like it. Like I theorized at the scene, the kid decided to get out of town, so she went back to the center to score some quick cash. The victim surprised her in the act, and she panicked. She may not have intended to shoot Gabriel, Kate, but we're pretty sure that she did."

I got out of the car and started pacing. Back and forth, forth and back, from one end of my car to the other. "If she thought far enough ahead to wipe the outside of the gun and the cash box, why didn't she wipe the magazine?"

"No one said she was a professional killer."

Martinez's theories made more sense than I cared to admit, but deep down inside, I didn't believe them. At least not all of them. Rainbow going back to the center to steal cash? Sure. Rainbow panicking when she was interrupted in the act? Absolutely. But Rainbow following Gabriel to his office, pulling the gun out of her backpack, and then shooting him point-blank in the chest? Not a chance.

I spent the rest of the night brainstorming theories with Michael and begging forgiveness for saddling him with Ed and Lonnie. Michael had modified the latch on their cage, so the prison break problem was solved at least for the time being. Managing his clients' reactions to the little fur beasts? Well, that hadn't gone nearly as well.

After several complaints and two threats to call the health department, he'd decided to relocate the little monsters to the storage room. The boys weren't happy, but it would do for now. Later this weekend, I'd implement plan B, which was to sweet-talk Dale and

Dharma into picking up their new pets on their way back to Orcas after the fundraising event.

It was the obvious solution, now that I thought about it. Dale and Dharma ran an animal rescue. Surely they had space for two tiny rodents. How much trouble could Ed and Lonnie be compared to sixty-four donkeys, thirty-four goats, and a Jack Russell Terriorist?

Problem theoretically solved, I wrapped my arms around my husband's shoulders. "I love you, you know."

He took my hand and glanced meaningfully at the staircase to the bedroom. "Then prove it."

I did. Multiple times. With pleasure. For one of very few times in six frustrating, no-baby-making months, there was nothing mechanical about it.

SIXTEEN

SATURDAY PASSED AND BLED into Sunday without further progress. I taught yoga classes, visited Ed and Lonnie at the pet store, and circled the blocks around Teen Path HOME hoping to find Rainbow, or at least someone I recognized who could lead me to her. Other than a locked door and a sign reading *Closed until Further Notice*, I found nothing. If Martinez had better luck, she didn't call to let me know about it. I considered calling Dharma and Dale to get their advice, but what would they tell me? Keep looking? I already planned to do that. Starting that morning at Gabriel's memorial.

I pulled into Queen Anne Memorial's parking lot at nine-forty and parked near a small group of teens gathered on the lawn near an ancient cedar tree. Henderson was with them, interviewing two girls I recognized from the center. I tucked my head down and hurried to the facility's entrance, hoping he wouldn't notice me.

Avoidance was futile, I knew. Henderson would inevitably confront me inside. But that was the lesser of two evils. If he stopped me now, I'd never make it through the front door. I needed one hundred percent of my willpower to keep from jumping back inside my Honda and driving away.

I hadn't attended a funeral since my father's death almost five years before. I kidded myself that I'd recovered—and for good reason. I'd gone on with my life. These days, I had Michael, Bella, and Serenity Yoga to keep me on kilter. So I was caught off guard when PTSD-like memories assaulted my senses. The sickeningly sweet smell of burgundy roses and ultra-white lilies. The sour taste of bile on the back of my tongue. The murmur of black-clad voices commenting about how peaceful my father's corpse appeared.

They were wrong. Dad hadn't looked peaceful, not in the slightest. He'd looked dead.

My stomach lurched. Maybe coming here hadn't been such a great idea after all.

A large man holding a clipboard and wearing a somber expression stopped me at the door. His energy felt hard, unyielding. A black-clad bouncer outside a melancholy nightclub.

"I need your name and identification, ma'am."

The request snapped me out of my memories. (Thank goodness.) "Wh … What?"

"Name and identification, ma'am." He added, almost as an afterthought, "Please."

Sam's voice came from beside me. "It's okay, Rex. This is my plus one, Kate Davidson. I asked Cherie's mother to add her to the guest list this morning." His eyes were underscored with purple-gray crescents, but the tired expression he flashed my direction was crystal. *Go with it.*

I went with it.

Bruiser (whose real name was evidently Rex) ran an index finger down the clipboard and stopped at the bottom. "Yes, I see the name handwritten here at the bottom. I'm afraid I'll still need identification."

I reached inside my wallet and pulled out my temporary driver's license. Bruiser eyed it skeptically.

"Sorry, this is all I have," I said. "My wallet was stolen, and the permanent one hasn't arrived yet."

He narrowed his eyes and peered at the black-and-white photo, then at my face, then back at the photo again. I flashed him an innocent smile. He handed the license back and pointed to a guest book. "Please sign in here."

I complied.

Sam took my arm and led me inside the chapel. I whispered, close to his ear but far enough away to avoid touching his blond mustache, "Thanks for vouching for me. What is that guy, a bouncer?"

Sam sighed. "Close enough."

"At a funeral?"

"You never would have gotten past him without me. Cherie's determined to make this a private affair."

"How did you know I'd be here?"

For the first time that morning, Sam's eyes sparkled. "Puh-lease, Kate. You're hardly unpredictable. Rene told me about you two's little adventure to Tacoma. Once I realized you were investigating Gabriel's death, it was a no-brainer that you'd crash the memorial. So I came early and convinced Cherie's mother to add you to the guest list."

"Thanks." Frankly, I was embarrassed that I hadn't thought to ask for Sam's help in the first place. "I'm glad she agreed."

"Cherie's mom wasn't hard to convince. Cherie's the problem." His cheeks turned pink. "And I might have lied and told her that you were a close friend of Gabriel's and mine in college. Don't make me regret vouching for you."

I didn't make any promises. Then again, I don't think Sam expected me to. "I still can't believe they're checking IDs at the door," I said. "What's that about?"

Sam sighed. "That's all Cherie. Requiring identification is an easy way to keep out Gabriel's clients."

"How so?"

"A lot of Teen Path HOME's clients are runaways. Others have outstanding warrants. Do you honestly think most of those kids outside would be willing to show identification?"

"You mean some of them won't be able to attend the service?"

"None of them will. Not even the ones who are willing to show ID. No one gets inside unless they're on the guest list."

I selfishly thought of Henderson, who was outside with the kids. "What about the police?"

"You mean that cop outside?"

"Yes. His name is Detective Henderson."

"Cherie already told him to get lost. I'm sure he could have forced the issue, but he didn't. I suspect he'll stay outside."

Which was good news, at least for Martinez and me. I wouldn't have to evade Henderson's questions if he didn't know I was here. "I get why Cherie wouldn't want Henderson to be at the service," I said. "He didn't know Gabriel, and the police have been treating Cherie as a suspect. But keeping the kids out seems cruel. Most of them don't have cars. It probably took multiple bus transfers for them to get here this morning. They wouldn't have come if the ceremony wasn't important to them."

"I agree, but there's no talking Cherie out of it. Believe me, I tried. She's convinced Gabriel's clients are responsible for his death."

"She seriously thinks one of the kids outside killed him?"

Sam's lips thinned. "Does she think one of them held the gun? No, at least I don't think so. Indirectly, though? Absolutely. She's positive his death is their fault."

"Where's the logic in that?"

"According to Cherie, it's simple cause and effect. If Gabriel hadn't wanted to help those kids, he wouldn't have worked at Teen Path HOME. If he hadn't worked at Teen Path HOME, he and Cherie wouldn't have fought. If they hadn't fought, he wouldn't have been at the center the night he was murdered."

"That's ridiculous. Even if Gabriel's death *did* have something to do with Teen Path HOME, he was a grown man. No one forced him to be at the center after closing. It's not fair to blame anyone but the killer."

Sam held up his hands. "You're preaching to the choir here, Kate, but Cherie won't budge. Arguing with her just makes her worse. She's not rational. I'm afraid she might be mentally unraveling."

I frowned. "Do the kids outside know they can't come in?"

"Yes. The Teen Path HOME board president is here, and he talked to them. He asked them to respect Cherie's wishes."

"I met him once. His name's Greg, right?"

Sam nodded.

"Will they listen to him?"

"I think so. Greg has worked hard to build positive relationships with the kids. They respect him. He said they promised to not make a scene, but they're not leaving, either. They're planning to create their own ceremony outside."

I glanced at my watch. "Maybe I should talk to them."

A low, dirge-like bell chimed three times. "Not now, Kate. The service is about to begin."

I followed Sam to a row of chairs near the back and watched the rest of the mourners filter inside. The gathering was small—twenty-five or so people—which wasn't surprising since Bruiser was turning people away at the door. Chuck sat two rows up and a few chairs to the right, and Vonnie occupied the chair next to him. Greg sat close to the back with four other men and a somber woman I didn't recognize.

Shortly before the ceremony began, Cherie arrived at the front, flanked by an older couple I assumed were her parents. A procession of four men and two women wheeled a casket to the front. Closed, thank goodness.

The officiant's words were kind but generic; her delivery, rehearsed. I suspected that she was reading a fill-in-the-blanks script written for burying strangers. My heart ached, not simply for the loss of Gabriel's life, but for the loss of human connection after his death. He'd helped many. I assumed he'd been loved by many. But few of them were in this space. Most were gathered two hundred feet away, holding vigil underneath a cedar tree, barred from entry by an angry wife and a bouncer in a funeral suit.

When the officiant launched into a monotone recitation of Gabriel's obituary, I tuned out her words and visually eavesdropped on the audience. Cherie stared straight ahead, white knuckles clasped in her lap. An ice sculpture on the verge of shattering. Her parents leaned oddly away from her. Chuck slouched and glanced down at his smart phone. Vonnie openly wept. The board president and his entourage murmured amongst themselves.

At the end of the blessedly short ceremony, the officiant invited us all to stay for coffee and pastries. I leaned over and whispered to Sam, "Do you know which people here were closest to Gabriel?"

"No. We lost touch for a few years before he contacted me about donating to Teen Path HOME."

"How about family?"

He gestured to the front row. "As far as I know, Cherie was the only family Gabriel had left. His parents and his sister died in an automobile accident years ago."

"How tragic."

"Yes. They were good people. Their death was what made Gabriel decide to go into social work. He told me that once he realized how fleeting life could be, he needed to make sure every day made a difference." Sam's eyes grew moist. "I had no idea at the time how prophetic his words were. It doesn't seem fair."

"It isn't." I squeezed his hand. "I promise, Sam, I'll do everything in my power to make sure Gabriel's killer is punished. I'll start by talking to Cherie and her parents."

"Not today, Kate, please. Cherie is like a rabid porcupine. Anyone who gets close enough to touch comes away bloody. If I'd known how unstable she was, I'd have told you to stay home." He shook his head emphatically. "Talk to anyone else you want, but leave Cherie alone. I don't want Gabriel's funeral to end up being a circus."

If anyone other than Sam had made the request, I'd have ignored them. But Sam, perhaps more than most in this room, was grieving his friend. I wouldn't add to his pain.

"It won't be, Sam. I promise."

We made our way through the refreshment line, then loitered uncomfortably in the back of the room, sipping black coffee and nibbling on shortbread. Cherie and her parents stood in deep conversation with Bruiser.

"Are you okay alone for a couple of minutes?" Sam asked. "Some of the Teen Path HOME board members are here, and we need to talk. It should only take five or ten minutes."

"I'll be fine." I smiled. "I'll mill around and see if I overhear anything interesting."

It was a reasonable plan. A good one, even.

Until Cherie noticed me.

She squinted as if trying to place my face, then frowned and said something to Bruiser. He pointed at the guest book, said something back, and shook his head. Cherie's mother grasped her arm and motioned for Cherie to stay put, but she shook her off and strode in my direction.

"Do I know you?" It wasn't a question. It was an accusation.

"My name's Kate Davidson. I'm so sorry for your loss."

Cherie cocked her head to the side, eyes paradoxically dull and piercing at the same time. "I don't know anyone named Kate Davidson." She pointed to Bruiser. "Rex says that your name was handwritten on the guest list and the ID you presented might be fake."

"It's not fake, it's temporary. I'm a friend of—"

I was about to say I was a friend of Sam's, but she didn't give me the chance.

"A friend of my husband's?" She snorted unattractively. "Well isn't that special. I'm glad Gabriel had time for friends, because he certainly never had time for me." She made finger quotes with her hands. "When he wasn't angsting over one of his 'kids,' he was too busy sleeping around with—" Her eyes widened. "Wait a minute. I *do* know you. You're that woman who was mooning around outside Gabriel's office two weeks ago." She poked my sternum with her index finger. Hard. "You're *her*, aren't you?"

The other mourners stopped talking and stared. I felt my face redden. "I'm sorry, I think you have me confused with someone else."

Cherie's voice grew thirty decibels louder. "Oh, believe me. I'm not the confused one here. How dare you come to my husband's memorial acting like you're part of my family. You're the one who destroyed it." Spittle sprayed from her lips to my face. "You're the reason Gabriel came home after midnight every night. You're the reason we fought the night he died." Her voice caught. "You're the reason he forgot about me."

I took several steps back and held up my hands, instinctively protecting my face. "Listen. I honestly don't know what you're talking about. I'm here with Sam."

The crowd's murmurs grew louder. Somewhere in the distance, I heard a voice say, "Shouldn't somebody stop her?"

I doubt Cherie heard any of it. Her eyes were wet with feverish fury. "I knew Gabriel was cheating on me, but the lying bastard denied it—he denied me—until the day he died. You stole him from me." She raised her right hand to slap me, and I braced for the blow.

An instant before impact, Cherie's father grabbed her wrist. Her mother stepped between us, the way I did whenever Bella lunged at the UPS man.

Sam appeared at my side. "I told you not to interrogate her!"

"I didn't, I swear!"

Cherie's mother stroked her daughter's hair and spoke in low, soothing tones. "Sweetie, I need you to come with me now. The funeral director wants to know what to do with the flowers." She smiled at me, not unkindly. "Excuse us."

Cherie grumbled as her mother drag-walked her away. "Tell the funeral director he can take those flowers and stuff them inside Gabriel's cheating corpse."

Her father—whose name I remembered from the obituary was Andre—waited until the women were out of sight before turning to me. "I'm so sorry. My daughter's not well. Did she harm you?"

"No, just spit on me a little. I'm not who she thinks I am, though." I turned to Sam. "She came up to me, I swear. All I did was introduce myself and tell her that I was sorry for her loss."

Andre took a deep breath in, then slowly released it. "It's not your fault, Miss…"

"Davidson, Kate Davidson." I didn't correct him that I was actually a Mrs.

"Miss Davidson. You're the third woman Cherie's accosted since her mother and I arrived in Seattle yesterday."

"The third?" Sam asked.

"Yes. And I strongly suspect there'll be a fourth before the day is over. We knew she was having difficulties, but we had no idea they were this severe."

I glanced at Sam, silently asking permission to continue. He nodded.

"Difficulties?" I asked.

"Cherie has always been hard on herself. Hard on everyone around her, for that matter. She suffers from clinical depression, though it often manifests as anger."

"Seriously?" Sam said. "Gabriel and I roomed together in grad school. Cherie practically lived at our place. He never mentioned that she had mental health issues."

"Ah," Andre replied, "you must be Sam. Gabriel spoke very fondly of you." He reached out and shook Sam's hand. "I suspect he never said anything about Cherie's mental health issues back then because he didn't know about them. She'd had them under control since high school. We thought she'd put all of that behind her, but in hindsight, I'm not surprised that her condition has flared up again. Life didn't exactly turn out the way she'd planned."

"You mean Gabriel's death?" Sam asked.

Andre sighed. "I wish it were that simple. Grief, she would eventually overcome. This is much trickier. I'm afraid Cherie suffers from terminal disappointment."

"Disappointment?" I asked.

"You don't know Cherie, do you?" Andre replied.

"No." I almost volunteered that I didn't know Gabriel very well either, but I stopped myself.

"Cherie and Gabriel were high achievers in college. She was convinced they'd both be CEOs of Fortune 500 companies someday."

Sam nodded. "Everyone who knew them back then thought they'd be famous."

"They probably would have been, if Gabriel hadn't decided to change careers and go into social work. Cherie was disappointed, but she supported him every way she could. They lived on her salary and spent their savings on his tuition." He shrugged. "Then she got laid off last year."

"Cherie lost her job?" Sam asked. "Gabriel never told me that, either."

"She didn't want him to talk about it. She wouldn't like me talking about it, either, but I think you and your friend deserve an explanation. Cherie's been looking for work, but positions at her level are rare, and she's overqualified for most others. She started spinning back into depression and lashing out at Gabriel. Gabriel responded by avoiding her. Lately, he's spent most of his time at the youth center."

"That doesn't sound like Gabriel," Sam said. "He and Cherie were practically inseparable."

Andre shrugged. "People grow apart. Honestly, given what I've experienced in the last couple of days, I don't blame him. I'm Cherie's father and I don't want to be around her either."

"Excuse me for asking," I said, "but Cherie mentioned an affair."

"Yes. Gabriel's supposed affair has become Cherie's obsession. Her mother and I can't figure out if it was real or the figment of her paranoid imagination. We'll probably never know for sure."

Cherie's story was tragic, and part of me understood her resentment. Michael and I had both chosen careers that seemed uniquely designed to keep us barely above poverty level. But we'd known that going in. Losing your job, your status, and your husband's attention might build a lot of resentment. Add mental illness and an extramarital affair to the top and you had plenty of motive for murder.

I was trying to come up with a delicate way to ask Andre where Cherie had been the night of her husband's death when he noticed that his wife was gesturing for him to join her.

"Excuse me," he said. "I'd better go. Again, please accept my apologies."

I waited until he was ten steps away before I spoke. "I'm sorry, Sam. I didn't mean to cause a scene."

"It's okay. It wasn't your fault."

"Do you think Cherie was right? Was Gabriel having an affair?"

Sam stared desolately at the carpet. "I don't know, Kate. Before today, I would have said no way. Never." He shrugged. "But now? Who knows? There was so much Gabriel didn't tell me. I don't know what to believe anymore." He gestured to the parking lot. "I'm going to get out of here. I've had about as much drama as I can take for one day."

"I think I'll hang around for a few more minutes, if you don't mind," I squeezed his shoulder. "Thanks again. I owe you one."

I meant it. Even if I didn't learn anything else, the memorial had been enlightening. The fights I'd witnessed between Gabriel and his wife hadn't been isolated incidents. They were two snapshots in an expanding album of marital discord.

A vivid scene unfolded in my imagination ... a furious Cherie slams down the phone and vows to confront her husband in person. She speeds from her house to Teen Path HOME, screeching to a stop on the dark, empty street in front of the center. She pounds on the door until Gabriel lets her in. She storms to his office and begins searching for evidence of his supposed affair. She screams at him. She shoves him. He shoves her back. Maybe he even slaps her. She picks up Rainbow's gun and—

And that's where the scene unraveled. How would Cherie have gotten Rainbow's gun?

Martinez's voice echoed inside my head. *She wouldn't have. The physical evidence points to the teen.*

That's because we haven't found all of it yet, I silently grumbled back.

I wandered through the diminishing gathering in hopes of learning something else useful. Chuck and Vonnie were gone. They must have had left during The Great Kate and Cherie Standoff. The mourners still present treated me like a pariah, stopping conversation and avoiding eye contact upon my approach. A side effect, I assumed, of my confrontation with Cherie. Hanging around any longer would be a waste of time.

I wiggled my fingers at Bruiser and stepped outside. I immediately felt lighter, and not simply because of the cool breeze on my skin or the sun, which was momentarily peeking through the overcast sky. Inside the memorial center, the energy had been heavy. Almost strangling. Outside, I could breathe.

Henderson was gone, but two young adults remained near the cedar tree. I recognized Echo by her duct tape-covered pink coat. She was talking to Jace, Rainbow's ex-boyfriend.

Or rather, Jace was talking at Echo.

His body language wasn't frustrated, like it was when I first saw them together outside of Teen Path HOME, but it wasn't friendly either. If I had to give it a name, I'd have called it arrogant. He had the power in their relationship, and he knew it.

Echo, in contrast, was jittery. Desperate. Her frayed jeans were so filthy they almost looked black.

When I got within hearing distance, I could tell that Echo was pleading. "You know I'm good for it. I just need a bump." She smiled and traced her index and third fingers down Jace's chest. "I can give you an advance payment."

Jace shoved her away. "I told you, no more free rides, of any kind. Get the green. You know where to find me." He turned his back to her and strode across the parking lot, toward the sidewalk.

I jogged after him. "Jace! Wait a minute. I need to talk to you."

He flinched, then half-turned to face me. "How do you know my name?"

"I'm a friend of Rainbow's."

He rolled his eyes and resumed walking.

"Hold up!" I yelled. "I need to find her."

He stopped moving, but the look he gave me was scathing.

"Do you know where she is?" I asked. "It's important. She's in trouble."

"Don't know, don't care." He loped five steps away, then turned back for one final proclamation. "If you do see Rayne, tell her she'd better hope the cops don't arrest her. Narcs don't do well in juvie."

"Narcs? What are you talking about?"

He left without answering.

Echo's voice came from behind me. "You're looking for Rainbow?"

"Do you know where I can find her? She needs help."

The girl scratched her fingernails up and down her arms. Sweat dotted her forehead. "Lady, we all need help. Haven't you figured that out yet? The help I need comes in the form of a C-note."

I stared into her bloodshot eyes, conflicted. I couldn't afford to give away any money, much less a hundred dollars. But that wasn't what stopped me. If I gave Echo money, she'd use it to buy drugs. I had zero doubt. Could I, in good conscience, enable that?

Echo's fingers twitched. "I haven't got all day. It's cash or deuces, lady. Take your pick."

"How do I know your information is legit?"

"I'll take you to her."

My internal struggle wasn't nearly as difficult as it should have been. I told myself that paying Echo for information about Rainbow wasn't the same as feeding her addiction. She'd find a way to get her fix regardless. Perhaps my "donation" would help both teens. If I paid Echo the money, I'd locate Rainbow and prevent Echo from prostituting herself, at least for one night.

It was a convenient lie, but I convinced myself anyway.

I pulled out my billfold and removed two twenties. "You'll get the rest when I see Rainbow."

Echo reached for the money, then hesitated. For the first time, I glimpsed kindness underneath her veil of addiction. "Are you going to turn her in to the cops?"

I considered lying, but Echo—even in the obvious throes of drug withdrawal—would know I was scamming her. Once I blew her trust, it would be gone for good.

"I have to. It's the only way I can get her help."

Echo's eyes met mine, then flicked to the pavement. "She didn't kill Gabriel."

"I know. Can you help me figure out who did?"

She hesitated, and for a moment I thought she'd say yes. Instead, her expression grew cold. "Not my problem. Give me another twenty. Sixty down, forty on delivery. We'll have to drive."

Not without backup, we won't.

I'd been reckless in the past, but I'd learned my lesson. I sensed Echo was inherently gentle, but I didn't know her. I wouldn't risk getting into a car with her alone.

I pulled out one of my business cards, folded a ten-dollar bill around it, and handed it to her. "This is the last of my cash. I need to get more. Consider fifty dollars my down payment. Do you have a bus pass?"

"Yes."

"Good. Meet me at the address on this card in an hour. The number five bus stops across the street. We'll drive from there. I'll give you another fifty when you take me to Rainbow."

Echo snatched the cash with trembling fingers. "Make it two hours. I need to get something first." I had a horrible feeling that "something" was a tiny bag of white powder.

"Fine. Two hours it is. Wait for me in front of Serenity Yoga."

We parted company. Echo hurried to the bus stop; I got in my car. I ignored the voice in my head saying I'd made a horrible mistake.

SEVENTEEN

WHEREVER ECHO WAS PLANNING to take me, we wouldn't be going alone. I stopped at home and picked up Bella, then drove to Pete's Pets to grab Michael. I expected at least token resistance from my safety-oriented husband, but he was surprisingly compliant.

Michael quickly showed Tiffany how to set up the Thanksgiving pet toy display while I said a quick hello to Ed and Lonnie. The little guys scampered up to the door of their cage and sat on their haunches like two tiny soldiers in formation.

"Sorry, guys. You have to stay here. I promise, as soon as I find Rainbow, I'll focus on getting you a better home. I know you miss Gabriel."

Michael poked his head into the storage room. "I'm ready when you are. If this Echo character is as twitchy as you describe, we shouldn't make her wait."

We left through the pet store's emergency exit, which led directly into the parking garage where I'd left Bella. I would have brought her inside Pete's Pets with me, but I was afraid that another dog might already be in the store and I didn't want to risk her creating a scene. Bella had never harmed another animal, but suffice it to say that one of her ferocious displays wouldn't earn Michael any repeat customers.

"I still can't believe you're not trying to talk me out of this," I said to him. "You hate it when I get involved in murder investigations."

"That's not true. I understand why you try to solve crimes. It's for all the same reasons I fell in love with you. You're smart and curious, you have a keen sense of justice, and you're drawn to help people. But you're also impulsive, and that impulsiveness puts you in danger. Frankly, I'm delighted that you invited me along this time instead of going off on your own." Michael's expression turned serious. "Besides, I want to help Rainbow, too. I need to make up for Wednesday night."

I stopped at the car and released Bella from her back seat prison. She danced a quick happy dance at Michael's feet. "You need to let that go, Michael."

"How can I? I was a jerk. I didn't even give Rainbow a chance. I got on my high horse, assumed she was a thief, and insisted that you call the police. I should have kept my mouth shut until you'd spoken to Dale. If I had, everything might have turned out differently."

"You weren't wrong, Michael. Rainbow did steal my wallet, and if we'd let her stay overnight without calling the police, we could have gotten in trouble. Dale explained that."

"But I still wasn't right. Rainbow's not much different than Gabriella was. She's been abused, she's scared, and she has nowhere to go. I broke the law big time to help Gabby, and it cost me a hell of a lot more than the few bucks Rainbow took from you. I practically shoved the kid out into that storm."

"You can't blame yourself. Rainbow made her own decisions."

"So did I. And I'm deciding now: you and I are helping her. Together."

I wrapped my arms around my husband's waist and gave him a squeeze. "I love you, you know."

By the time Bella, Michael, and I reached the yoga studio's front entrance, Echo was already huddled outside, looking impatient. Her hands were significantly less jittery than earlier, due no doubt to a recent "bump" obtained from her favorite drug dealer. She flinched away from Bella, then narrowed her eyes at Michael. "You didn't say you were bringing a search party."

She was right. I hadn't told her I was planning to gather reinforcements because I was afraid she'd veto the idea. She still might, but that was a risk I'd have to take. Michael and Bella's attendance wasn't optional. For all I knew, Echo was the killer. If she wouldn't allow Michael and Bella to come with us, I wouldn't go either.

The bravado in my voice wasn't false. "This is my husband, Michael. He and the dog come with us, or we don't go." I pulled out the fifty dollar bill I'd withdrawn from the cash machine. "Do you want this or not?"

She gave me a foul look, then reached to snatch the bill out of my fingers. I pulled it away. "You'll get this after we find Rainbow. That was the deal."

"Fine. Let's go. Who's driving?"

We opted to take Michael's SUV. I climbed into the back with Bella while Echo rode shotgun. Michael slid the key into the ignition and looked expectantly at the young woman. "Where are we headed?"

She stared out the passenger-side window. "Woodland Park. We have a campsite there."

I shouldn't have been surprised. The universe, after all, tends to bring us full circle. I spent the ten-minute drive reminiscing about the last time I'd gone with a homeless person to Woodland Park. The experience hadn't been pleasant. My friend George—Bella's first owner—had been murdered, and in trying to figure out who killed him, I'd naïvely followed a homeless man named Charlie to Woodland Park.

The park had been deserted that cold, rainy afternoon. Frighteningly so for a female yoga teacher accompanying a mentally disturbed man significantly larger than she. Charlie had eventually taken me to the park's fenced-in horseshoe area. I'd assumed that he had chosen the horseshoe pit as his home rather than one of Seattle's more populated homeless encampments because he craved isolation. Charlie wasn't exactly a people person.

A lot had changed in the past three years.

The homeless problem in Seattle had gotten significantly worse, or at least significantly more visible. Astronomical rents, decreased social and mental health services, and a flourishing opioid crisis had dramatically increased the number of Seattleites without stable housing. Local homeowners blamed the city council, whose primary response had been to ignore and enable the problem.

The issue had been simmering barely below boiling for over a decade. The tipping point came when the city closed the Jungle, a homeless encampment located on a 160-acre greenbelt under Interstate 5. In spite of the Jungle's poor sanitation and abysmal crime rates, over four hundred people in Seattle's unhoused community called it home.

Or, at least, they had. After a few well-publicized murders in the Jungle, the area had been cleared out, cleaned up, and fenced off.

The individuals who lived there were ordered to relocate. And relocate they did.

Tent and RV encampments had popped up all over the city. Simply put, the Jungle was now everywhere, including Woodland Park. So when Michael drove past the fenced-off horseshoe area, I was only mildly surprised to see a half-dozen tents and approximately twice that many souls inside it. I doubted Charlie was among them.

"Is this it?" Michael asked.

"No," Echo replied. "You can't see our place from the road. Keep driving." She directed us to a lot near the park's southernmost restroom. "Park here. We'll walk the rest of the way."

I clipped on Bella's lead, and the three of us followed Echo out of the lot and down a narrow trail crowded by dense underbrush. Pine needles scented the air and crunched under our feet. Bella alternated between pulling me forward and stopping every few seconds to sniff the ground and mark her new territory.

"How long have you been camped here at the park?" I asked.

Echo shrugged. "I'm not sure. A couple of months, I guess."

"It's pretty far from Teen Path HOME," I said.

"Not really. It's only a twenty-minute bus ride. I got sick of being harassed by the suits downtown, and Aurora's walking distance for when I need to ... well, you know." She didn't meet my eyes.

She was referring to Aurora Avenue North, a major thoroughfare that formed the park's westernmost border. Aurora was the home of fast food restaurants, gas stations, used car lots, and pay-by-the-hour motels. It was also a mecca for drug dealing and prostitution. I had a feeling Echo participated in both.

I pointed to a sign near the path. *No camping. No access from 11 p.m. to 7 a.m.*

"The police don't stop you from setting up camp here?"

She shrugged. "They come around and talk to us every now and then, but they haven't made us leave, at least not yet. They'd rather have us here than out in the neighborhoods where people can see us. A maintenance guy locks up the restrooms at night, but during the day we have access to toilets and running water. And as long as we stick together, it's pretty safe. Downtown gets sketchy at night."

"You're sure Rainbow's here at the encampment?" I asked.

"She was this morning. She's too freaked out to leave."

"Because of the police?"

"Yes. She thinks they'll find her if she tries to leave town, but she's not safe here anymore either. The cops have already harassed everyone within three miles of Teen Path HOME. It won't be long before they start hitting the encampments farther away. I figure it's better for you to find her than them." Echo stared at her hands. "Besides, if Jace finds out I'm hiding her, he'll cut me off."

I consciously kept the judgment out of my voice. "Jace is your dealer, isn't he?"

She didn't reply.

An uncomfortable thought churned in my belly. "Does Rainbow deal too?"

Echo harrumphed. "Rainbow? Are you kidding? She's so clean, she can't even crap without squeaking." Her face grew solemn. "She'll never survive prison. I hope you can help her."

In her own skewed way, Echo had Rainbow's best interests at heart. Echo wasn't a bad person, just a flawed one trapped in a terrible situation. There had to be some way I could find Rainbow without further enabling Echo's addiction.

"Echo, I have a deal for you," I said. "Instead of giving you fifty dollars in cash after we find Rainbow, why don't Michael and I take you to a store and buy you a hundred dollars worth of supplies?"

Her shoulders stiffened. "Supplies?"

"Food, soap, clothes … Whatever you need."

Echo's face screwed up in anger. "What, now you're going all social worker on me? I got enough of that crap from Gabriel. What's next? An offer to drive me to rehab?"

The thought had crossed my mind.

Echo must have read my expression, because she stopped walking. "If I want your lame do-gooder advice, I'll ask for it. It's too late to change our deal now." She thrust out her palm. "Give me the rest of the money."

I didn't move.

"Now. Or the tour stops here."

Michael touched my arm. "Give it to her, Kate. Rainbow's our priority."

I reluctantly pulled out the money and handed it to her. Irony bittered the back of my tongue. I'd just given money I couldn't afford to an addict, who would spend it on illegal substances that I abhorred. All so I could find a runaway who didn't want to be found. Worse yet, said drug user would likely give the money to the runaway's ex-boyfriend, who'd dumped her and taken off with their camping supplies, which was why she'd broken into Teen Path HOME and gotten into this mess in the first place. There was a life lesson—or a who's-on-first comedy skit—in there somewhere.

But not for me. At least not now. For now, I just felt like a shit. I had a feeling we all did.

Two minutes later, it was show time.

We emerged from the trees into an opening with a dozen or so tents arranged in a circle, like pioneer wagons preparing for battle. The pine scent faded, replaced by the musky smell of rotting garbage and unbathed humans.

The circle's center was littered with cardboard boxes, fast food containers, propane cook stoves, and empty potato chip bags. Two brightly painted cylinders hung from a navy blue tent on the opposite side, one with colorful swirls around pink and red hearts. The solar lanterns I'd seen Echo creating at Teen Path HOME.

A forty-something bearded man approached us. "Got any spare change?"

"Now's not a good time," I said. Bella lifted her lip and added a low growl.

He held up his hands and backed away. "Okay, lady, never mind. No need to sic Cujo on me."

Bella lifted her chin, then gave three quick air sniffs. With a low, happy woof, she charged toward the tent with the lanterns. I stumbled behind her; Michael and Echo jogged behind me. Bella skidded to a stop outside the tent, nuzzled the entrance, and whined.

A blonde head peeked through the opening.

Rainbow.

Her face broke into a surprised smile. "Bella!" Then she saw Michael and me. The smile vanished, replaced by something that looked an awful lot like panic. She reached for her pack, preparing to bolt.

Echo grabbed her arm. "Stop. They're here to help you."

Rainbow shook off Echo's grasp, but she didn't run. "Three hundred dollars. I gave you three hundred dollars to hide me, and still you ratted me out the second you finished shooting my money up your veins. You're a selfish junkie, just like my mother."

Echo didn't flinch. "I never said you could stay here forever. Be glad I didn't snitch to the cops."

"What's the difference? These two aren't going to hide me. They wanted to turn me in before Gabriel was even shot."

She whipped toward me, face so red it was practically purple. "I didn't do anything except protect myself from my psycho stepfather. But it doesn't matter, because no one believes me."

She was wrong. I believed her. One look at my husband's face and I knew he believed her, too. Rainbow had obviously been through four very tough days. The jeans and sweatshirt I'd given her were filthy. The bright green Seahawks slipper socks sagged over her shoes. She looked impossibly thinner than she had on Wednesday, and her eyes were shiny with stress. But I saw no signs of a recent life-or-death struggle. No dried blood on her outfit, no defensive wounds on her hands. No guilt in her voice, either. Just fear. And betrayal. And anger.

"At least I won't have to go back to that scumbag," she scoffed. "I'd rather be some prison hag's wife than get raped by Sergeant Psychopath." She held out her hands, daring me to cuff them. "Go on," she said. "Book 'em, Danno. You know you want to."

I kept my voice deliberately calm. "Put your arms down, Rainbow."

"Why should I? You're turning me in, aren't you?"

"No."

Michael's eyes widened. "We're not?"

I ignored him and kept my eyes pinned on Rainbow, preparing to grab her if she tried to run. "*We're* not turning you in; you're turning *yourself* in. But first you're going to talk to my attorney friend, Dale. He's going to help get you out of this mess. We all are."

Rainbow didn't reply, but she didn't argue either.

I took Michael's hand. "Rainbow, you're not alone anymore. Michael and I are your friends. Let us help you."

EIGHTEEN

FORTY-FIVE MINUTES LATER, RAINBOW and I sat across from each other at my kitchen table while Michael stir-fried an early dinner for Rainbow of mixed vegetables and tofu. I suspected that she would have preferred something less healthy—a cheeseburger and fries, perhaps—but meat wasn't part of our vegetarian kitchen.

Michael plated a steamy concoction of bright orange carrots, dark green broccoli, snow peas, and brown rice. The scents of garlic and ginger made my stomach rumble, even though I'd eaten lunch just a few hours ago. Rainbow eyed the plate warily.

Michael handed her a fork. "Go on, eat. I didn't drug it, I promise."

Rainbow gulped down the food like she hadn't eaten in days, which, in retrospect, she probably hadn't. I held off asking questions until she'd finished her second large helping, then invited her to follow Michael and me to the living room. She perched on the couch, one eye on me, the other on the door, as if preparing to make a run for it. Bella hopped on the couch next to her, sighed, and laid her chin on Rainbow's thigh.

I sat on a chair across from her, hoping against hope that I could make her see reason. "You know you can't keep running, right? If you're lucky, the police will catch up with you. If not, you'll end up like Echo, selling your heroin-riddled body to any scumbag who offers you a twenty."

"And try to enjoy it, because those will be the good days," Michael added. "Before long, you'll be dead."

Our words were abrupt, but now wasn't the time for niceties.

Rainbow gripped the loose skin around Bella's neck. "I don't want to go to prison. It's not fair. I didn't hurt Gabriel."

"I know you didn't." I wasn't placating her. Rainbow wasn't the predator in this story; she was the prey. "But what you and I know doesn't matter. We have to convince the police. As far as I can tell, there's a single road out of this mess for you, and that's to prove that you're innocent. Working with my attorney friend Dale is your best bet. But I won't lie to you. He'll make you turn yourself in."

"If I turn myself in, they'll take me to jail."

I nodded. "To juvenile detention, yes."

"For how long?"

"I don't know. For a while, likely, unless Dale can arrange bail." What I didn't tell her was that the odds of Dale getting bail for a runaway arrested for murder were less than his odds of winning the next Lotto jackpot without holding a ticket.

"I know it sounds grim," Michael said. "But the only way this can end well for you is if you go to the police. The longer you run, the guiltier you look. Will you do it?"

Rainbow stared at Bella's black fur as if the answer lay hidden somewhere deep in her undercoat. After several long seconds, she gave a single nod yes.

"Good." Michael reached for the phone. "I'll call Dale."

"Not yet, honey. We need to talk first." I assumed Dale was still two hours away in Olympia, but I couldn't risk it. I turned to Rainbow. "I've helped solve a few mysteries myself, so I don't plan to let Dale do all of the work. But if I'm going to help you, I'll need information. Dale's a good guy, but once he enters the picture, he won't allow you to tell me anything."

It wasn't a guess. I'd seen Dale handle murder investigations two times before. Three, if you counted the time I was his client. Dale's rules of attorney-client privilege left no room for anyone else, including a self-proclaimed yogi detective.

Rainbow released Bella's fur and frowned. "Look, I get that I have to turn myself in. I don't have anywhere else to go, anyway. And I'll talk to this Dale friend of yours. But I don't promise to let him be my attorney. I couldn't afford him even if I wanted to."

I considered telling Rainbow about her trust fund but decided to leave that particular Pandora's box closed, at least for now. "We'll figure out the money later."

Rainbow's tone left no room for argument. "It doesn't matter. I'm not going to let some ... " She paused. "Some man I don't even know boss me around. I got enough of that from the drill sergeant." Her expression grew stony. "My life, my decision."

My stomach dropped to my toes. How could I have been so naïve? I'd assumed Rainbow would jump at the chance to have an attorney—any attorney—in her corner. But why would she? Adults hadn't exactly had her back before now.

"Rainbow, you need an attorney, and Dale's the best. I've trusted him with my life before. So has Michael."

She glanced sideways at Michael, who nodded solemnly. She turned back to me. "If you and this lawyer dude are so close, why would he stop me from talking to you?"

"Because anything you tell me won't be privileged. I might be called to testify against you in court."

Rainbow's jaw tensed, but her face grew ashen.

"I know that's frightening, but I hope your case won't get that far. I have a … " I paused at the word. "I have a gift, I guess you could say. My solve rate is pretty darned good."

"Then why do I need a law—"

I didn't let her finish. "Trust me. You need an attorney, and Dale's as good as they get."

The three of us were silent for one second, then two, then three. Finally, Rainbow spoke. "I said I'll talk to him. No promises after that."

It was the best I was going to get, for now. "Okay. We'll call him in a minute. First, tell me what happened Wednesday night after you left Michael and me, and don't leave out any details." I grabbed my notebook and pen from the end table. "Do you mind if I take notes?"

She shook her head, then reached down to ruffle Bella's ears. She stared at my canine best friend for several seconds. I assumed she was gathering the courage to continue. "It all started when I overheard you and Michael talking." Her eyes flicked between Michael and me, as if she expected us to chastise her. "I wasn't trying to eavesdrop or anything, I promise. I just wanted to show you that your cat is a sweetheart." I withheld the impulse to roll my eyes. "But when I overheard you tell Michael that you'd call the police, I freaked. I knew the cops would send me back to my stepfather." She avoided my gaze. "I meant what I said, Kate. I'd rather die than live with him alone. I figured my best option was to get out of town, so I bolted."

Michael wore an expression of pure unadulterated guilt. "I'm sorry about that, Rainbow. I made a mistake. We ran after you, but we couldn't find you."

"I jogged down to Market Street and hitched a ride from there to downtown. I walked the rest of the way to Teen Path HOME."

I blurted out a stupid question. "You hitchhiked? Don't you know how dangerous that is?"

Rainbow cringed. "I couldn't exactly stand around waiting at a bus stop. I knew you guys would try to catch me."

"Why Teen Path HOME?" Michael asked.

"I needed money to get out of Seattle. I'd already spent the cash that I swiped from Kate's purse." Her upper lip trembled. "I'm sorry for taking your money, Kate. I didn't know you well then. I know that doesn't excuse stealing from you, but ... " Her voice trailed off.

"Don't worry about that, Rainbow," I replied. "We have bigger issues than a couple of twenties you swiped from my billfold."

"It was more than a couple of twenties." She opened her pack, pulled out a small spiral notebook, and flipped through the pages. Midway through, she stopped and held her index finger against the paper. "I took forty-seven dollars and fifty-three cents from you," she replied.

"You wrote it down?"

"I'm keeping a tab. I'm going to pay back everything I stole someday, I promise."

I didn't reply. The promise sounded genuine, if naïve.

"I swear, I only take what I need. I don't have a choice. I can't get a legitimate job without someone finding out I'm a runaway, and I won't sell drugs. Not after what they did to my mother. That leaves stealing and prostitution. Stealing is the lesser of two evils."

I couldn't disagree with her.

She continued. "I would have taken the cash and left your wallet under the table, but I was afraid someone else would swipe it and use your credit cards. I couldn't exactly turn it in to lost and found."

"Is that why you kept it?" I asked.

"Yes. I was waiting for an opportunity to get it back to you when you wouldn't realize I'd swiped it. I would have thrown it out, but the photo inside seemed important.

Part of me didn't want to know what had happened next, but I prodded anyway. "So you went to Teen Path HOME to get money?"

"That and food. Chuck has a petty cash box for kitchen supplies and a stash of protein bars he gives out to his workers. There's a window in the kitchen that doesn't completely lock, so getting what I needed from the kitchen was a sure bet."

She unconsciously placed her hand on her backpack. "I should have grabbed the money and run, but I needed to get something else, too."

"Your drawing." My voice sounded flat.

"You know about that?"

"Yes. The police do too. Didn't you realize that taking your own artwork was like leaving a calling card?"

She chewed on her lower lip. "I wasn't there to hurt anyone. I was just swiping some petty cash. I didn't think Gabriel or Chuck would even bother reporting it. If they did, what difference would it make? I was planning to head out of town in a day or two. The cops don't exactly send out a search party for a few hundred dollars. The drawing has meaning for me, you know?"

"It's okay," Michael said. "What happened next?"

"My drawing was part of a display outside Gabriel's office, so I went there and grabbed it. Gabriel's door was open and a few lights were on, but I honestly didn't think much about it. I figured they left the lights on to scare off burglars." Her cheeks turned pink. "Anyway, after I rolled up the drawing and stashed it in my pack, I heard a shower turn on upstairs. That was the first time I realized I wasn't alone. I figured someone else must have come in through the window like I did."

"How many people know about that window?" I asked.

"No one talked about it, but I'm pretty sure most of us who worked in the kitchen knew."

"If it was so obvious, why didn't somebody fix it?" Michael asked.

"It wouldn't have been obvious to the staff. Casing easy entry points is a survival skill for us street kids. We're always on the lookout. Adults who have money and a comfy place to sleep at night don't pay attention."

"I don't know, Rainbow," I replied. "Certainly Chuck would have noticed. He's in that space every day."

Rainbow stood. For a moment, I thought she was preparing to flee. "Rainbow, where are—"

"Don't worry, I'll be back sooner than you think." She left her pack behind and walked to the kitchen. Bella trotted behind her. The door to the back yard opened, then closed again.

Michael stood. "I'll go outside and keep an eye on her."

A minute later, I heard an upstairs window slide open.

What the …

I stood to check out the sound and saw Rainbow waving at me from the top of the staircase.

"Hey there, Kate." She winked.

Michael and Bella meandered back through the kitchen.

"Unbelievable," he said. "She scaled right up the trellis and crawled in through the bathroom window."

"Believe me now?" Rainbow asked. She flopped back onto the couch. Bella jumped up, turned a quick circle, and sank down beside her again. "I blocked that window latch open four days ago, and you never noticed. I told you, casing easy entrance and exit points is a survival skill."

I glanced at the stairwell, concerned about how quickly Rainbow had broken into my supposedly secure home.

She followed my gaze. "Don't worry about the window. I fixed it so it won't open from the outside again."

Don't worry, indeed. I was calling a locksmith. Pronto.

Rainbow picked up the conversation as if it had never been interrupted. "Like I was saying, I heard the shower turn on upstairs, and I realized I needed to get out of there. I hustled back to the kitchen, found the petty cash box, and pried it open with a butter knife. Then I pulled out my gun, shoved the money into my pack, and headed to the cabinet where Chuck keeps the protein bars."

"Why did you take out the gun?" I asked.

"It wouldn't do me much good buried under a pile of food. I was going to put it back after I snagged the protein bars, but I got distracted by Ed and Lonnie."

"Ed and Lonnie?" Michael asked. "The rats?"

She nodded. "Someone must have forgotten to latch their cage again. Ed was chasing Lonnie across the kitchen floor toward the compost bin. It freaked me out, because Chuck said he was going to put out rat poison, and I figured he might hide it in the compost container."

Her fingers tensed around Bella's scruff. "The only way I could be sure Ed and Lonnie were safe was to catch them, and I couldn't do that with a loaded gun in my hand, so I laid the gun down on the counter and ran after them."

I wanted to scold her. To shake her, even. Leaving a loaded gun out in the open—especially while committing a crime—was hugely irresponsible. But how could I? I'd made plenty of stupid choices in the past, especially when I was trying to help an animal in need.

"Those little suckers are fast, though. I knocked over the compost bin trying to grab Lonnie. Gabriel must have heard, because he slammed into the kitchen a few seconds later. His shirt was unbuttoned and his hair was dripping."

"Did he recognize you?" Michael asked.

"Totally. He tried to grab me, but I got past him. I barely had time to snag my pack before I scrambled out the window. There was no way I could have gotten the gun." Her eyes welled with tears. "I left Ed and Lonnie behind like a selfish coward. I didn't even tell Gabriel they were loose. They probably ate some awful poison because of me."

"Don't worry about the rats," Michael said. "They're fine. The little monsters are destroying my pet store for now."

A smile brightened her face. "Good. That's good."

I wished I felt as relieved as she looked. "Rainbow, that gun you left behind was used to shoot Gabriel."

"I know. Echo told me. That's why the police think I killed him."

"You left it on the kitchen counter?"

"Yes."

"The police found it stashed outside, behind the dumpster. It was inside the petty cash box."

Rainbow frowned. "When I left, the gun was in the kitchen. Someone must have found it and taken it outside."

Michael set his Guinness on the end table and leaned forward. "Rainbow, here's what I don't get. You stole the money so you could leave town. Why didn't you?"

"The weather was awful that night, and my clothes were soaked. I left my coat here, remember?"

How could I forget? I still felt guilty about it.

"Once I got back outside, I was freezing. I needed to get somewhere dry. I was fresh out of options, so I caught a bus to Aurora and started looking for Jace."

"I thought you two had broken up," I said.

"We had, but I hoped that when I told him my stepfather found me, he'd help me out anyway. We have history, you know? I didn't realize how truly pissed he was at me until I saw Echo. I'm dead to him now."

"What happened between you two?"

She scoffed. "Heroin happened. And oxy. And meth."

"Jace uses drugs?" Michael asked.

"Worse. He's a dealer." Rainbow shuddered. "I hate dealers. Heroin destroyed my mom. Jace claimed he hated drugs as much as I did. We both swore when we left Tacoma that we would never get near anything stronger than alcohol or nicotine. Ever." She laughed. "What a crock. Jace still doesn't use, but he started selling to the kids outside Teen Path HOME a month after we got here. That's slimier than dealing to junkies outside an NA meeting. At least I put a stop to that."

"How?" I asked.

Her face turned pink. "The specifics don't matter. I amped up the pressure enough to make him uncomfortable. It didn't work for long, anyway, at least not the way I wanted it to. Jace kept dealing, and the kids at Teen Path HOME kept buying. He just moved his operation to Aurora."

Bella nudged Rainbow's hand, and the teen absently stroked her fur. "Jace and I had a huge fight the day before Gabriel was killed. I said something stupid and he figured out that I was the person who'd made things so hot at Teen Path HOME. I knew Jace would be pissed if he found out, but I never dreamed he'd pull up camp and ghost me."

"You said you looked for him on Aurora," Michael said. "Did you find him?"

"No. If he was dealing that night, I didn't see him. I wandered around for about forty-five minutes until I saw Echo get out of a car. She'd just gotten done with one of her … Well, you know. One of her clients. She was pretty messed up, but she said she'd let me spend the night in her tent if I paid her twenty bucks. So I did."

"If you hate drugs so much, how can you stand being around Echo?" I asked.

"Echo's an addict, like my mom. It's a disease. Dealers like Jace are the problem. Besides, I was freezing, and it was only supposed to be temporary. I was going to give Dean a day or two to lose interest, then I was planning to get out of Seattle. But then Gabriel got killed and the police started looking for me. After that, I was too scared to go anywhere. Echo told me the rent had gone up, so I gave her the rest of the money I stole from Teen Path HOME." Rainbow's jaw clenched. "Lot of good that did. She sold me out to you two the first chance she got."

I paused for a moment, thinking. Rainbow's story made sense. Not that the police would believe it. "I have a couple more questions, then we'll call Dale. When the police found the gun, it had been wiped clean. Did you do that?"

"No. Why would I? I wasn't planning to leave it behind."

I glanced through my notes to make sure I hadn't missed anything important. Mouse flattened herself to the floor and slinked past me. Rainbow made clicking noises with her tongue and reached out her hand. The calico tentatively leaned toward the teen, sniffed her outstretched fingers, then jumped on the couch and curled up between her and Bella. The sound of contented purring filled Michael's and my shocked silence.

"I don't believe it," Michael said. "That cat likes you."

Rainbow smirked. "Believe it or not, some people actually think I'm pretty cool."

"Of course they do. That's not what I meant. I figured the other night was a fluke. Mouse doesn't like anyone but Bella, and Kate and I have the scars to prove it. What are you? A cat whisperer?"

She shrugged. "I've always been good with animals. When I was little, Mom told everyone I'd been kissed by St. Francis. That's why I wanted to be a veterinarian."

There was that use of the past tense again. At the age of sixteen, Rainbow had already written off her future. I would have corrected her, but the way things were going, it seemed she might be right.

She massaged the fur between Mouse's ears, leaned down, and gave her a kiss. Michael lifted his hand as if planning to pet the cat himself, then reconsidered and lowered it to his lap.

"I only have one more question," I said.

"Go for it."

"Did you see anyone besides Gabriel at the center?"

"No. No one. I didn't hear anyone else, either."

I glanced at Michael. "Anything else you can think of?"

He shook his head.

I placed my hands on my thighs and stood. "Okay then, Rainbow. Hang out here for a minute while I make a call. It's time to bring in Dale."

———

Luckily, Dale answered his cell phone. He was scheduled to judge a goat agility event that evening, but given the gravity of Rainbow's situation, he decided to head back up to Seattle right away. Dharma agreed to take over his duties at the festival and rent a car to drive back to Orcas the next day. She would have preferred to come to Seattle with Dale, but one of them needed to go home to manage the rescue. Dale claimed it was no problem, but it sounded like a major hassle for both of them. Reason number 326 why I counted myself lucky to have them as family.

Rainbow was exhausted, so I gave her some private time upstairs in Michael's and my bedroom. Bella and Mouse opted to join her. I would never have been able to nap in Rainbow's situation, but then again I'd never been on the run. I doubted she'd slept much since Wednesday.

Tiffany had already worked well past the end of her shift and there was nothing left to do now but wait, so Michael went back to Pete's Pets to take over until closing. I paced the living room, shoulders knotted like tennis balls.

Two hours later, I heard Dale's rattletrap Plymouth pickup pull into the driveway. Four loud taps on the door followed.

Bella tore down the stairs on full German shepherd alert, but not in her typical I'm-about-to-murder-the-mailman manner. Instead, she yelped with glee and performed her trademarked open-the-door-and-let-him-in dance. Rainbow rubbed her eyes and trudged down the steps behind her. Mouse was nowhere in sight, no doubt hiding underneath the bed.

I grabbed Bella's collar and pulled her away from the door. "Okay, girl, I get it." I teasingly raised my voice loud enough for Dharma to hear in Olympia. "The crazy goat man is here."

I flung the door open with a dramatic flourish. Bella planted both front paws on Dale's shoulders and covered his white beard in slobbery kisses. Rainbow paused in the middle of the stairway and eyed Dale warily.

Dale returned Bella's greeting with a hearty neck scratch and tossed her a goat-shaped cookie. He spoke in his affected Southern twang. "Well hey there, Missy Bella! It's good to see you, too. It's only been three days, you know." He wore overalls, a flannel plaid shirt, and a *Stubborn Old Goat* baseball cap. The smell of goat manure emanated from his work boots. He tilted the cap my direction and played along with my joke. "Read the hat, Miss Kate. I may be stubborn, but I ain't crazy." Dale's eyes then fixed on Rainbow. "I take it this young'un here's my client. Nice to meet you in person, Ms. Rhodes. I hear you've gone and gotten yourself in a heap of trouble."

Rainbow wrinkled her nose, crossed her arms, and scowled. She wasn't fooled by Dale's affectation. Then again, not many of us were. Playing Southern goat farmer was Dale's way of putting strangers at ease. With Rainbow, it had the opposite effect. I mentally kicked myself. I should have warned her about Dale's alternate persona. Better yet, I should have told Dale not to assume it. He was already one strike down and the inning hadn't even started.

"What's with the *Beverly Hillbillies* impersonation?" Rainbow grumbled. "Are you really a right-wing whack job or do you just get a kick out of acting like one?"

Dale took off the hat and tossed it onto the couch. The slouch disappeared, but the smile on his face was genuine. When he spoke, the twang had vanished. "Actually, you're only half right. The accent's real enough, or at least it was. I grew up in the South. Marlington, Kentucky, to be precise. I lost the drawl in law school, which was a couple of decades before you were born. As for my political affiliations, they're none of your business."

Rainbow didn't reply. Bella glanced back and forth between them, confused by the tension between her two favorite humans.

Dale sighed and scratched his beard. "Sorry if my little charade offended you. Frankly, most people enjoy it. Let's start over." He moved to the stairway and reached out his hand. "I'm Dale Evans. You, my smart young friend, must be Rainbow."

Rainbow hesitated, but she eventually gave Dale's hand a cautious shake. "You're an attorney?"

"I am. And if what Kate tells me is correct, you need one."

Rainbow's scowl spoke volumes.

I understood her reticence. The first time I met Dale, I was taken aback by his appearance, too.

I moved past Dale and approached her on the staircase. "Rainbow, you said earlier that you trusted me. Is that still true?"

She nodded.

"Then trust me on this: Dale's right. You need an attorney, and there are none better." I gestured to the couch. "Can we at least sit down and talk?"

She didn't reply, but she trudged downstairs and perched on the sofa. Dale commandeered the chair across from her, with Bella snuggled on top of his feet. I hovered behind Dale, nervous. If Rainbow refused his help, what would happen to her?

Dale got right to business. "Let me be straight with you, Rainbow. If everything Kate told me is true, you're in a lot of trouble. But before you give me your side of the story, you need to retain me as your attorney. Do you want to do that?"

Rainbow studied him seriously. "You don't look like an attorney."

He waved a hand over his informal attire. "Didn't anyone ever tell you not to judge a book by its cover? I drove straight here from a farm animal fundraiser. I have a monkey suit in the truck, and I'll put it on before we leave the house. I've been a defense attorney longer than you've been alive, and I've successfully represented hundreds of clients, most of whom I liked a lot less than you. Honestly, though, you have choices. There are lots of good attorneys out there. If you don't want me to represent you, you can hire someone else."

"I'm only sixteen."

"Your age doesn't matter. Everyone has a right to legal representation. You can have an attorney assigned to you, or you can hire one. Generally, your parents would be responsible for finding you a lawyer, but according to Kate, they're not likely to be of much help."

"Lawyers are expensive, right? I don't have any money. I gave everything I had to Echo."

That was my opening. "Actually, you do. Have money, that is." I told Rainbow and Dale about the letter Rene had pilfered from Dean's end table. "I have no idea how much money is still in your trust fund, but it has to be more than ten thousand dollars. I called the executor's office, but it's closed until tomorrow."

Rainbow's eyes flashed with a mixture of surprise and betrayal. "You mean that trust fund was mine all along? Mom lied to me? Why would she do that?"

"I don't know," I replied. "Maybe she felt betrayed by her parents. Maybe she felt guilty for using the money. Maybe she didn't want you to know that your good grades supported the whole family. That's a lot for a kid."

Rainbow scoffed. "More likely she was afraid that I wouldn't let her use my money on booze and drugs." Irritation morphed to confusion. "I still don't get it, though. How could I have stopped her? I'm a minor."

"You might have more control than you think," Dale said. "I won't know until I get a hand on those trust documents. That is, if you'll give me permission to talk to the executor."

"Yes, of course. How else would I pay you?"

Dale smiled. "I'm not worried about payment. That money was set aside to secure your future, and I'm not about to take it. But I do want to look at the documents. Later on, if I need to hire a private investigator or by some miracle a judge grants you bail, that cash might be helpful. Does that mean you're retaining me?"

For the first time since I'd recommended Dale, Rainbow looked certain. "Yes. Absolutely."

"Great." Dale slapped his hands on his thighs, stood, and faced me. "Kate, that means it's time for you to leave the room. I need to have a confidential conversation with my client."

NINETEEN

I took Bella for a long walk around the neighborhood to allow enough time for Rainbow to tell Dale her full story. By the time I returned home, Dale had contacted Detective Martinez and arranged for Rainbow to turn herself in. He sent Rainbow upstairs, ostensibly to grab her backpack, and sat me down on the couch. Bella padded upstairs behind her.

Dale waited until he heard the door close behind them, then spoke. "I asked Rainbow to give us a few minutes."

"Is she going to be okay?"

"Honestly? I'm not sure. She's a tough kid. A heck of a lot tougher than you led me to believe. I'm darned near positive that she's telling the truth about what happened that night, but I'm not sure the prosecuting attorney will believe her. It may well come down to establishing reasonable doubt at her trial."

"And until then?"

"Until then, no judge in his right mind is going to grant that kid bail. She's a proven flight risk." He paused. "Kate, you should prepare yourself. Even if I succeed in getting her a not guilty verdict, she might spend most of the next year in juvenile detention awaiting trial."

Part of me—the naïve part—wondered if that might not be a good thing. At least she wouldn't be living on the street. In juvie, she'd have a bed, three meals a day, and the chance to earn her high school diploma. She'd have access to a library, a place to shower, and clean though not exactly fashionable clothes.

Then I remembered who she'd be spending that year with. Rainbow hadn't been immune to criminal activity and violence. Not by a long shot. But she hadn't been confined with criminal offenders 24/7, either. After a year spent locked away in the under-eighteen equivalent of maximum security, she might never be the same.

"Dale, a year in juvenile detention might destroy her."

"I know, Kate-girl, I know. Believe me, I'll do everything in my power to prevent it, but some things are beyond my control. Getting bail for a runaway accused of a capital offense is one of them."

"Does she know?"

"Yes. I told her. I'm always up front with my clients. She doesn't like it—hell, I don't like it—but she understands. She's mighty mature for a kid of her age. I have a feeling she was forced to grow up fast."

I glanced up the stairway, toward the bedroom. "She can crawl out of the bathroom window up there. Maybe we should check on her to make sure she doesn't—"

Dale held up his hand. "She's fine, Kate. She's not going anywhere. She says she's too tired to keep running." He gestured toward the couch. "Before Rainbow and I head to the station, I need to talk to you about something else. Once this circus gets started, I'm going to be totally focused on Rainbow. But you and I both know she's not the only person in this house who needs my help."

At first I was confused. Had Rainbow told him that I'd handled the gun used to shoot Gabriel? And why would it matter? I'd already told Martinez, and the gun had been wiped anyway. Then I realized that Dale wasn't talking about legal help. He meant the IVF treatments. I'd been so caught up in Rainbow's issues that I'd temporarily forced my fertility struggles out of my conscious awareness.

Dale sank onto the couch and patted the cushion next to him. I sat, but my body was anything but relaxed.

"Why didn't you tell me that you and Michael needed money for fertility treatments?" Dale asked.

I avoided eye contact. "You've already done so much for us. It seemed wrong to ask."

"How could you think such a thing? Frankly, I'm a little hurt." He shook his head. "I'm even more hurt that Dharma thought she needed to ask my permission before she said yes. We're supposed to be family. Your baby will be my grandchild, too."

I liked his use of the future tense. "Dale, you and Dharma aren't married. She couldn't very well give away your money."

"It's not *my* money; it's *ours*. Dharma should know that. She's my life partner. We would have gotten married long before Michael and you did if Dharma didn't think it would hex us."

"Hex you?"

"She claims marriage destroyed her relationship with your father. She's convinced it would destroy us, too."

"What do you think?"

"That she doesn't give herself enough credit. I love Dharma, past mistakes and all, but she's changed a lot since you were a baby. She would never leave a husband and child behind again. Still, when that woman makes up her mind ... " His white whiskers creased into a wry smile. "There's a reason she ended up rescuing a herd of donkeys. They're just as stubborn as she is. Fortunately, I'm old enough to have learned the fine art of compromise. Dharma and I have sworn to be 'not married' together for the rest of our lives. I drew up a no-nup agreement and everything."

"No-nup? Is that a thing?"

"It is for Dharma and me. As for whether it would stand up in court? Well, that wasn't the point. The point was that I would commit to Dharma in whatever way worked for her." He shrugged. "This did."

The idea made sense, considering the odd match that was my mother and Dale.

"So tell me, Miss Kate, where should I send the check?"

"Dale, I don't know how to thank you."

"You don't have to. Family helps each other." He wrapped me in a huge hug. "Do you want the money now or later?"

"Later, after I set up an appointment with the clinic."

"Good. Glad that's settled. Now let me put on that monkey suit so I can take our young friend to Detective Martinez."

———

By the time I woke up at seven the next morning, Michael and Dale had both come home and left again. Dale must have snuck in sometime after I'd fallen asleep at one, which meant I was completely in the dark about what had happened at the police station. I paced back and forth across the living room carpet, feeling anxious and at loose ends. Rainbow had the best representation available, and that was great news. But as Dale had admitted himself, he could only do so much. I wanted to help.

Every cell in my body ached to call Martinez, but interfering between her and Dale right now might cause more harm than good. I considered going back to the Woodland Park encampment to press Echo for more information, but what would I ask her that I hadn't already asked Rainbow? More than that, I desperately wanted to question the other kids who'd worked in the kitchen. How many of them knew about that broken window latch? Rainbow hadn't seen anyone other than Gabriel at Teen Path HOME the night of the murder, but that didn't mean he was the only one in the building.

I called Teen Path HOME and got the same frustrating voicemail message I'd gotten earlier. The center was closed "until further notice." I would have tried Fred Fredrickson next, but Dale was planning to follow up on Rainbow's trust. Put simply, I was stuck.

So I tried to be productive.

I ground and pre-medicated Bella's kibble, tried for the thousandth time to pet Mouse, then spent five minutes disinfecting and bandaging the fresh, deep red cat scratches bisecting my hand. Daily futile bonding attempt complete, I headed off for the studio. I walked in the door at nine, which gave me ninety minutes to putter around until my students started arriving for the ten forty-five class. I decided to spend fifteen of them picking Rene's brain.

When I walked into Infant Gratification, Rene was helping a mother of triplets determine the optimal accessorizing strategy for two three-month-old girls and their same-aged brother. Ten minutes of babbling over baby baubles later, Rene had talked her into an animal theme. Each child would wear a unique creature from the safari collection, thus allowing the siblings to coordinate while having their own signature look.

The boy would be giraffes, the blonde girl would be lions, and the brunette would be elephants. The enthusiastic mother purchased three of almost everything: coordinated hats, infant jewelry, booties, onesies, rattles, toys, bottle holders, and blankets. She even bought three pairs of those horrible bejeweled tennis shoes.

I held back a gasp when Rene announced the four-figure price tag, but the new mom's smile remained as bright as her gold credit card. She maneuvered the stroller out through the door as Rene called, "See you next month, Evelyn!"

"Next month?" I asked, horrified. "She spent my wardrobe budget for the entire year!"

"Evelyn comes in at least once a month. Wait till she sees my Christmas collection. She'll go gaga."

"But she's already spent over a thousand dollars on infant accessories."

Rene eyed me drolly. "And your point is?"

I would have come up with a snappy retort, but a surprising revelation shocked me silent. I'd spent the last ten minutes in the same room with adorable triplets and their doting mother, and for the first time since discovering I was infertile, I didn't feel jealous. I didn't feel angry, either. Ditto bereft.

I felt...

Normal.

I was concerned about Rainbow, sure. But I felt like Kate again. I would have chalked it up to being distracted by Gabriel's murder, but I sensed that the change went deeper than that. I still didn't know whether or not I could get pregnant, but I was finally able to take action, and action brought optimism. For now, that was enough.

Rene interrupted my thoughts. "Earth to Kate, is anyone home?" Her brows knit together. "Are you all right?"

"Honestly? I am." I quickly filled her in on Dale's generous offer and my decision to begin IVF treatments.

"For what it's worth, Kate, I think it's fabulous. I know it's hard for you to accept help, but if you don't at least try IVF, you'll always regret it."

"Thanks. You're right."

The right corner of Rene's mouth lifted into a smirk. "I always am."

"Then maybe you can help me with something else. I'm fresh out of ideas on what to do next to get to the bottom of Gabriel's murder."

"Sam told me about the hubbub at Gabriel's memorial. I meant to call and grill you last night, but the twins were beyond fussy. Before I can brainstorm, I need to get caught up. What did you learn?"

"A lot, actually."

I filled her in on everything that had happened the day before. Talking to Echo and Jace outside the funeral home, finding Rainbow at the homeless encampment in Woodland Park, arranging for Dale to represent her, and his taking Rainbow to the station to turn herself in. It had been less than twenty-four hours, but in many ways it felt like a lifetime.

"Wow, Kate. That's a lot for one day. I'm impressed. You're better at locating suspects than the police are."

"Don't be too impressed. I got lucky. Echo overheard me ask Jace about Rainbow, and I paid her off. Not exactly earth-shattering detective work. The problem is, I don't know where to go from here."

Rene leaned back in her chair and crossed her arms. "Tell me more about your suspects so far."

"I don't have many, at least not many good ones. On the surface, Rainbow is by far the most likely killer. She saw Gabriel the night he died, she admits that he interrupted her in the middle of a burglary, and her gun was the murder weapon."

Rene cringed and scrunched her face in a classic don't-kill-the-messenger expression. "Don't get upset with me, Kate, but I have to say something. Rainbow's stepfather was right about one thing: the artwork in her room was disturbing."

"Meaning?"

"Meaning there are lots of maybes. Maybe you shouldn't put so much blind trust in that kid. Maybe she's hiding violent impulses underneath an innocent mask. Maybe something unimaginable happened that night."

"You think she killed Gabriel?"

"It's possible, isn't it?"

I sighed. "Of course it's possible. But Dale thinks she's innocent. So do I." I picked a stuffed bunny off the counter and twirled his floppy blue ears around my index finger. "If she did kill him … " The words tasted bitter on the back of my tongue.

I thumped Mister Bunny Ears back on the counter. "Sorry, Rene, I don't buy it. Rainbow could be fooling me about a lot of things. She may be a fabulous liar. But energy doesn't lie, and her energy isn't that of a killer. She's telling the truth, at least about Gabriel being alive when she left."

"Fine. Let's assume she's innocent for now. If she left her gun in the kitchen like she claims, then anyone could have picked it up and used it."

"I know, but how does that help us?"

"It covers means. Let's talk about opportunity. Who had access to the building after closing? I know Sam has a key, so I suspect the rest of the board does, too. Plus full-time staff. Who else?"

I shook my head. "The killer wouldn't have needed a key to get inside. Rainbow snuck in through a window with a broken latch. Pretty much anyone could have gotten in that way."

"Okay," Rene replied. "A lot of people had means and opportunity. We'll focus on motive. Who might have wanted Gabriel dead?"

"I've been thinking about that. The motives I've come up with so far seem pretty flimsy."

"So what? We're brainstorming."

"Okay. Let's start with Gabriel's wife. Cherie was convinced that Gabriel was having an affair, and she was definitely unhinged at the memorial. I think she might be having a nervous breakdown."

"Sam thinks she's losing it, too," Rene said. "So Cherie is suspect number one."

"Suspect number two is the mistress."

"Any idea who that might be?"

"I don't even know for sure that a mistress exists. But Vonnie seemed awfully broken up about Gabriel's death at the memorial service."

"Vonnie?"

"She teaches art classes at Teen Path HOME. She and Gabriel seemed a little too friendly the first time I saw them together, but it makes complete sense if she was his lover."

"Why would Gabriel's lover kill him?"

"Honestly? I'm not sure. Maybe he was going to break it off with her. They could have met at the center that night to talk about it. Maybe they got into a fight, and ... " I shrugged.

Rene raised her eyebrows, but she didn't comment.

"What about Rainbow's stepfather?" I asked. "That guy was a jackass."

"I didn't like him either. But why would he want to kill Gabriel?"

"The oldest motivator in the world. Money. He needed to get Rainbow home so he could tap into her trust fund. Maybe he went back to the center looking for Rainbow and ran into Gabriel instead. Gabriel might have confronted him. Backed him into a corner, so to speak."

"That's a lot of maybes, Kate."

"True. But the stepfather certainly would have known how to use his own gun. Besides, the more I think about him, the more I'm convinced he's hiding something."

"Rainbow's money," Rene replied. "But we already know that."

"The money, sure. But I think he's hiding something about April, too. Why did she take off again so quickly when she learned Rainbow was gone? Shouldn't she have stuck around and tried to find her daughter?"

Rene nodded. "Speaking as a mother, I certainly would have."

"That makes Dean suspect number three. And we should add Chuck as number four while we're at it."

"Chuck?"

"He runs Teen Path HOME's kitchen. He and Gabriel had an altercation the first time I met him. Gabriel told me that Chuck wanted his job. Maybe he was willing to kill for it."

Rene didn't look convinced. "I don't know, Kate. Killing someone for a crap job at a youth center? Seems kind of weak."

"It's not a crap job, though. Chuck wanted to be Teen Path HOME's director. Maybe he wanted it enough to kill." Which, now that I said it out loud, sounded about as realistic as someone killing me to take over Serenity Yoga. Why would Chuck risk a lifetime in prison to trade one low-paying job for another? I sighed. "Honestly, Rene, every motive we've discussed so far seems weak."

Rene's eyebrow's narrowed. "That's because we're missing something."

"Obviously. But I have no idea what it might be. I'd bet Bella's enzymes that one of the kids at Teen Path HOME has information that will help us find the killer, but I have no idea which one, or how to find them for that matter. I didn't recognize anyone at Echo's campsite, and I'm not comfortable wandering up and down Aurora looking for one of the few homeless teens that I'd recognize. It's too close to the studio. One of my students might see me and assume I'm a drug addict or a prostitute."

"Definitely a drug addict," Rene said. "You don't dress nice enough to be a prostitute." She winked to let me know she was kidding.

I ignored the gibe and kept talking. "I was planning to talk to Vonnie and Chuck at the funeral, but Cherie created that scene before I got a chance. By the time it was over, they were gone."

"So call them."

"I considered that, but I looked online last night, and they're both unlisted."

"That's not surprising, actually. Many of the homeless kids Teen Path HOME serves are mentally ill or addicted to drugs. The staff members probably don't want to risk having them contact them at home." Rene frowned. "But if you know Chuck and Vonnie's names, can't you search property records or something?"

I sighed. "I suppose, but Chuck already hates me, and I'm about to accuse Vonnie of being Gabriel's mistress. If I'm not careful, they'll take out a restraining order on me. Talking to them at the center would be much less threatening."

"So where does that leave us?"

"Until the center reopens, I'm screwed."

Rene's lips slowly lifted into a Cheshire Cat grin. "Why, Kate, I think you've discovered our next step."

"What's that?"

"We're going to get the center reopened."

"And how exactly are we going to do that?"

"By attending tomorrow night's emergency board meeting."

TWENTY

RENE CALLED SAM AND confirmed that Teen Path HOME's board was meeting at the president's home the next evening. Sam wasn't exactly ecstatic to have Rene and me tag along with him, but he didn't argue about it much either. I doubted that either Rene or I could influence the center's reopening, but I was eager to attend the meeting nonetheless. Gabriel's murder would undoubtedly be agenda item number one.

In the meantime, Rainbow was safe, and she had a skilled advocate protecting her. For now, it was time for me to attend to my own life. My conversation with Rene had taken longer than I'd anticipated, but I still had twenty minutes before my All Levels Yoga students would begin arriving. I used that time to call the fertility clinic and make an appointment. Their next opening for an IVF consultation was two weeks away, so I grabbed it. The five-figure deposit they required made my stomach churn, but with excitement as much as with apprehension. Michael and I were finally going to make a baby.

Three group classes, two private clients, and a month's worth of bookkeeping later, I left for home with a smile in my heart and a skip in my Birkenstocked step. Things might just turn out okay.

My unusual optimism vanished the moment I entered the kitchen. Dale and Michael were seated at the table wearing disheartened expressions. Dale stared idly into a half-filled coffee mug. Michael's shoulders were slumped. Bella—who read energy almost as well as I did—lay curled up near Michael, worry creasing her beautiful face. Mouse glared from the top of the refrigerator, silently passing judgment on them all.

"Hey guys," I said. "This doesn't look good. Is Rainbow okay?"

Dale slowly shook his head. "No, she's not okay at all."

Michael pulled out the chair next to him. "Sit down, Kate."

I sat.

"It's Rainbow's mother, April." Michael slowly closed his eyes, then opened them again. "She's dead."

"Oh no." I covered my face in my hands. "Does Rainbow know?"

"Yes," Dale replied. "Martinez broke it to her last night. They identified the body on Saturday, but no one knew how to contact the kid."

"You found out about this yesterday? Why didn't you wake me up when you got home and tell me?"

"It was late, and I was too exhausted to talk to anyone," Dale said. "Rainbow, well, she didn't take it well. That tough façade of hers just crumbled. I've been on this earth longer than I care to admit, but I've never felt so heartbroken. I don't care to see anything like that ever again."

"Nobody takes a parent's death well," Michael said. "Especially not a teenager. Couldn't they have given her a tranquilizer or something?"

"Rainbow didn't want to take drugs, and I wasn't about to let Martinez force them on her without a court order. She's been traumatized by narcotics enough for one lifetime."

"Back up for a minute," I said. "You said April's body was *identified* Saturday. When was it found?"

Dale took a slow sip of coffee. For the first time in the three years I'd known him, he seemed old. "A week ago."

"Why did it take so long to identify her?"

"The body didn't have a wallet or any form of identification. She'd still be a Jane Doe in the Tacoma morgue if it weren't for Detective Martinez. She thought Rainbow might be hiding out with April, so she created a missing person report. When she entered the information into NamUs, she got a hit."

"NamUs?" Michael asked.

"The National Missing and Unidentified Persons System. It compares missing person reports to records of unidentified bodies. Frankly, April should have been entered into the system right after she disappeared."

"Why wasn't she?" I asked.

"No one reported her missing."

I shook my head, not sure whether I should feel depressed or disgusted. "According to Dean, the police wouldn't have looked for April anyway. This wasn't the first time she'd taken off."

"He's probably right," Dale replied. "Still, would it have killed the man to go through the formality? I sure as hell wouldn't let Dharma take off without a fight."

Michael reached across the table and took my hand. "I wouldn't let this one go anywhere, either."

I appreciated the sentiment, but I wasn't sure the circumstances were comparable. I wasn't a heroin addict. Neither was Dharma.

How steadfast would Dale and Michael be if it were the third time either of us had disappeared? The fifth? The tenth?

"Did April die of a drug overdose?" I asked.

Dale nodded. "Heroin, according to the tox screen. Which was precisely why I wasn't about to let anyone drug that teenager."

"So the death was accidental." My heart sank. Rainbow had lost her one remaining family member to a horrible, self-imposed accident.

Dale hesitated. "Probably."

The nerve endings on the back of my neck prickled. "What do you mean?"

"I mean we don't know for sure, at least not yet. The body showed obvious signs of long-term drug abuse, so an accidental death by overdose wouldn't be unexpected. But the body was moved post-mortem."

"Moved? To where?"

"To the crawl space of an abandoned house not far from where she lived. The investigators found evidence of squatters on the main floor. There were used needles and drug paraphernalia all over the place. Whoever they were, they're gone now. April's body could have remained hidden in that crawl space indefinitely, but a builder decided to check out the property. When he went inside, the smell, well..." Dale didn't complete the sentence.

I remembered the drawing taped above Rainbow's bed. A two-story house mired in quicksand. *Refuge.* "Was the house dark green, by any chance?"

Dale tilted his head, perplexed. "I have no idea. Why do you ask?"

"Rene and I noticed an odd drawing of a dark green house in Rainbow's bedroom. I think she may have known that her mother crashed in that house when she was using."

"Are you insinuating that Rainbow killed her own mother?" Michael asked.

"No. Anyway, the timing's off." I flashed back to Rene's and my road trip to Tacoma. According to Dean, April had temporarily returned home on Halloween, which meant she'd still been alive two weeks ago, long after Rainbow had run to Seattle. Dean, however, lived in Tacoma. He admitted that he'd searched Rainbow's room. He must have seen her artwork. If he recognized the dark green house in the drawing, he might have made the same assumption I had: that April crashed there when she wanted to escape.

"Has Martinez spoken to the husband?" I asked.

"I'm not sure," Dale replied. "She pulls the not-in-my-jurisdiction card whenever I ask about the investigation into April's death. I don't buy it, though. April may have died in Pierce County, but Martinez is invested. She won't let the case go unnoticed. Neither will I, for that matter. We owe it to Rainbow to find out the truth. But like I told the kid: suspicious circumstances or not, it's likely that her mother OD'd, exactly like the tox screen indicates."

"And she performed a *Walking Dead* stunt to get herself into the crawl space?"

"She may have been with someone—another addict or a dealer—when she died. They might have panicked and hid the body." Dale shrugged. "We may never find out. Crimes this old are notoriously hard to solve."

"This old?" Granted, the body had gone unidentified for a week, but that was hardly cold case material.

"According to the autopsy report, April's been dead for well over two months."

Electric surprise jolted my spine. "Wait a minute, did you say two *months?*"

My mind flew back to Tacoma again. Rainbow's stepfather wasn't just an abuser. Not just an alcoholic, either. He was a liar. April hadn't returned home two weeks ago. She hadn't prodded him to start looking for Rainbow. Her corpse had likely been stashed in that crawl space before Rainbow even ran away.

I leaped from my chair, startling Mouse. She dove from the refrigerator and tore off to hide in the office. "I'll be right back. I need to make a phone call."

I left the two puzzled-looking men behind and jogged upstairs to call Martinez. I had a new theory, and if it was right, it might get Rainbow out of juvie. I needed to talk it through with Martinez.

My logic went something like this:

Dean had told Rene and me that he'd seen his wife on Halloween. Unless she'd visited him from the afterlife, that story had been an obvious fabrication. The question was, why would Dean lie?

A few more questions and my mind jumped to the answer. Dean and his wife had been living off Rainbow's trust fund for years, but he'd recently upped the ante by trying to extract an extra ten thousand dollars from it.

Why?

Because time was running out on his little charade.

Why?

Because his wife was dead.

Why?

Because he murdered her.

Killing April with a heroin overdose was pure genius. His one mistake was that he'd hidden the body, but he needed to do that to buy enough time to get his ten-thousand-dollar payoff before the trust administrator found out she was dead.

Why did he kill her?

I couldn't answer that one—at least not yet—but Dean certainly wouldn't be the first domestic abuser to escalate to murder. I couldn't prove any of it, but I'd bet my IVF funds that Martinez could, provided I gave her all of the relevant information. If she ever picked up the phone, that was.

"Pick up, pick up, pick up," I whispered to the empty room.

Voicemail.

"Dammit!" I left a message saying I had urgent information and asking Martinez to call me. Immediately.

Bella trotted into the bedroom and jumped on the bed. I flopped down on the mattress next to her and continued mapping out motives. Not just for April's murder, but also for Gabriel's. April's death could have been the result of a final, violent argument gone horribly wrong. But what if the motive was more pedestrian? Perhaps Dean beat April one time too many. Perhaps she'd decided to leave him, taking Rainbow and her trust fund money with her. Dean may have figured that if he killed April but pretended she was still alive, the money would keep pouring in.

And it had, for a while.

Then Rainbow ran away and Dean discovered that the trust fund payments were tied to her GPA. He was forced to start looking for her. When he found her, and Gabriel got in the way...

I made an imaginary gun with my thumb and forefinger. "Bang."

Martinez had rejected my theory of Dean as Gabriel's killer before. She thought the circumstances were iffy and the motive was weak. But Dad used to say that once a murderer makes his first kill, the second is easier. Maybe after you've murdered your wife, a weak motive is enough.

Michael's voice came from the doorway. "Kate? Are you okay? Dale's afraid he said something to upset you again."

I ruffled Bella's ears and stood. "Not at all. I needed to think through a theory. I was hoping to talk to Martinez about it, but she's not picking up. Let's go back downstairs and discuss it with Dale. I think I know who killed Gabriel."

Dale wasn't nearly as enthusiastic about my theory as I'd hoped. "It's an interesting idea, Kate, but nothing you've told me so far links this Dean character to Gabriel's murder. It's all wishful thinking on your part."

"But he lied to me!"

"Yes, and that's compelling evidence that he's hiding something about *April's* death. It says nothing about Gabriel's."

"But it's worth looking into, right?"

"Yes, of course, but don't get your hopes up."

"Frankly, I don't see reason for hope in any of this," Michael argued. "There's no happily-ever-after here. Not for Rainbow. Her mother is dead. If we prove that her stepfather killed Gabriel, she'll get released from juvie and immediately be placed into foster care. Avoiding the foster system was part of the reason she ran away in the first place."

He was right. Now that her mother was dead, Rainbow had no safe harbor. Her biggest fears had been realized.

Every fiber of my being wanted to drive to the juvenile detention center, hug Rainbow, and promise her that everything would be okay, even if I had to lie to her. I couldn't. The rules for visitation with incarcerated minors were strict. As her attorney, Dale could visit her. Other than that, visitors were limited to close family members. Rainbow's stepfather—a man she loathed and who might have killed her mother—was her only family, and thus far she'd refused to see him. For the immediate future, Dale would be her single contact with the outside world.

I had to get her out of there.

———

I tried to call Martinez two more times that night and once the following morning, without success. I considered storming the precinct, but Dale convinced me to stop harassing the detective and let him handle it. I agreed, but I didn't like it. If Dale couldn't convince Martinez to interrogate Dean soon, acid would burn a hole in my stomach. I spent the day teaching two mindless yoga classes, bumbling my way through a misguided private session, and staring out the window, so distracted that I almost didn't notice the long line of students waiting to get in for Some Like It Hot Yoga's grand opening. Almost.

At six-thirty, Sam and I left for the Teen Path HOME board meeting in Medina, an East-side neighborhood populated by plastic surgeons, middle-aged trust funders, and Microsoft executives. The twins had chosen that afternoon to come down with the sniffles, so Rene—after making Sam and me pinky-swear to tell her everything that happened—reluctantly chose to stay home rather than saddle a sitter with two cranky toddlers.

Our destination was a gorgeous, red-brick Tudor sitting on a grassy half-acre lot. Its huge picture windows overlooked an ornate marble fountain, and its three-car garage had more square footage than the ground floor of Michael's and my Ballard bungalow. A dark gray Mercedes, a red Toyota hatchback, and a metallic green SUV were parked in the three spaces in the driveway. Sam pulled his red Camaro next to the mailbox and turned off the ignition.

"Rene may have talked me into bringing you along, but tonight's meeting is important, Kate. I can't afford any scenes like the one at Gabriel's memorial."

"Is Cherie going to be here?"

"No, but I didn't tell anyone I was bringing you, and I don't expect it to go over well."

"Why not?"

"We all agreed that except for Chuck, who's the acting site manager, tonight's meeting would be closed. We have important business, and there's too much friction between us to behave well in front of strangers. Three of the seven board members have already quit since Sunday."

"Quit? Why?"

Sam sighed. "Rats leaving a sinking ship. Gabriel had an amazing vision for Teen Path HOME, but it's had its share of troubles. His murder was the final straw."

"Gabriel and Rene both mentioned that the center was having issues, but Gabriel wouldn't elaborate, and Rene says you've refused to give her any details. Now's not a good time for secrecy, Sam. Whatever's going on might be important."

Sam turned off the engine and pushed open the door. "You'll hear all about it during the meeting, I'm sure. If not, I'll tell you on the way home. We need to get inside."

I followed him down the sidewalk to an ornate wooden door, where he announced our arrival by banging a brass knocker shaped like a lion.

The door cracked open, revealing a fortyish blonde woman wearing dark red lipstick and a form-fitting black dress. "Yes?"

"We're here for the board meeting," Sam said.

She smiled and opened the door wider. "Sorry, Greg told me he was only expecting one more person. Please come in. Everyone's waiting in the living room. Can I pour you each a glass of wine?"

We thanked her and followed her into a large, warm space with a mahogany leather sectional, two overstuffed chairs, and a brightly burning gas fireplace.

Four people were waiting. Greg sat in an arm chair at the room's front. An Asian woman in a conservative blue suit and a balding white man wearing wire-rimmed glasses shared the couch. I recognized them. They were two of the five people who had been seated with Greg at Gabriel's memorial. Chuck perched on the edge of a dining room chair that had obviously been pulled in for the occasion.

Chuck spied me and stood. "What's the yoga teacher doing here? When I agreed to attend this meeting, I was under the impression that we were going to discuss reopening the center. I don't have time to listen to some harebrained presentation about one of Gabriel's pet projects."

"Sit down, Chuck," Greg said firmly.

The balding man peered at me through narrowed eyes. "I recognize you. Aren't you the woman who created that scene with Cherie at the funeral?"

"It was a misunderstanding, I—"

Greg interrupted before I could finish. "Sam, who is this woman?"

"Actually, we've met before," I replied. "It was a few weeks ago at Teen Path HOME. My name's Kate." I reached out my hand, but Greg didn't take it.

Sam flashed me a forced smile that clearly said, *Please let me handle this*. In a move so uncharacteristic of me that I could scarcely believe I did it myself, I took a step back and faded into Sam's shadow.

"Everyone, this is Kate Davidson. She's a friend of my wife's, and she's very interested in the work we do at Teen Path HOME. I brought her here tonight hoping we could convince her to fill one of our new board vacancies."

Chuck leaned back and crossed his arms. "That's a bunch of rubbish. She's a paid employee, exactly like I am. As you've informed me multiple times, according to the corporate bylaws no employees are allowed to join the board."

Sam affected surprise. "You're paid for teaching those yoga classes at Teen Path HOME? I thought you were a volunteer." He shrugged. "Sorry. I probably should have checked about that before I invited her."

"Yes, you should have," Greg replied. "This is a closed meeting. She'll have to leave."

"She can't. We came together in my car," Sam replied.

The blue-suited woman let out a resigned sigh. "I don't see the harm in letting her stay. I strongly suspect tonight will be our last meeting, anyway."

The woman who I assumed was Greg's wife reentered the room, carefully balancing two glasses of golden Chardonnay in one hand and carrying a second dining room chair in the other. She handed a glass to each of us and set down the chair.

Greg sneezed.

She gave him a veiled look. "Allergies bugging you again?"

Greg wiped at his nostrils. "Yes. Someone in here must own a cat. Such foul creatures."

I didn't inform him that someone was me. I'd already lost enough brownie points for one evening. Frankly, I was surprised that I'd brought in enough cat dander to matter. Mouse wasn't exactly a lap cat.

"Do you need anything else?" his wife asked.

Greg shook his head.

A minute later, all of us—except for Greg's wife, who had disappeared upstairs—were seated in a crude semicircle. "I call this meeting to order," Greg said.

They began with the procedural formalities: roll call, reading of the prior minutes, and a discussion of old business. After about five minutes, Chuck grumbled, "Is all of this parliamentary procedure nonsense necessary?"

The woman set down her glass. "I agree. Let's dispense with the formalities." She ignored me and spoke directly to the men. "Gentlemen, we have a problem. My job as fundraising chair has never been easy, but Gabriel's death has made it next to impossible. As you know, half of the board has already quit. We've also lost three of our major donors, and four more are threatening to cut funding substantially. Having a murder on site is simply too controversial."

Sam groaned. "I was afraid of that."

"Imagine how many more would have jumped ship if they'd heard that one of our staff members was peddling illegal drugs out of the center," Greg said.

One of the staff members? I tried not to show it, but the skin on my arms tingled.

"Oh, for Christ's sake," Chuck growled. "Would you please let this drug nonsense go already? You have absolutely no proof that anyone is selling drugs out of Teen Path HOME. None. Many of our clients are drug addicts, sure. Those backpacks they carry are probably filled with marijuana, prescription narcotics, and lord knows what else. Some of the kids are undoubtedly dealers. They have to earn money somehow."

The woman frowned. "Are you condoning criminal behavior?"

"Of course not, but it's hardly surprising. What's preposterous is thinking that one of our staff members is involved." He stared Greg down without blinking. "How many surprise inspections did you perform, anyway?"

"Three," Greg replied.

"And you found nothing." Chuck made a circle with his right thumb and fingers. "Zippo. Nada. You received one anonymous call claiming that an adult involved with Teen Path HOME was supplying the kids with drugs and you went totally off the deep end. If the donors get wind of this nonsense, you have no one to blame but yourself."

In a moment of bell-ringing clarity, the puzzle pieces clicked into place. Of course. The anonymous caller they were referring to was Rainbow. She'd hated Jace's drug dealing, especially when he did it at the center. She'd tried to stop him by, in her own words, "amping up the pressure." Saying a staff member was dealing drugs at Teen Path HOME would definitely make everyone in charge pay attention, which would make it harder for Jace to operate on site without getting caught. I suspected Rainbow had made up the part about adult involvement in order to deflect attention from Jace. She'd just wanted him stopped, after all, not caught.

Unless…

What if she hadn't made it up? The theory made a lot of sense, actually. According to Rainbow, Jace hadn't dealt drugs until they'd run away to Seattle. Jace had obviously gotten connected with a supplier somewhere, and awfully quickly for a kid who had no history of drug use. His connection had to have been someone he trusted. What if it was an adult he'd met at Teen Path HOME?

I remained silent, but my mind was far from inactive. It whirled, scouring my memory for every adult I'd met who was involved with Teen Path HOME. Could one of them be a criminal? Could he or she even be in this room?

Sam's voice jolted me back to the conversation. "Settle down, everyone. I understand your point, Chuck, but the board had no choice but to investigate. Janice, do you think the donors are backing out because of the drug rumors?"

The woman—whose name was obviously Janice—shook her head. "I don't think any of them have caught wind of that, at least not yet. Right now, they're freaked out by Gabriel's murder. That was enough to send some of them packing. If the rest learn there's another PR disaster waiting in the wings, they'll be gone too. Most of them are on their way out already."

Greg's upper lip twitched. "Frankly, I'm not so sure I want to be associated with this debacle anymore either."

The balding man adjusted his glasses. "You're overreacting. Even if our suspicions were correct, that crisis is history now. The killer fixed our drug problem."

Sam wrinkled his forehead. "Exactly what are you insinuating?"

"I'm not insinuating anything. I'm flat-out saying it. No more Gabriel, no more drugs at the center. Gabriel's murder proves he was involved."

"With something, yes," Chuck replied. "But not necessarily drugs. I can think of at least one other reason Gabriel would have been cavorting late at night with an underage female."

Janice frowned. "You think he was sleeping with that girl the police arrested?"

"Well, he was obviously doing something hinky with the kids. Why else did he meet with them on site after hours?"

Janice leaned forward. "Meeting with clients after hours is a clear violation of the center's policies. If you knew Gabriel was doing so, why didn't you tell us about it before?"

"Because I didn't figure it out until now," he replied. "But in hindsight, it's obvious. Do the math." He held up an index finger and counted off the points one by one. "One: Gabriel's wife was constantly calling and dropping by the site, complaining because Gabriel was never home. Two: He was always the last person to leave. Three: He was killed on site. I don't know what time he was shot, but it was obviously after closing. And four: He was waaaay too chummy with those kids. Didn't anyone but me think that having pets in his office was weird? He was grooming those kids. We all should have seen it."

"Come on, Chuck. They were rats." Greg wiped at his nostrils as if the mere thought of fur made his nose run. "He wasn't exactly using puppies to lure toddlers off playgrounds."

The exchanges continued, but for the next few moments, I was immersed in my own thoughts. Could Chuck be right? When Rainbow saw Gabriel, his hair was wet and his shirt was unbuttoned. She'd assumed that he'd been upstairs showering, and she might have been right. But what if he hadn't been alone? Gabriel had told me the first day we met: *These kids are vulnerable, and it's easy for people to take advantage of them.* Had Gabriel fooled all of us? Had he fooled me?

Sam's voice brought me back. "I knew Gabriel for almost two decades. He was a good man. He would never have done anything inappropriate with a teenager."

"Your friendship with Gabriel blinded you," the balding man replied. "At best, he had poor boundaries. At worst, he was a criminal who took advantage of the youth he was supposed to be helping. Maybe he peddled drugs to them; maybe he used them for sex. Hell, maybe he did both. How would we know? We gave that man way too much power. I warned you that we needed to hire an executive director to provide oversight. Putting one of the counselors in charge of operations was asking for trouble."

"What money would we have used to hire one?" Janice asked. "The capital improvements we made to the kitchen drained the reserve funds."

Chuck stood, as if being taller would give him more power. "What good would an expensive bureaucrat have been? Every penny diverted to 'directing' would have been a penny not spent helping those kids. Look, we're all avoiding the important issue here. Gabriel is dead. The kids who depend on Teen Path HOME aren't. Let the cops deal with what happened to Gabriel. And if we find out that someone *is* dealing drugs at the center, we should report it and let the cops deal with that, too. Our job is to serve those kids, and to do that, we need to reopen."

Sam gestured for him to sit down. "Chuck is right," he said. "No more talk about Gabriel." He turned to the balding man. "How much money do we have left in unallocated operating funds?"

245

The balding man looked pointedly at me, then wrote a figure on a piece of paper and handed it to Sam. "Our current financials are confidential. Don't say the number out loud."

Sam took the paper from him, frowned at it, then handed it to Janice, who stood and walked it to Greg. After they'd all had the chance to see it, Sam spoke. "It's low but not abysmal. Here's my proposal: I'll personally throw in another fifty thousand."

"That's a great start," the balding man said, "but—"

Sam held up his palm. "I'm not done. We'll hold off reopening until Monday, to give Cherie a chance to grieve and to allow the negative press to die down some. For the next two months, we'll maintain reduced hours, say from eleven to five on weekdays."

"And after that?" Chuck asked.

"After that, we'll see. Janice can start canvassing for new donors. People are twitchy right now, but the news is fickle and memories are short. I'm betting that if we can get through the next couple of months, we'll make it. If I'm wrong, well, we'll deal with that then. In the meantime, those kids need us."

In the end, Sam made a motion to reopen Teen Path HOME the following Monday, as he'd suggested. Greg's eyes were clouded and Chuck wasn't happy about the reduced hours, but the motion passed unanimously.

I felt simultaneously satisfied and frustrated. Satisfied because the kids I'd grown to care about would be receiving services again soon. Frustrated because Monday was six days away. If my theory about Rainbow's stepfather being the killer didn't pan out, Rainbow would spend six more days in juvenile detention before I could talk to anyone else at the center.

Fortunately, I had a new theory. If Rainbow's anonymous phone call hadn't been a ruse, Jace wasn't the only person involved in peddling illegal drugs at Teen Path HOME. He'd had an adult overseer. Every atom of my psyche resisted the idea that Gabriel was involved, but it was still a distinct possibility. If so, I might be out of luck. His killer could be an anonymous drug cartel member, already back over the border.

But if he wasn't . . .

If Gabriel had been killed because he'd uncovered the drug operation, I had multiple possibilities. Jace, for example. Killing Gabriel with Rainbow's gun would have been poetic justice. He'd get rid of a witness and implicate his "narc" of an ex-girlfriend at the same time.

And how about Chuck? He was awfully eager to see Teen Path HOME reopen. Was that because he cared about the kids, because he wanted to prove that he deserved Gabriel's job, or because he had an entirely different empire he wanted to resume building?

Vonnie had found Gabriel's body. She'd supposedly stumbled upon it when she opened Teen Path HOME the morning after his death. What if she'd known it was there all along? I'd assumed she was upset at Gabriel's funeral because she was his mistress. What if it was because she felt guilty for pulling the trigger?

There were dozens of other possibilities, of course. Anyone associated with Teen Path HOME could have been involved. The drug angle wasn't my favorite theory so far, but it was one I could act on. The first step was convincing Dale and Martinez.

TWENTY-ONE

WHEN I GOT HOME, I filled Dale and Michael in on everything I'd heard at the board meeting. Dale agreed that the drug angle was worth pursuing. And why not? He'd spent the entire day working on Rainbow's case without discovering anything else promising. Martinez continued her strange silence on the subject of Rainbow's stepfather and the lies he'd told about April's reappearance. Each time Dale had asked her about April, she'd claimed ignorance, sticking with her out-of-my-jurisdiction mantra. Dale didn't believe her, but he couldn't get her to budge from her story.

I wasn't pleased.

Neither was Michael. "If Martinez doesn't get off her butt soon, I'm going to storm the juvenile detention center and break Rainbow out of there myself."

I pointed to Michael but spoke directly to Dale. "What he said."

Dale sighed. "Believe me, guys, I'm doing everything I can. I don't want that kid locked up any more than you do. But be careful what you wish for."

"What do you mean?" I asked.

"Once she's out of juvenile detention, where will she go? If your suspicions are correct—if Rainbow's stepfather killed her mother, or if he even covered up her death—he may end up doing serious prison time of his own. She has no other family."

"What about the trust?" Michael asked.

"That's the good news," Dale replied. "Rainbow has money. Not enough to make her rich, but enough to keep her housed for a few more years and pay college tuition."

"So she's sixteen and she can support herself," I said. "Can't she get emancipated?"

"Her grandparents wrapped that money up tight. She doesn't get a dime unless she stays in school and maintains a GPA over 3.5. I met with the trust administrator today. He's a stodgy old fart, about as flexible as the steel rod shoved up his fanny. Until Rainbow proves that she meets the scholastic requirements again, he won't give her a cent. He even expects her to pay back the monthly stipends that creepy stepfather of hers embezzled after she ran away. Besides, Rainbow's not ready to be on her own. She needs a responsible adult to guide her. Even if I *can* get her declared an emancipated minor, I don't think I should."

"Which leaves what? The foster system?" I asked.

Dale didn't reply.

"She'll run away again, Dale. I know it."

Dale's expression was grim. "I suspect you're right."

I turned to face Michael. He stared at the table, studiously avoiding my gaze. Not a word passed between us, but Michael's nonverbal communication was crystal. He was a good man. A solid man. Even a great man. But he didn't know Rainbow. Neither did I, for that matter, and we were getting ready to start our own family. Our only spare bedroom was currently our office, and hopefully it would soon become a nursery. Housing Rainbow for a few weeks—even a few months—that we could do. But Rainbow needed stability, at least until she graduated from high school. How could we commit to raising a troubled teen for the next two years? Answer? We couldn't. Fortunately, I had another idea.

I nodded to let Michael know that I understood, then squared my shoulders with pretend confidence and faced Dale. "Well then, I guess you'll have to convince Dharma that Rainbow belongs with the two of you on Orcas."

Dale's expression remained impassive. "I'd been wondering how long it would take you to volunteer us."

"So you've thought about it?"

He avoided the question. "I left behind a lucrative law practice to start over, you know. And I was happy. No stress; no responsibilities. Just me, the goats, and a whole lot of land out in the country. Then I met you and all hell broke loose. I ended up with Satan's own Jack Russell Terrier and your mother's herd of stubborn, unadoptable donkeys. Now you expect me to branch out into Dale's Goats, Dharma's Asses, and the Orcas Home for Wayward Teens?"

I suppressed a grin. "Maybe you can call it D & D's Happy Menagerie."

Dale's white whiskers trembled, but not in ill humor. "You are *exactly* like your mother, you know. And that's not always a good thing. Dharma's been bugging me about Rainbow since that first night you told us about her."

The grin I'd been suppressing blossomed on Michael's face. "So Dharma thinks Rainbow should live with you?"

I knew why Michael was grinning. Generally speaking, what Dharma wanted, Dharma got. In this case, though, Dharma's desires weren't enough. If she and Dale were going to foster Rainbow, Dale needed to want it too.

"What do you think, Dale?" I asked.

"I think we're too old." He leaned back and laced his fingers together across his belly. "Before Rainbow would be allowed to stay with us, Dharma and I would have to get approved as foster parents. That would be a heck of a lot easier if we were twenty-five years younger and married. Second, Rainbow may not want to live out in the boonies with a couple of old farts like us."

"Buuuut…" I drew out the word, hoping Dale would come up with an acceptable answer.

He sighed. "But Dharma and I talked it over, and if Rainbow wants to live with us and the state will allow it—and those are two big ifs—we'll take her in." He shook his finger at me and smirked. "I'm warning you, though, this is the last orphaned *anything* I'm going to let you or your mother saddle me with. Rainbow told me all about those two rats you've got stashed at Michael's pet store. Don't even think about trying to unload them on me."

I considered pressing my luck, but I smiled and reached out my hand instead. "Deal."

I left our conversation feeling cautiously optimistic but still surprisingly uneasy. Even if Rainbow agreed to live with Dale—and frankly, I agreed with Dale that it might be a hard sell—the point would be moot unless we got her out of juvenile detention.

I lay awake the rest of the night listening to Michael's deep breathing, Bella's soft snores, and Mouse's rumbled purring from across the room. Michael left for the pet store the next morning at eight; Dale for the courthouse ten minutes later. I tried—unsuccessfully—to cover the purple-blue smudges under my eyes with concealer and burned a month's worth of calories pacing a bald spot in the living room carpet. Bella paced beside me, as if we were practicing an odd form of indoor off-leash healing.

At nine, I abandoned Dale's mandate to leave Martinez alone and picked up the phone. My number must have flashed across her caller ID, because when she answered two rings later, her voice sounded resigned. "For goodness sake, Kate. Dale called a half hour ago and told me about the supposed drug dealer operating out of Teen Path HOME. I'll look into it, but you need to give me more than thirty minutes."

"Great, but that's not why I'm calling. Rainbow's mother is dead."

Silence. Then, "I know that."

"You're looking into the stepfather, right?"

"I already told Dale—"

Insomnia-fueled frustration made me irritable. "I know, I know. Not your jurisdiction." I started pacing again. Bella ignored me, attention focused on devouring her chew. "How can you not get how important the timing of April's death is? Dean claimed that he saw his wife two weeks ago. Why would he lie, unless he was covering up that he killed her?"

I spoke faster, as if getting the words out quickly would make them more compelling. "And Dale told me there was evidence that April's body had been moved, which means that she didn't die a natural death."

"We don't know that, Kate. The coroner—"

I didn't let her finish. "I get that April's death and Gabriel's murder aren't necessarily connected, but can't you at least look into it?" I paused, finally waiting for a response.

"Are you finished yet?" Martinez asked. Her voice didn't sound friendly.

I waited a beat. "Yes."

"Good. Because if you'd let me get out a full sentence, you might actually learn something."

Oops.

"Kate, I know I haven't paid enough attention to your ideas in the past, but that's not completely one-sided. You don't listen to me either. Do you think I'm completely incompetent?"

"Of course not, but—"

"Good. Because I'm not. Contrary to what you seem to think, I'm actually pretty good at my job. I didn't tell Dale anything yesterday afternoon because I didn't want to tip my hand. Besides, I didn't have anything definitive yet to tell him. I interrogated Rainbow's stepfather until almost midnight last night before I got him to confess."

"Wait a minute. Dean confessed? To Gabriel's murder or to his wife's?"

"Neither. To hiding the body. He knew all about that abandoned house. His wife usually stayed there when she took off."

"How did he know that?"

"He figured it out from some drawing."

I'd been right. Rainbow's art had revealed more about her life than she'd intended.

Martinez continued. "The husband said April usually left home for a few days at a time. When she didn't come back after a week this last time, he went to the house to drag her back himself. He broke inside and found his wife's body slumped next to the fireplace, needle still stuck in her arm."

"Why hide the body?" I asked. "Why not call the police?"

"The trust fund. He figured if he hid the body, he could milk the fund for another six months or a year. If Rainbow hadn't been on the run and the developer hadn't come by the drug house, he might have been right."

"Disgusting."

"Yep. But it's far from the worst I've heard. And his story matches what the coroner found. Rainbow's stepfather is no Prince Charming, but I don't think he killed his wife. He for sure didn't kill Gabriel."

"How can you know that?"

"He has an alibi. Mister Wonderful was arrested on a drunk and disorderly the night of Gabriel's death. He was locked in a Tacoma jail cell from eight p.m. that evening until noon the next day. Sorry, Kate. He's not our killer."

My heart deflated. "I swear Rainbow isn't the killer either."

Martinez sighed. "I hope you're right. I like the kid too. But for now, the evidence disagrees. I'm still investigating Gabriel's wife and I'll look into the potential drug angle, but I'm not optimistic about either. If it makes you feel any better, you got Rainbow a great attorney and a jury will be sympathetic. The poor kid never stood much of a chance. The DA will be hungry to make a deal, so Dale will likely get her a light sentence. He might even be able to plead her down to manslaughter. She'll get out in time to restart her life."

I didn't argue with the detective, but I didn't agree with her either. Light sentence or not, a conviction for a violent felony would ruin Rainbow's life. I thanked Martinez for her time, hung up the phone, and spoke to my canine companion. "Well, Bella, that settles it. I'm moving on to plan B."

TWENTY-TWO

MARTINEZ WAS A GOOD cop—a great one, maybe. But like Dad—like Sherlock Holmes, for that matter—she was programmed to follow logic. *Elementary, my dear Watson,* and all of that. Good in theory, but in my experience, logic rarely led to the answer.

Like Bella, I trusted my gut. And my gut insisted that Rainbow was innocent. I'd come up with lots of ideas about who'd killed Gabriel, but as both Dale and Martinez had noted, they were built on flimsy assumptions. If I was going to prove Rainbow's innocence, I needed to create a solid foundation.

I resolved to contact Sam that night and beg him to connect me with Cherie and Vonnie so I could explore my jilted lover theories, but until then, it was time for Jace and me to have a pointed discussion about his vocation. With a little patience and luck, Echo would lead me straight to him. All I had to do was hang out near her campsite, watch, and wait.

Michael's stern voice reverberated inside my head. *Don't you dare stake out Woodland Park on your own.*

Imaginary Michael was right, which is why I was planning once again to take Real Michael with me. As plans went, it was a great one. Or so I thought.

When I dropped by the pet store, Tiffany informed me that Michael was on a supplier visit for the rest of the day. I considered asking Tiffany to come with me instead, but the *Baby Now Loading...* T-shirt she wore nixed that idea. I didn't think staking out Echo would put Tiffany in any danger, but I wasn't willing to risk her unborn child. Besides, Michael was relying on her to staff the pet store in his absence.

No problem. Rene, my other partner in crime fighting, was always up for an adventure. A hand-written sign on Infant Gratification's door nixed that idea, too. *Closed due to toddler virus. Back when the twins stop coughing.*

I considered asking Rene to bundle up the twins and join me anyway, but a stakeout with colicky sixteen-month-olds seemed counterproductive. Ditto driving home to grab Bella. Stealthiness wasn't exactly her strong suit.

Sorry, Michael, I tried.

I altered my plans and headed for the Honda alone, mentally rehearsing the excuses I'd give Michael. My solo adventure was in no way irresponsible. I wasn't planning to interrogate Echo, simply follow her. Following wasn't dangerous, right? And if she led me to Jace like I hoped she would, well...

I'd deal with that problem when the time came.

I pulled a knit cap and sunglasses out of the trunk, drove to Woodland Park's northernmost parking area, and stopped where I could easily see Aurora Avenue North. If Echo walked from her campsite to meet Jace on Aurora, I'd see her.

The question was, would she see me? I doubted it, especially if I scrunched down low enough in the driver's seat. When Echo, Michael, and I had driven to Woodland Park the day we found Rainbow, we'd been in Michael's SUV. There was a small chance Echo would remember my Honda from Gabriel's memorial, but I doubted it. She'd been too focused on getting her next high to notice a beater automobile in a public parking lot.

I slumped down until my scalp was barely visible over the dash, peered out through the steering wheel, and waited.

And waited.

And waited.

Ninety minutes later, I'd seen three joggers, five dog walkers, four squirrels, and a half-dozen or so transients from the park's homeless encampments. No sign of Echo.

Way to waste an afternoon, Girl Detective.

An hour after that, I was ready to call uncle. My stakeout had been an obvious waste of time.

I sat up, turned the key halfway in the ignition, and caught a glimpse of bright pink.

Echo's jacket. Moving toward Aurora. Alone.

Nervous anticipation bubbled beneath my sternum. Showtime. I grabbed my knit cap off the passenger's seat, tucked my hair underneath it, and slid on the sunglasses.

When Echo was almost out of sight, I tossed my keys into my jacket pocket, left the Honda behind, and followed her. She crossed northern Woodland Park's wide grassy expanse and meandered between the evergreen trees and the low fence bordering Aurora. I stayed on the park's inner path, trying to look inconspicuous while still keeping her in my peripheral vision. When the fence melted into the sidewalk along Aurora, I turned a sharp left and followed a block's distance behind her. We continued this way for three quarters of a mile, past dive bars, cheap eateries, and used car lots. Sixty-fifth Street, 70th, 80th … *Come on, Echo, where are you headed?*

Two buildings before 83rd Street, she turned right and entered a convenience store parking lot. She continued past the entrance and took another sharp right around the north side of the building. A few steps later, she disappeared from my sight.

The hair on the back of my neck vibrated. *What are you up to, Echo?* I'd driven past this store multiple times. There was nothing on that side of the building except more parking spaces and a large garbage bin. Was she dumpster diving? Meeting someone? Waiting to ambush a five-foot, three-inch yoga teacher? I stopped walking and stared at the window of a Thai fast food restaurant, pretending to examine the menu while actually looking for Echo in its reflection. The scents of garlic, ginger, and peanut sauce made my stomach rumble.

Okay, Super Sleuth. What's your next move?

If I followed the path the teen had taken, she'd see me as I approached. If I cut behind the building and snuck up on her from behind, I might lose her. If I stood here staring at Thai food photos much longer, she'd be long gone before I made up my mind.

Ultimately, I chose option two. I turned right on 82nd Street, jogged down the alley behind the convenience store, and crouched behind a large blue dumpster. Echo was leaning against the building about twenty-five feet away, smoking a cigarette and looking impatient. From my new vantage point, I could see the convenience store's driveway, side parking lot, and north-facing wall. The front lot and the store's entrance were out of my view, but as long as Echo stayed put, I'd be okay.

I squatted lower to avoid being seen and tried to ignore the stench of dog waste wafting from the dumpster. Echo glanced at her watch, ground out the cigarette with her shoe, and immediately lit another.

Five minutes passed, then five more. Echo chain-smoked; my thighs cramped. Dozens of cars pulled into the store's driveway and left it again, but no one ventured to our side of the building. I gave up on squatting and kneeled on the wet pavement, trying not to imagine what other fluids might be mixed with the rainwater soaking my knees. Five minutes more. The leg cramps diminished, replaced by bone-chilling cold. I yearned for hot chocolate with a triple shot of Schnapps. And a restroom.

Three minutes after my toes had turned numb, a dark gray Mercedes pulled through the driveway and disappeared out of view, presumably having parked. Foggy recognition tickled my subconscious. Who did I know with a gray sedan?

I was so caught up in trying to place it that at first I didn't notice the gangly, confident-looking teenager ambling toward Echo.

Jace. Finally.

I was plotting how to inconspicuously tail him when my conscious and subconscious minds collided. Rapid-fire images flashed through my head. The loading zone at Teen Path HOME. The parking area in front of Greg's garage. The convenience store's driveway. All had one item in common: a dark gray Mercedes. I shifted from kneeling to crouching and watched, one eye on Echo and Jace, the other on the driveway, scanning for the car's departure.

Echo dropped her cigarette and walked toward Jace. Jace meandered toward Echo. In one fluid motion, their palms touched. A flash of green passed from Echo to Jace; a clear plastic bag passed from Jace to Echo. The Mercedes stopped at the driveway, readying to turn right onto Aurora. I stared at its back bumper and mentally repeated its license plate.

A few seconds later, Echo walked back toward Woodland Park. Jace sauntered the opposite direction. The Mercedes successfully turned right on Aurora and headed north, not slowing as it sped past Jace. I pulled a pen out of my jacket pocket and made a note on my palm.

Three letters, three numbers.

Gotcha.

I abandoned my hiding place and jogged the three-quarters of a mile back to my car. I didn't try to avoid Jace or Echo, though I doubted either of them noticed me. It didn't matter. I no longer believed either of them was the killer. The killer was behind the wheel of a dark gray Mercedes. A dark gray Mercedes that had just dropped Jace off at his new territory.

It was all theoretical, of course. There were likely thousands of Mercedes sedans driving around Seattle, and although the timing was right, I hadn't actually seen Jace get out of the passenger seat. But by the time I arrived home, I believed my new theory as much as Bella believed that the mailman was a dog-torturing psychopath. And if I was right—if this Mercedes was the same one that had been parked in Greg's driveway the night of the board meeting—it belonged to one of five people: Chuck, Greg, Greg's wife, Janice, or the balding man whose name I'd never been told. Now all I needed to do was to figure out which one.

Whoever it was, they certainly weren't following the supposedly sacred hands-off policy that the center espoused. At best, they were driving around town with an underage client. At worst, they were pushing life-ruining drugs to the teens they were supposed to be helping.

I screeched into the driveway and dashed through the kitchen to my office, barely acknowledging the exuberant canine bouncing around me. I might not be a computer expert like Sam or an Internet wizard like Michael, but I'd learned one thing from both of them during my short time as an unwitting sleuth: you can find almost anything with a computer and a search engine.

I pulled up a browser and typed in the phrase *how to find owner of car*. Not elegant I'll admit, but then again, it didn't have to be. Such is the terrifying power of the Internet. The very first site gave me what I needed: a search engine that would find the owner of any licensed vehicle, provided the searcher had a vehicle identification number, the title, or the license plate number.

I clicked on the link, scanned the warning asserting that unauthorized use of the search engine would subject me to criminal fines and/or civil liabilities, and clicked the checkbox affirming that yes, I understood the possible risks of my actions. I would have added *and I don't give a crap*, but that wasn't an option.

The next item stumped me: *To conduct searches, please select from one of the authorized purposes below. If none of the below purposes are applicable, you may not conduct searches.* I scanned the drop-down menu and checked the box next to *Driver safety and theft*. Carting around drug dealers had to be unsafe for the driver, right?

A quick electronic payment later, I knew exactly who was running drugs out of Teen Path HOME. If my theory was right, that same person had killed Gabriel.

Now all I had to do was prove it.

TWENTY-THREE

"I'm not sure this was such a great idea, Kate. Maybe Michael was right. Martinez and Henderson could have handled it."

Sam paced back and forth in front of the pool table at Teen Path HOME, boots making muffled thuds with each step.

Thunk, thunk, thunk, turn.

Thunk, thunk, thunk, turn.

Over and over and over again.

I took a deep yogic inhale, coordinating my breath with his steps in an odd, waiting-to-catch-a-killer mantra.

Inhale—Thunk, thunk, thunk, turn.

Exhale—Thunk, thunk, thunk, turn.

For the first time in my amateur sleuthing career, I wasn't going to unveil a murderer by accident—or by myself. This time, I'd involved all of my loved ones in creating the plan. Michael hated the idea. He was concerned about Sam's and my safety. Rene complained about being left out. "But you two will get to have all the fun without me!"

I told them both the same thing. "You can't be there. The trap will work best if Sam and I set it alone."

So here Sam and I were. Alone. Sort of.

I perched uncomfortably on the couch while Sam grumbled. "I hope he doesn't come. This was a terrible idea."

The front door squeaked open. "What was a terrible idea?" Greg closed it behind him, locked eyes with me, and froze. "What is she doing here?"

Sam stopped pacing. "Kate is my source."

I stood and tried to look confident. "I'm afraid Sam wasn't completely honest with you. I didn't think you'd come if you knew the truth."

Greg's face turned pomegranate red. "Sam, when you called me this morning, you told me you'd learned who was selling drugs at Teen Path HOME. You assured me that I'd want to discuss it in person—alone. You didn't say anything about bringing the yoga teacher."

"Don't be cranky, Greg," I said. "You should be glad I'm here. If it weren't for me, Sam would have called the police. I convinced him we could come up with a more … equitable solution."

Greg's eyes narrowed. "A more equitable solution to what?"

"To the problem of what to do with you." Sam's low growl startled me, and I jumped. He strode several steps forward, not stopping until his nose was inches from Greg's. "All that time you spent being a 'positive role model' to the teens. All those 'surprise inspections.' They were all smokescreens. You've been funneling drugs through the kids. What I don't get is why. These kids trust us. They rely on us. Why would you take advantage of them that way?"

Greg appeared genuinely startled. "Sam, what are you talking about?" Then, dawning clarity. He stumbled back toward the kitchen. "Wait a minute, you think I—"

"Save it," Sam snapped. "Kate saw you."

That wasn't entirely true, of course. I'd seen Greg's car, not the driver, but it was close enough. "You got sloppy yesterday," I said. "I saw you with Jace Foster, right before I witnessed him selling heroin to a street kid named Echo."

"That boy had heroin on him? I assure you that I had no idea. I saw him hitchhiking, which is terribly dangerous, so I gave him a ride. I certainly didn't search him for drugs before I let him get in the car. Driving the kid across town may have been ill-advised, but it wasn't illegal."

"You've done a lot more than give Jace a ride," I said. "I confronted him after you took off. He told me everything." I felt no guilt about the deception. Lying clearly violated yoga's principle of satya (truthfulness), but if confronting a killer wasn't an exception, it should have been.

"Whatever that boy told you, he was lying," Greg said.

Sam's shoulders tensed.

I kept talking. "I should have known you were up to no good the first time I met you."

"At my house the other night?" Greg sounded genuinely confused.

"No, at Teen Path HOME. I was there the day the rats got loose, remember?" I gestured toward the stairway. "When you came charging downstairs, you ran into me and knocked me over."

"So? That was an accident."

"Gabriel had just given me a tour of the second floor, and you weren't in any of the rooms he'd shown me. You must have been in the hygiene area."

"What's your point?"

"Gabriel told me that the hygiene area is restricted to staff members and clients whenever the center is open. He specifically said that even board members couldn't tour it except after hours. So why were you hanging out in there? It's kind of creepy, if you ask me."

Greg's face, red to begin with, turned purple.

I gave an exaggerated shudder. "Either you have a fondness for spying on teens without their clothes on, or—"

Greg clenched his fists. "Shut up. Shut your filthy mouth right now."

I held up an index finger. "*Or*, you had another reason to hang out with the kids alone. Were you recruiting new dealers or trying to find new customers?"

Greg sniffed and wiped at his nose. His hand came away bloody. In a burst of insight so powerful it felt almost physical, I understood. Greg's constant nose irritation had nothing to do with animal dander. It was caused by white powder of an entirely different nature.

I pointed to the inflamed skin under his nostrils. "I had it all wrong, didn't I?"

Greg's face relaxed. "Of course you did. That's what I keep say—"

I didn't let him finish. "Not about you recruiting the kids. You're totally guilty of that. I was wrong about why you were in the hygiene area that day. You needed privacy, didn't you? You couldn't exactly snort up in the loading zone. That's probably why you got so agitated with Chuck and Gabriel, too. I understand cocaine is a powerful stimulant."

The muscles on either side of Greg's jaw bunched.

"It all makes sense now," I continued. "Sam and I couldn't figure out why a successful man like you would risk losing everything to run a small-time drug ring. We decided it must be some sort of deluded power trip. But we were wrong, weren't we?"

Greg didn't reply, so I kept speaking. "It has to be hard to pay for that nice car and a fancy home in Medina while feeding a cocaine addiction. Extra cash must come in handy. Not to mention the opportunity to get your own supply at wholesale prices."

"Is she right, Greg?" Sam asked. "Are you an addict?"

Greg stared at the carpet.

"Why didn't you get help?"

I waved my hand through the air. "Give it up, Sam," I replied. "His motives don't matter. Nothing from the past does. The future, that's what's important." I turned back to Greg. "If you want to have one, you need to make a choice."

Greg's lips barely moved. "What choice?"

"Why, which punishment you'd like, of course. You can let Sam go to the police—in which case you'll lose that home, that car, and that lovely wife." I lifted my lips in a fake smile. "On the plus side, an attractive guy like you will probably get lots of action in prison." I paused for a count of three. "Or we can keep our mouths shut, and you can pay a fine."

"You're blackmailing me?

"I prefer to think of it as creating a partnership for our mutual benefit. You need me to keep quiet. I need to pay for fertility treatments. You'll have to resign your position on the board, of course. That way the kids will benefit, too. When the center reopens, they'll get the services they deserve without a slimebag like you taking advantage of them. Everybody wins." I shrugged. "Everybody except you, I guess."

Greg stood between the pool table and the front door, mouth open in a wide O. "Are you seriously going to let her do this, Sam?"

Sam huffed. "Believe me, I don't want to. I'd rather call the police and let you rot in prison. But as you've pointed out numerous times, another scandal could close Teen Path HOME permanently. Kate's plan is the lesser of two evils."

Greg's glare shifted from me, to Sam, and back again. When his eyes met mine, they held angry resignation. "How much?"

"That depends," I replied. "How much were you paying Gabriel?"

"Gabriel? That fool wouldn't take money. He wanted to ruin me. That's why I—" He stopped speaking.

"That's why you killed him." I finished.

"Kate, don't make accusations you can't prove." Sam's face remained expressionless, but the tightness in his voice left no room for doubt. He thought I was pushing too hard.

He might well have been right. I didn't like the way Greg's eyelids were twitching or how his hand hovered near a bulge on the right side of his jacket. Was that a gun in his pocket, or was he happy to see me?

Greg growled, like Bella warning off the UPS driver. "You're not blackmailing me about just the drugs, are you?"

Sam nudged me. "Kate ... "

I ignored him. Too hard or not, I couldn't stop pushing now. I sneered at Greg. "What do you think?"

Greg rolled his eyes. "I think Gabriel was an idiot. If he hadn't threatened me, none of this would have happened."

"Gabriel figured out you were using Teen Path HOME to distribute drugs?"

Greg scoffed. "No. He got it all wrong. He came outside looking for that stupid homeless girl and saw me parked in the loading zone. I was with one of my younger ... " He paused, as if searching for the right word. "One of my younger *employees*. Gabriel thought I was using that fourteen-year-old boy for sex!" His voice grew higher as he repeated the word. "Sex! He accused me of being a child rapist! I was outraged." Greg paced back and forth in front of the pool table, much like Sam had done earlier. "The kid jumped out of my car and ran off, but I was stuck. I couldn't let Gabriel call my wife or, worse, the police. Do you know what happens to accused child molesters?"

I sensed it was a rhetorical question, so I didn't reply.

"Gabriel told me to get out of the car and follow him to his office, like I was some miscreant teen he'd caught smoking pot under the bleachers. I considered running him down with my car, but I'd never have been able to hide the damage." He shrugged. "So I followed him. What choice did I have?"

I knew that Greg's admitting all of this was a terrible omen, but I kept pressing. I needed him to confess to pulling the trigger. "Gabriel had taken Rainbow's gun to his office, hadn't he?"

"It and the cash box were on top of the desk, like they were waiting for me." Greg unbuttoned his jacket. "That gun was the perfect solution to my dilemma."

Sam poked me again. "Kate, wouldn't this be a good time to tell Greg about that yoga guy?"

Greg wrinkled his lips, dumbfounded. "Have you gone batty? What does yoga have to do with any of this?"

I knew exactly what "yoga guy" Sam was referring to. We'd agreed that "Patanjali"—the author of yoga's key philosophical text—would be our safe word. But I pretended ignorance. "He's right, Sam," I said. "It's not relevant right now." I turned back to Greg. "Why did you hide the gun and the cash box behind the garbage dumpster? You had to have known someone would find it."

Greg smiled, but the expression didn't go past his lips. "I certainly hoped so. Neither of them could be traced back to me; I'd wiped them. And if some homeless kid found the gun and got their prints all over it, they'd be the most likely suspect."

"You were hoping to frame one of the kids?" Sam asked. "What kind of a monster are you?"

"It wasn't personal. They would have been collateral damage, like you two are going to be." Greg pulled a revolver out of his jacket pocket and pointed it at me.

Sam didn't hesitate. He pushed me aside and stepped between us.

"For the love of Patanjali," I yelled. "Don't shoot!"

Everything next seemed to happen in blurry, strobe-light flashes of motion. The doors to the kitchen and conference room slammed open simultaneously. Multiple voices yelled.

"Freeze!"

"Police!"

"Drop your weapon!"

Detective Martinez leapt from the kitchen and leveled her gun on Greg with both hands. Detective Henderson froze in a similar position in the conference room doorway.

Greg's eyes grew huge, then narrowed at me. "You set me up! You both set me up!" His finger tightened on the trigger.

In that moment, the world stopped spinning. I'd made a terrible mistake. Greg was going to shoot Sam, who'd made himself my human shield. It was my fault. Sam had asked me to back off. He'd hinted that I should say our Patanjali safe word, and I'd ignored him. If he got hurt, I'd torture myself every day for the rest of my life. A life that would be blessedly short, given that Rene would slaughter me.

Martinez's stern voice commanded, "Drop your weapon. Now."

Interminable milliseconds ticked by, filled by the thwock, thwock, thwock of my heart.

"Drop it!" Henderson boomed.

Greg's expression slackened. His shoulders slumped. The fire in his eyes extinguished. The gun clattered to the floor, and he slowly raised his hands.

As Martinez cuffed Greg's hands behind his back, the world went dark.

———

Ten minutes later, Sam and I were both ensconced on the couch. I'd woken up almost immediately after I passed out, but I still felt shaky. The standoff with Greg had been much too close. Sam had almost paid the price.

"Jesus, Kate," Sam said. "You could have said that Pata-whatever word a little earlier. Were you trying to get us killed?"

"I'm so sorry, Sam. The situation escalated a lot faster than I thought it would. I was trying to get him to admit to pulling the trigger."

Sam had reluctantly agreed to participate in Martinez's and my plan to catch Greg, but none of us had fully anticipated the risk. I hoped it had been worth it.

Henderson returned from the kitchen and handed us each a glass of ice water. "You went down like a rock, Kate. Are you sure you don't want me to call the paramedics and have them check you out?"

"No, I'm fine. I panicked there for a minute and forgot to breathe. Then when it was all over … " I shrugged. "I think I collapsed in relief." I fingered the wire that was taped between my breasts. "Did you get the entire conversation?"

"We did. But Kate, we agreed that at any sign of danger, you'd say the name of that yoga guy."

"Patanjali," I said.

"Whatever." He sighed. "You do realize that 'at any sign of danger' meant before you had a gun pointed at you, right?"

"I did, but—" I was about to say that I did, but I'd screwed up and gotten carried away in the moment. Doing so would have forever cemented me in the number-one position on Henderson's idiot list.

Sam didn't give me the chance. "It's not her fault," he said. "That gun came out of nowhere. She had no way of knowing Greg was armed." It was a lie, of course. I'd seen Greg's hand twitching near that bulge in his jacket. I was pretty sure Sam had seen it too, but his look warned me not to contradict him. My hero, yet again.

"Did Greg say enough for you to get a conviction?" I asked.

"Enough to probably convince a jury, but it will never come to that. Slimebags like him always cut a deal." Henderson winked. "You got him, kid."

Martinez appeared beside me. "You two all right?"

"Kate probably has a few bruises, and I think I need a new pair of underwear," Sam replied. "But other than that, we're fine."

I wrapped my arms around him and squeezed. "I'm sorry, Sam. That was a lot closer than I intended. You're my hero. You risked your life to protect me."

He gave me a droll look. "Sweet-talk me all you want, Kate. I'm still telling Michael and Rene that we almost got shot."

Henderson winked. "Tell them not to worry, Sam. Next time we'll put you in a bullet-proof vest."

Sam turned green, but he didn't reply.

Martinez chuckled and left to speak to another officer.

Henderson turned to me. "I have to admit, you surprised me tonight. For a yoga teacher, you've got balls. Do you remember the first time we met?"

How could I forget? "The night I discovered my friend George's body?"

"Yes. You puked all over my crime scene. I thought you were an imbecile."

I cringed. "And now?"

He clapped me on the back, lips lifting into a dangerously close impersonation of a smile. "You're growing on me."

I smiled back. The feeling was mutual.

TWENTY-FOUR

I STOOD OUTSIDE THE closed door to my office, uncharacteristically hesitant. What if the conversation didn't go as I hoped? I was still recovering from one devastating disappointment. I wasn't sure my heart could handle another.

Seven months had passed since the night Sam and I cornered Greg at Teen Path HOME. Detective Henderson had been right.

We'd gotten him.

Greg had formally confessed to killing Gabriel and setting up a drug distribution ring at Teen Path HOME. He'd named his suppliers and agreed to testify against them in exchange for a maximum twenty-year prison sentence. I thought he deserved life without the possibility of parole, but Martinez assured me that this was a good outcome. His testimony would break several key links in Seattle's opioid supply chain, at least temporarily. If it made it harder for kids like Echo to get their hands on heroin, I supposed it was worth it.

I hadn't seen Echo or Jace since that day in the convenience store parking lot. In a likely misguided attempt to help Echo, Michael and

I had searched for her at Woodland Park a few days after my confrontation with Greg. Her tent was gone, replaced by that of another homeless youth. The only evidence of her time in the encampment was the two solar lanterns. Sad symbols of the beauty and light that Echo might never find. If anyone knew where she'd gone, they weren't willing to tell us. I'd likely never know if Echo and Jace left together, or if they simply scattered like leaves in the wind, the way so many of Seattle's homeless youth do.

Some Like It Hot Yoga had, as I'd feared, poached a good chunk of my customers, but I was beginning to believe Serenity Yoga would eventually pull out of it. Class attendance had taken an alarming dip during our competitor's cheap promotional period, but it had been steadily growing since it ended. I'd redefined our offerings, and I was in the process of designing our first yoga teacher training program. Initial interest was encouraging. Yoga teacher training might be exactly what the studio needed to thrive. If not? Well, Tiffany's daughter was due soon. Fatherhood would soon take up much of Chad's marketing time.

Teen Path HOME reopened, but without me as an employee. The yoga program continued, however. Another teacher from Serenity Yoga had taken my place, and she was doing fabulously. I'd wanted to continue my classes there, but Chuck's first act as the center's new director had been to fire me. He said that given my recent history, he didn't trust me to keep appropriate boundaries with the teens.

To be completely honest, he was right. The proof was on the other side of this door.

I tapped my knuckles against the wood three times.

"Come in."

Rainbow stared at the desktop, refusing to meet my gaze. She pretended to be concentrating on her newest drawing, but that was a ruse. Her energy was troubled. Bella curled around Mouse on the teen's double bed. Worry creased her brow. She sensed that something was wrong with Rainbow, too.

I grabbed a piece of kibble from a bowl on the desk and called, "Ed, Lonnie! Come!"

Eight feet's worth of tiny claws scratched along a network of Plexiglas tubing. Michael had created the maze-like structure, which spanned the room and connected two extra-large metal cages. One held a sign that read *Gym* and contained wheels, balls, and a variety of other exercise toys. The other, labeled *Bedroom*, was filled with nesting material and a collection of teeny tiny teddy bears that Rene had knitted for her two favorite vermin.

Ed and Lonnie screeched to a halt at the edge of the exercise cage and stood on their hind legs, exactly as Gabriel had taught them. Mouse opened her eyes, stared at them disinterestedly, then closed them again. Great calico hunter, she wasn't. Then again, why should she be? She had three human slaves and a German shepherd devotee who saw to her every need. We never chanced leaving Mouse alone in the room with Ed and Lonnie, but there would be no prison breaks. Michael had locked their new residence up tighter than Fort Knox. Not even Bella could figure out how to release them.

Rainbow laid down her colored pencils, tossed a few more kibbles to the boys, and then flopped on the bed next to Bella and absently stroked Mouse's belly. I picked up her sketch pad and thumbed through the most recent drawings. The first was of a blonde teen crouched on a sidewalk, face obscured by a hood, arm wrapped around a dog that was obviously Bella. She'd titled it *The Power of Love*. In the next, the same teenager crawled out from the jaws of a python. *Escape.* The third was of her Tacoma home, slightly tilted. A large crack bisected it through the middle. *Interrupted.*

Her current work wasn't finished. The girl in the drawing was viewed from behind. A cat that looked remarkably like Mouse rubbed against her ankles. The teen stared out a window, but at what? So far, the outside world was blank. What was she looking at? An escape? A refuge? A dream? A longing?

I tapped my finger against the page. "What are you going to call this one?"

Rainbow sighed. "Disappointment."

I sank on the bed next to her, carefully remaining outside of Mouse's strike zone. "Is that how you feel? Disappointed?"

"No. It's what I am. A disappointment." Her expression was troubled. "I'm a bad person, Kate."

"Oh honey, that's simply not true. How can you think that?"

She turned her face away. "You and Michael, you're good people. You both tried to help me that night I showed up at your yoga studio. You risked your life to make sure I didn't go to jail for Gabriel's death. When I didn't want to go to Orcas with Dale after Dean was arrested, you and Michael agreed to take me in. You've both been so good to me. I don't deserve it."

I understood what she was talking about, at least in part. As I'd feared, Dale's plan to foster Rainbow hadn't gone over well with the teen. She liked Dale, but she'd never met Dharma, and she was too fragile to start over in a remote place with relative strangers. In a move we all thought was a brilliant compromise at the time, Michael and I had agreed to foster her until the baby we hoped to conceive was close to arriving. After that, Rainbow promised she'd move to Orcas. For a teen in the foster care system, that much stability was almost a dream.

Almost.

Rainbow's eyes turned liquid. Her lips trembled. "I tried to be sorry when you lost the baby, Kate, really I did. But I'm not. I'm happy. You lost a child, and I'm so self-centered, all I can feel is glad." Her voice turned to a whisper. "I wanted you to have that miscarriage. I wished for it. It's my fault."

My own eyes started to water. "Rainbow, that's not possible. There is zero percent chance that you had anything to do with my losing the baby. The doctor warned us that the pregnancy would be high risk. We should have expected it."

Dale and Dharma had made good on their promise to pay for our IVF. The first attempt had failed. The second had ended in a heart-wrenching, early second-trimester miscarriage three days ago. Michael and I had talked it over, and we agreed. There would not be a third attempt. The process was too hard; the chances of success, too low.

I'd already broken the news to Dharma and Dale who were, of course, disappointed. Dale offered to pay for an egg donor, but Michael and I chose a different path. One we obviously should have shared with Rainbow much, much earlier.

Her tears turned into sobs. "I'm so sorry. I swear, I never wanted for you and Michael to be hurt. I just like living here."

I wrapped my arms around her. "Don't worry about us, Rainbow. We're fine." I was telling the truth. Michael and I were sad, but we weren't devastated. One dream had withered, but the seeds of a new one had germinated in its place.

Rainbow stopped sobbing, but she refused to look up. "When are you two going to try again?"

"We're not."

She pulled away from me, frowning. "Not ever?"

"Nothing's for sure, at least not permanently sure. We could still use an egg donor or a surrogate in the future, but Michael and I talked about it, and for now, we've decided to adopt."

Rainbow swallowed. "Oh."

"What do you think?"

"If it's what you guys want." She stared down at her hands. "I hear adoption can take a long time, especially if you want a baby."

"Sometimes. But in this case I think the process will go pretty fast. Dale knows a great adoption attorney who's prepared to draw up the papers whenever we want. It could be final in a couple of months."

Rainbow nibbled on her bottom lip, took a deep breath in, then blew it back out again. "I know we agreed that I'd go to Orcas when the baby came, but I don't want to. I like Dharma and Dale, but it would suck to change schools again right before senior year. I love this school, and I've been working hard. I'm back on the honor roll."

"I know. Michael and I are proud of you."

"And I can pay rent. Unless I screw up finals, I'll have a 4.0 GPA this year, which means I can access the trust fund money again."

My heart fell. She was suggesting that she become an emancipated minor. "That's not a good idea, Rainbow. You'll need that money for vet school. Besides, do you really want to live on your own?"

"I wouldn't be living alone, though." She held up her hands. "Hear me out. I've only got a year of high school left. Sam and Rene have a huge house. If I rent a room from them and help with the twins … "

Rainbow kept talking, but my ears refused to listen. I'd been mistaken. Rainbow didn't want to move out on her own. She wanted to bribe Sam and Rene—my two multimillionaire friends—into letting her live with them. They'd never take rent money from her, of course. The idea was preposterous. Living with Rainbow was a gift. The fact that she didn't realize this broke my heart into a million pieces.

No wonder the houses she drew were representations of chaos. She'd lived with Michael and me for over seven months and she still didn't feel stable. How could she? She was beginning to believe she didn't *deserve* stability. For the first time, I realized how truly selfish Michael and I had been. We'd deluded ourselves that we were doing Rainbow a favor by allowing her to live with us temporarily. We never fully considered how much emotional damage the uncertain living arrangement was causing.

That ended. Today.

"I'm sure Sam and Rene would love to have you, but I'd rather have you stay here."

Confusion clouded her pretty face. "But you won't have enough room once you adopt a ba—" Confusion disappeared, replaced by a slow, dawning clarity. "You mean you guys want to adopt me?"

"Yes. If you'll let us, that is. Michael and I want you to be part of our family. Legally. It's what we should have done in the first place. But I need you to know something before you decide. Your home here is secure. Even if you don't want to be adopted, you can live with Michael and me until you're a hundred and three."

Michael's off-key singing trickled in from the kitchen, carrying with it the scents of yogurt, chickpeas, and honey. Rainbow's favorite dinner: falafels with tzatziki, lemon potatoes, and rich, honey-covered baklava.

I reached out to touch her hand, forgetting that my fingers were entering my semi-feral cat's territory. Mouse hiss-spat at me, but for once she didn't draw blood. I'd take my victories where I could get them. "What do you think?"

Rainbow didn't answer, at least not verbally. Then again, she didn't have to. Her smile left no room for doubt.

"Let's go tell Michael," I said.

We walked hand in hand toward the kitchen, leaving behind the room that used to be my office. The room that I'd hoped would one day be my baby's nursery. The room that was now what it had always been destined to be: my teenage daughter's bedroom.

I'd wanted to make a baby with Michael so much that my soul hurt. But deeper than that—more importantly than that—I'd wanted to create a family. I'd wanted to leave a legacy. A permanent mark that said, *You were here. You were important. You made a difference.*

Whoever was in charge out there—God, the universe, or maybe plain old Mother Nature—had a different plan, and I was finally okay with it. As a famous rock star once asserted, you don't always get what you want. Sometimes—some amazing, wonderful times— you get something better. Sometimes you get exactly what you need.

And isn't that more important?

THE END

© Jason Meert

ABOUT THE AUTHOR

Tracy Weber is the author of the award-winning Downward Dog Mystery series. The first book, *Murder Strikes a Pose*, won the Maxwell Award for Fiction and was nominated for the Agatha Award for Best First Novel. *Murder Likes It Hot* is her sixth novel.

A certified yoga therapist, Tracy is the owner of Whole Life Yoga, a Seattle yoga studio, as well as the creator and director of Whole Life Yoga's teacher training program. She loves sharing her passion for yoga and animals in any way possible. Tracy and her husband, Marc, live in Seattle with their mischievous German shepherd puppy, Ana. When she's not writing, Tracy spends her time teaching yoga, trying to corral Ana, and sipping Blackthorn cider at her favorite ale house.

For more information on Tracy and the Downward Dog Mysteries, visit her author website at TracyWeberAuthor.com.